DANCING ON MY GRAVE
Book & Mug Mysteries #2

By Michelle L. Levigne

www.MtZionRidgePress.com

Mt Zion Ridge Press LLC
295 Gum Springs Rd, NW
Georgetown, TN 37366

https://www.mtzionridgepress.com

ISBN 13: 978-1-955838-52-8

Published in the United States of America
Publication Date: February 15, 2023

Chapter One

Monday, April 25

Eden Cole jumped down the last two steps of the back stairs of the Mug building and reached to pull open the private entrance. Conrad Price had called. He was across the street at Windows on the River and asked if he could run across the street and "have a consult." He rarely asked for help or sounded so quietly tense.

"Hey, thanks." Conrad hesitated for a moment before stepping inside. He looked over his shoulder. Maybe he thought someone on Apple was watching him? His gray eyes seemed to have extra wrinkles around them, and his windblown, white-blond hair didn't mask the new creases in his forehead.

Eden thought she glimpsed a navy uniform as the door closed but couldn't be sure. She wouldn't put it past that idiot, Carruthers, to be giving Conrad a hard time. The Fontaine family had managed to hold onto its many properties during the last economic downturn, in contrast to the Cadburns. That automatically made them enemies, partially because the Fontaines were some of the nicest, most generous people in town. And far better landlords. Carruthers, being in the pocket of the head trustee, seemed to consider it part of his duty as a police officer to harass anyone who wasn't on Trustee Roger Cadburn's "nice" list. Even he wasn't such an oaf that he would give Sarah Fontaine a hard time, so all that frustrated self-righteous nastiness landed on her grandson, Conrad, who now ran Fontaine Realty since his grandfather Albert had died.

"So … how can I help you?"

"Not really sure where to start. Lots of stuff going on." He followed her up the stairs to the office on the second floor she shared with her cousins, Troy and Kai. He waited until they reached the landing and stepped through the supply room into the office. They were alone for the moment. "Did you know I was adopted?"

"Uh … no. Why would it come up?" She flinched like she always did when she encountered someone who was adopted or a foster child. The reaction came from a longing to run into someone who had the same history, with holes torn in it, so they could compare notes and say, "What? You too?" And maybe find some clues to the mystery surrounding the Venetian glass heart lockets she and her cousins guarded.

He nodded thanks and settled into the chair she gestured him to at the long conference table in the center of the office, surrounded by workstations and multiple computers. "I just found out I've got an older brother, Steven. He's been looking for me."

"Is that good, or bad?" She gestured with her smartphone, and when he nodded, she turned on the voice recorder and set it down on the table between them. "What does he want? How did he find you?"

"That's what I need to find out. I'm responsible, you know? Grandpa left me in charge of the family business. Need to protect it, and Grandma. Kind of convenient that Steven shows up out of nowhere just a few months after he died."

"Yeah, convenient." She leaned back, cataloging the details of Conrad's features. His parents, Julia and Rick, had moved to Montana before Eden and her cousins settled in Cadburn. He didn't look anything like his maternal grandparents, Albert and Sarah Fontaine. Especially not Albert's blue-black curls and hawklike nose. Eden had assumed he took after his father's side of the family, whom she had also never met. Obtaining family pictures and details of Conrad's adoption went to the top of her mental list of tasks. Eden could guess what he was going to ask her to do. "Find out his story and see if the details match yours? Find out where he's been, how he was raised, what he's been doing for the last thirty years? Especially if he's got money problems or a criminal record. Hopefully he's been looking for you for a while now and the timing has nothing to do with that big newspaper story about the business."

"Uh yeah ... pretty much." Conrad nodded, with a crooked smile.

"Do you know if it was a sealed adoption? Depending on what kind of privacy your birthmother asked for, that could take up most of my time. It's the place to start, because once I get inside, I can work my way outward again, in different directions."

"No idea. I didn't know I was adopted until ..." He glanced away and rubbed the back of his neck. "A lot of ugly family history's been coming out since Grandpa died. A week after his funeral, three uncles showed up out of nowhere. Didn't even know I had uncles. I just thought it was Mom and Aunt Caroline. Now I've got three uncles and about a dozen cousins, and my uncles haven't talked with my grandparents since before Mom met Dad. My uncle Frank is a real – he's a piece of work. He told me I was adopted, I wasn't a Fontaine, so I should keep my big mouth shut, step out of the way, I had no authority —" He stopped. Took a couple deep breaths. Shrugged stiffly. "That's what got me looking, asking questions. Boom, out of nowhere, I've got a brother."

"Wow, that's ... gotta be painful." Eden smothered a smile, wishing it could be that easy for her and Troy and Kai to get answers and relatives, even nasty ones, showing up out of nowhere. "Well, you've got my interest and my services." She held out her hand to shake.

Thursday, April 28

From: Conrad.Price@FontaineRealty.com
To: Reb.Sheridan@NEO-Cuy.net

Need to bounce something off you.
I found out I'm adopted.
I have a brother named Steven and he contacted me out of the blue.
I'm looking at a family reunion.
But should I?
Yeah, I'm kind of ticked Mom never told me. Putting off that phone
    call as long as I can.
I'm curious. And with that big mess after Grandpa's funeral, I really
    want some answers. I want to have someone I really belong to.
Yeah, I know what you'll say, and it's like kicking Mom and Grandma
    in the teeth to feel this way. But those uncles showing up out of
    the blue, telling me I'm not family, that kind of knocked me loose.
    Know what I mean?
I always wanted brothers.
So am I being a jerk?

Becca Sheridan rubbed a few incipient tears from her eyes and smiled at the computer screen. This had to be bothering Conrad more than he wanted to admit, if he would write an email instead of waiting for their twice-monthly video call. Granted, usually he included his grandmother Sarah in the calls. Sarah refused to use email, video-conferencing, or even a smart phone, so the only other way Becca could communicate with her was by snail mail. She understood why Conrad wouldn't want to bring up this problem in front of Sarah.

"Please, Lord …" She leaned back from the computer and pressed her hands over her aching eyes. Probably bloodshot.

Too long of a day sorting through piles of scrambled records with contradictory information. If it weren't for the teenie-weenies, as she referred to the youngest children at this missionary school in Bosnia, she would have waved a white flag of surrender and fled back to the good old USA months ago. What had she been thinking when she volunteered for this short-term missionary service project, helping schools get organized and update their systems? Well, other than trying to feel useful, and not quite a slouch, compared to her parents, teaching and running an international school in Japan when they should be settling into retirement.

The children, though, more than made up for the frustration and homesickness. Except for the times she let herself daydream, and wonder if that spark of warmth between her and Conrad would still be there when she returned to Cadburn Township in July. And if that warmth would lead to someday, maybe, hopefully, a teenie-weenie of her own. Their own.

"Please, Lord, give me the words to help Conrad," she whispered, as she sat forward again and reached for the mouse. "Give him wisdom and perception, and please, let this be a good family reunion for him, to make up for the bad one?" She snorted, and refused to speak aloud the prayer she was desperately trying to leave in God's hands. *Please keep Conrad safe from Simone. She only wants him to hurt me.*

Tuesday, May 3

From: Conrad.Price@FontaineRealty.com
To: Reb.Sheridan@NEO-Cuy.net

You were right, Grandma waved her wooden spoon in my face, but she didn't quite whack me. Then she cried a little. Then she made me get on the phone and call Mom, with her listening in.
They both think I owe it to myself to find out more about my past.
What past? I was adopted when I was three months old.
Grandma is past furious with my uncles, letting that particular family cat out of the bag. She and Mom won't say what sent them packing. Gotta be bad.
Need to bounce something else off you, since you're so great with advice. Remind me to put you on retainer as my adviser for the rest of my life? Not just business stuff, but … everything?
I've got at least one decent cousin. Or else he's trying to play a con on me. Raymond. He called and wants to talk about knocking the uncles' heads together until they make up with Grandma.
I can go for that. If it's real. How can I know?
So along with worrying what my new brother really wants, I have to figure out if my cousin is for real or playing me.
Yeah, tell me I'm a pessimist. Lecture me about learning to pray for a change. I know!
But fixing the family could be good for Grandma. She's been so lost since Grandpa died. Help me with that, too?
When are you getting back?
We've got a date. The day after you're home. Meet for lunch at the Mug, we'll put our halves of the Mizpah together and give it back to Grandma and have a talk that's long overdue.

Becca grinned. Well, wasn't that a couple of answers to a big handful of prayers? She laughed and started her email by reminding him that she had told him several times already, her plane was arriving 2am July 1. Rufus and Devona were picking her up at the airport. They insisted, claiming that sharing the duplex made them more roommates, with a nice sturdy wall between them, than sibling landlords and tenant.

Then she reminded him, yet again, that they had plans to meet at Book & Mug on July 2, to plan a family picnic with Sarah, Rufus and Devona. And hopefully plan much more, for just the two of them. His constant reminders that they had a date as soon as she returned to the country had to mean what she hoped they meant. Didn't they?

"Please, God, let them both be for real, this brother and this cousin?" she whispered, as she sat back and studied the screen, and thought about how to encourage Conrad.

> *You know I'm praying for you. All of you.*
> *As for your cousin, take a leap of faith. He could be the advance scout, and all your cousins want to make things right. You have to feel sorry for them, growing up without Miss Sarah. I remember her in the nursery at church and leading the cherub choir when I was 8. My favorite Sunday School teacher. They've been deprived.*
> *Give Raymond a chance. You might like the guy.*
> *The same with your brother Steve. Did you take the problem to Eden? Both problems? Have her do some investigating for you?*

Tuesday, May 10

Becca tried to be calm, but Simone was at it again. She needed to head the glittery, tippy-dippy schemer off at the pass. Forget the pass, put up a roadblock long before the pass.

The nerve of that nasty, skinny ... fortunately, or maybe not so fortunately, she didn't have the right words in her vocabulary to apply to Simone Radcliffe, who had been her nemesis since that ugly mess in high school between Alicia Monroe and JD Ryan. How many times did she have to insist that she had never encouraged that jerk, and he had been pretending to chase her to play mental games with Alicia? Simone had never cared about Alicia until she was able to use her as a club and a weapon to hold over Becca's head.

This was too much, even for Simone. What kind of game was she playing, emailing to scold Becca about something that Conrad ate that he shouldn't have? Was she insane, insisting Becca had deliberately set her up to try to poison Conrad? Since when was Conrad allergic to almonds, so he got sick, supposedly anaphylactic shock, from eating cranberry almond chicken salad? And what was Simone doing using Becca's special recipe that she won an award for in Home Ec? How had Simone learned that Conrad loved her chicken salad? He wouldn't tell her, would he? And just how had Simone gotten Becca's email address in the first place, to screech at her from thousands of miles away?

The girl was insane.

The problem was, supposedly Simone and Conrad had gone on a picnic, where she gave him a cranberry almond chicken salad sandwich, and he got sick.

What was Conrad doing, going on a picnic with Simone in the first place?

"God ... help?"

Writing the email to ask Conrad what was going on took two days.

The effort to be calm, to be casual, and try to treat it as a sick joke on Simone's part, did pay off.

From: Conrad.Price@FontaineRealty.com
To: Reb.Sheridan@NEO-Cuy.net

The girl's delusional. I wouldn't eat anything from her hand if she was wearing full-on HAZMAT gear.

And I would rather die than not eat your chicken salad. Yeah, her cousin Angelica has to be the one who gave her the recipe.

Did Lisa tell you? Worter & McIntosh hired Angelica. Lisa doesn't hold out much hope for her lasting very long. She thinks Angelica's father knows some nasty secrets from when he and McIntosh were in college, and that's how she got the job. The girl's been snooping from day one. That's probably how Simone got your email. I'm almost scared enough to ask Grandma to change to another law firm.

Make your chicken salad for our picnic on the 4th?

Friday, May 13

The crash-tinkle of a glass mug shattering on the tile floor caught Kai's attention, if no one else's. He laughed at himself for that ridiculous, nostalgic cautiousness. If those glass mugs, the first supplies he bought right after deciding on the name of Book & Mug were so precious to him, he would take them all out of circulation.

Then he stepped around the counter into the main seating area of the coffee shop to see what had happened. No one else turned. The mid-afternoon traffic in the Mug was loud enough, crowded enough, it was a miracle he had heard one mug breaking. Or maybe that was a sign of OCD taking over, as Troy and Eden both teased him from time to time. His stomach twisted when he saw elderly Sarah Fontaine standing two steps back from the counter, her mouth forming a little O of dismay, and staring down at her feet. Kai hurried over to her, shoving aside the mental tally of how many mugs were left. Sarah wasn't the type to let a broken mug make her look like she might burst into tears. She was more likely to blush a little with embarrassment, and immediately go to her knees to pick up the pieces, and wave away anyone who tried to help her.

"You okay, Miss Sarah?" he asked, catching hold of her hand, which shook a little. He wanted to take whoever put that hurt, lost look in her eyes and slap them around a few times

"Hmm? Oh, Kai. I'm sorry." She tried to laugh. "Distracted, I suppose. One of the perils of getting old and ..." She sighed, and her gaze slid over to the tables by the glass block wall that divided the coffee shop from the bookstore.

Kai turned to look. All the tables but one were empty, so it was a pretty sure guess Conrad Price or whoever he was talking to had startled Sarah enough she dropped her mug.

"You wants I should trow 'dem guys out on der ears?" he growled, in a very bad gangster imitation.

For a second she looked lost, then she shook her head and smiled and wrinkled up her nose at him. "You're a dear." She patted his hand holding hers. "No, it's all right. He just ... startled me."

"The guy talking with Conrad?"

"Do you know him?"

"Yeah, his name's Raymond ... not sure the last name. He's met Conrad here a couple times. Why? What's he done?"

"Why ... nothing, that I know of." Sarah's gaze fastened on Raymond. "He just looks so much like someone I used to know. I supposed I was startled by a little time travel, as Rufus calls it."

"You mean deja voodoo?" Kai grinned, relieved to see her normal creamy rose color coming back to her cheeks. He hadn't realized how pale she had gone until that color returned. Movement caught his attention, and he glanced up to see Devona stepping through the gap in the glass block half-wall, her smile widening, a happy flush touching her cheeks as she walked over to the table. Raymond sat up, his smile growing to mirror hers. "Now that's something I thought I'd never see. A guy who can get Devona to smile like she smiles over a box of rare books."

"Who?" Sarah caught her breath and her hand tightened its grip on his. "No, that's not right."

"I think they've only had one date, and I'm no expert on romance, but they seemed to hit it off great from the first time he came in here."

"No. No, he can't." Sarah tugged her hands free and took a step back. "I have to – Kai, would you be a dear and ask Devona to call me when she gets off work? I need to – and put that mug on my tab, would you?" Before he could respond, she turned and hurried to the door.

Kai's mouth dropped open. He had never, in the six years he had lived in Cadburn, ever seen Sarah Fontaine hurry anywhere. He watched until she vanished out of the front picture window, then slowly turned to watch Devona and Conrad and Raymond whatever-his-name was chatting, smiling, and totally oblivious to how they had knocked a dear old woman off balance. Sarah had never struck him as someone who would flee in the face of a problem, but something there made her afraid.

Friday, May 20

"Hey." About twenty pounds of tension fell off Becca's shoulders when Devona appeared on the computer screen, without her brother Rufus. A private conversation was just what she needed. "So, how's it been?"

"I need to ask you that." Devona's smile didn't seem quite as bright as usual. "Conrad says you've gone into silent mode on him. He's been writing every day. The news isn't saying there's any trouble over where you are. Power outages or something?"

"No, we're fine." She quelled a shiver that threatened to turn into paranoia. "That's funny you should say that, because I haven't heard from him. He usually sends me at least a cartoon or a Bible verse or something every day."

"Time to have Rufus dive into the office network again. Something odd is going on. Conrad was joking that maybe the uncles are trying to break into the system and steal the whole company out from under him, but …" She shrugged. "It isn't funny anymore."

"Tell him I haven't heard from him either, would you?" Becca said.

"You got it."

"I'm glad we're alone right now. The last time I heard from Conrad, he asked me to check with you. He's worried, but Miss Sarah won't tell him, and you nearly started crying when he tried to ask you. This Raymond guy … did he hurt you?"

"No!" Devona flushed and looked away and raked one hand through her long sable hair. "No." A deep breath. "Mama Sarah … asked me to stop seeing him."

"Why? Is he as much a jerk as his father? Or at least, like Conrad described his father?" Becca wished she could reach through the computer screen and hug Devona. Her friend seemed to shrink in on herself, and her eyes got big with misery.

"She won't say. She started crying—I couldn't push her." Another deep breath. Devona straightened her shoulders and rubbed one eye that looked suspiciously wet. "She just said it has to do with the family split, and she's so happy Raymond and Conrad are trying to maneuver things to fix the whole mess, and she says I'll understand when her sons—she calls them the three idiots and dirty diaper babies and a few other things that just made me want to laugh and cry at the same time. You know how she was when she was our Sunday school teacher."

"Yeah. I remember." Becca blinked away some suspicious wet warmth in her own eyes. She hated seeing Devona fighting not to show her unhappiness, and she could just imagine how much it hurt Sarah to ask her to break things off with Raymond. Devona had been so happy, the last time they video chatted. She had been gushing about Raymond, to the point Rufus had pretended to be ready to vomit. He wheeled away from the computer and vowed not to come back until the sugar quotient in the air went down to breathable levels.

"Mama Sarah says when the family is fixed, then I'll understand, and I'll be glad she stopped us from ..." Devona shrugged. She knuckled her other eye. "So, Conrad is worried?"

"You know he thinks of you and Rufus like his brother and sister. He's kind of hurting for Raymond, too. The guy is furious. He blamed Conrad, said he was paying him back for the way the uncles acted right after Albert's funeral."

"No, Conrad would never be that mean. He wouldn't hurt me, for one thing."

"Well, go talk to the big softie and let him know. Or smack him upside the head a few times until he straightens out. I really wish I was there. You need some girl time, and a movie marathon at my place, eating ice cream right out of the carton until we're both in a sugar coma."

"Oh, gads, I really need that." Devona sniffed and managed a more believable smile. "We definitely have to do that. Any chance of you getting home a month earlier?"

"I wish."

"Hey, who started without me?" Rufus called from offscreen, punctuated by the muffled sound of a door slamming shut.

"Who got home late?" Becca called back. "Later, okay? Email me, let me know how things are going?" she added, voice softer.

Devona nodded. Rufus wheeled into the computer room and she slid her chair aside so her brother could join her for the video call. The three chatted and shared news from both sides of the ocean. Rufus was concerned, as expected, over the silence on both sides for Becca and Conrad. He promised to dive into the computer network for Fontaine

Realty and voiced his suspicion that Becca's email was being blocked from coming in, as well as Conrad's emails being stopped from going out. Probably tied into the same computer problems and signs of hacking that he had been fighting for several weeks now. He found it suspicious that Conrad wasn't able to send or receive from Becca on his smartphone, rather than the problem being limited to the office computer network. While he enjoyed untangling computer problems, this was aggravating him to the point of physical violence.

"You?" Becca muffled a strangled sort of chuckle. She hoped Rufus was joking, but there was something in his eyes that hinted at seriousness. "I know you love your computers, but that much?"

"Physical violence to the computers. As in dumping them in Cadburn Creek and starting over from scratch." Rufus's irritation shifted to weariness. "Then moving on to leaving tire tracks on whoever's been messing with them. Major, nasty-talented hackers."

The tone of the conversation changed, lightening, as the siblings shared news from church. They shared messages given them from members of the Four Corners, the square dance club Becca had been serving as president. They reported on preparations for the Memorial Day weekend street festival in town, and the arguments in the last trustee meeting. They didn't have much news to report on Conrad's communication with his long-lost brother Steve, except that he was firming up plans to go meet face-to-face.

Becca was glad at least that family reunion seemed to be progressing on a positive note. She made a note to herself to pray hard about the Fontaine family situation, and especially Raymond and Devona's relationship. Her friend had been so happy. Whatever Sarah's reasons were for asking her to break it off, they had to be serious.

Chapter Two

Tuesday, May 31

From: Lisa.Pascal@NEO-Cuy.net
To: Reb.Sheridan@NEO-Cuy.net

Hey, something weird's going on here. Just gotta give you a head's up. That glittery twit is making her moves.

Simone keeps chasing Conrad around town. I've caught at least five arguments in the last two weeks, where she's all chirpy and tending toward gooey. You know how she is when she thinks a guy can't resist her? And then he just gives her this look like he's ready to pull out the silver crosses and holy water. You know? And then he says something like, "I don't know what you're talking about. We have no plans. And she goes all poor pitiful me, why are you being so mean? And you just hope she's finally gotten the message, but you know she hasn't because two days later, she's back at it again.

Weird, huh?

I mean, she's pushing the guy to the edge. He got mean the other day. And Conrad is not mean. But I swear he was prepared for her to attack this time.

She came skipping down the sidewalk to him while we were talking about how great the festival was, and planning on Worter and Fontaine teaming up for the Labor Day fest. She barged in and started talking about their plans for next weekend. Edged in like I wasn't even there. Typical for her. Conrad gave her the glare of doom. Like he uses on Prince Roger when he's especially stupid-nasty-arrogant at trustee meetings. You know how it is. Then he got this nasty smirk, and he reached in his pocket and pulled out a Payday bar, ripped it open, and started eating it.

Simone went into hysterics, screaming about him teasing her, and how could he be so stupid and mean. She shrieked for someone to give her an EpiPen and tried to drag Conrad over to a bench to make him sit down, before he fell over. She was all over him, trying to give him mouth-to-mouth like he was going to start suffocating any second. And he just went on chowing down on the Payday. Nothing was happening, other than people gathering around while she kept making a scene. Then she shifted gears, and goes into weepy mode, accusing him of playing games with her, setting her up to scare her, and asking if he was joking when he gave her a list of his allergies so – get this – she won't poison him next time she cooked for him.

Conrad nearly choked and he even spat a few peanuts when he asked when would he ever be stupid enough to let her cook for him. She claimed she did on Saturday. Impossible, because the Fontaine booth was next to ours and he was there the whole day with Miss Sarah. No sign of Simone. But honestly? She claimed Conrad spent the day with her.

I tell you, the girl is even more psycho than ever.

Monday, June 6

"All the indications are that there's something federal involved in the mix," Eden said. She kept her head bowed over the far-too-thin stack of printouts from all the research she'd been doing for Conrad and studied him from under her eyebrows.

She needn't have bothered being so discrete. Conrad didn't see her. He frowned, new furrows in his forehead and around his mouth, staring at a spot a few inches off the surface of the conference table between them. They were alone in the office upstairs from Book & Mug for the moment. Troy was due back in another half hour from a trip to Michigan. Eden looked forward to hearing if he had learned anything new from a tenuous lead about their hidden backgrounds.

"Most of what I've been learning has been the shadows cast by the information I can't get at. Kind of like deciding the shape of something from the hole it left when it passed through other things. I thought at first the difficulty came from the adoption records being sealed. Now ..." She slid the bulldog clip back onto her copy of the reports and sat back in her chair. "Either your brother is involved in something dangerous, and he's being protected --"

"Or he's dangerous in and of himself, and the further I have you dig, the more danger you could be bringing on yourself." He nodded and only flicked his gaze up to meet hers for a moment.

"I didn't say that." Eden offered him a smile. The business smile, as Kai called it. Cool and calm and confident, that could slide over into threatening at a moment's notice, and freeze demanding creepazoids in an instant. Who needed guns when she had her killer glances?

"You don't have to. Those business smarts Grandpa trained into me come in handy, figuring out people and situations. You've gotta be good at reading people when you work real estate. All the horror stories you hear about the renters-from-hell, you don't want that happening to you, so you learn to sniff out the delinquents and troublemakers and vandals before you sign the lease." He leaned back in his chair, and raked his fingers through his thick, pale curls. "And figure out how to say no to the really big troublemakers without giving them an opening to sue you for prejudice or something else."

"I have a few remote connections to people with access to higher security clearance," Eden began.

"No, it's okay. I've got a few ideas I need to follow up on first. Steve mentioned something ... still need to figure out if it'll help with my other problems, or just make them worse. The only way I can do that is to meet him face-to-face."

"You sure?"

"The way I see it, this can only do me good. Get out of town, away from the whole political machine before Prince Roger can drag me in."

"Does that mean you're planning on running for trustee?" Eden perked up. "Finally?"

"I'm considering it. The best way to keep my nose clean is make it hard for him to set me up for some public humiliation, like he used to do when we were kids." Conrad shrugged. "Then there's the whole mess with Becca."

"What's wrong with her?"

"Total silence. Devona has passed on a few messages from her, but she's not getting my emails and I'm not getting hers. More Internet stupidity. And then Simone is back to the mental games she was playing in middle school before she went mental. She's constantly having meltdowns in public, talking about plans we made and I bailed on. It's getting harder every day to avoid her."

"Yeah, that's a good reason to get out of town," she murmured.

"And Rufus doesn't need me breathing down his neck while he's trying to fix the company computers."

"He's the best."

"You ought to know, you trained him."

"I can't take all the credit." Eden shook her head. "The guy's a genius, he just needs a few road signs. Sometimes you have to whack him over the head with the road signs, because like a lot of geniuses, he can be oblivious, but ... yeah, he's got a great future ahead of him. Just as long as the CIA doesn't drag him away into some clandestine operation."

"Yeah, he's a good kid. Glad he's family. He and Devona are good for Grandma. I'm glad their mom came into her life when she did, needing a family. She and Grandpa sure needed her, when my long-lost uncles cut them off."

Wednesday, June 8

"Where's Conrad?"

That sharp voice made the hairs bristle on the back of Kai's neck, so he didn't want to turn around to face the speaker. However, he was the only one at the counter right now, and the coffee shop was quiet enough in the lull during the dinner hour, he couldn't pretend he hadn't heard.

Yep, Simone Radcliffe stood there, skinny arms crossed, wearing enough jewelry and makeup, she was on her way to a wild night on the town. So why had she stopped in Book & Mug? Wednesdays were quiet, now that the poetry club had disbanded for summer break.

"Uh, sorry? I know a couple Conrads," he lied.

"Conrad Price." She turned her head, visually sweeping the quiet seating area fast enough to make her chandelier earrings jangle. How did she wear such heavy things without pulling her lobes out like some African tribesman, and how was she not deaf from all that noise right next to her ears? "We had a date, and he's stood me up."

Kai clearly heard the unspoken *again,* expressed in a brief grimace.

"Sorry, haven't seen him come in yet. Where were you supposed to meet?"

"At Windows." She sighed loudly and hooked her thumb over her shoulder, at the building across the street. As if she doubted Kai knew what she was referring to.

Windows on the River was on the second floor of the building, which Conrad owned. He rented out the large room for banquets and meetings. Simone's tap dance club and the square dancers club Becca Sheridan led met there.

"If I see him –"

"Tell him – no, don't tell him anything. I've left more messages than he deserves. He's not standing me up again!" With another clash-jangle of her earrings, she turned and stomped to the door.

"That makes no sense." Olivia, his head barista, stepped up to the counter with a bus pan of dirty plates and mugs she had gathered up from the two bus stations on the other side of the shop. "Conrad got a to-go yesterday before he hit the road. He said he was heading out of town, for a week, at least."

"Yeah?" Kai frowned at the building across the street. He could just make out the sign for Windows on the River, and the door at street level leading to the lobby for the offices and the stairs. "That's weird, because I know I saw Conrad going in there this morning."

"Maybe he changed his plans?"

"Conrad?" Rufus wheeled around the counter, having just come out of the elevator. "Nope, he's in Virginia. We were on the phone for a couple hours last night, trying to untangle the new roadblock in his email. He gave me the passwords for the bank accounts for some heavy-duty digging. Something's weird, like people are trying to hack the company. He's been emailing people and they aren't getting through. He's gotten some angry phone calls, because people have been asking for quotes or help with property, and he doesn't respond. I think he's right. His uncles are trying to get in the back door and take over, prove he can't handle things now that Pop Albert's gone."

"Say what?" Olivia leaned back against the counter. "I know there was some nastiness over at the office on Vista. Some yelling, someone trying to get in and take things, but ... what uncles? I thought it was just Miss Sarah and Conrad, now that Mr. Fontaine's gone."

"There was a big mess back when Aunt Caroline, and Aunt Julia, and my mom were in school. The brothers had some big fight with Pop Albert and just left town. Cut him off. And they cut off Mama Sarah and her girls when they didn't side with them. They were all in college at the time, down at OSU, so it was easy to just pack up and not come home again." Rufus shook his head, his gaze distant. "It had to have been pretty dang ugly, because nobody really talks about it. At least, not until they showed up after the funeral, and just expected everything to be handed over to them. Excuse me? Thirty years of silence, and you expect the big welcome home feast? Nuh uh."

"How do you know all this?" Kai said. "You said ... aunts?"

"My grandmother died when Mom was in middle school, and the Fontaines took her in, raised her. Conrad and Mama Sarah are all the family we've got, what with Dad being an only child."

"When are your folks coming home?" Olivia asked.

"Oh, they'll be home on furlough next winter, a whole six months."

"Furlough." Kai snorted, grinning. "Sounds like a prison sentence, not missionary work."

"Yeah, well, sometimes it feels like it. At least, for us. They're really enjoying working as support staff."

Several times while closing down the coffee shop for the night, Kai thought about the conversation. Some of the things Eden had mentioned, while protecting the privacy of Conrad as her client, made sense now. He felt sorry for Sarah and Conrad, but he could only imagine what it was like to have a family squabble that ugly, to make Conrad suspect his uncles of playing dirty like that. Thank goodness he and Troy and Eden had stuck together for as long as he could remember. He felt a little sick trying to imagine a disagreement that would split them, so they wouldn't talk for years.

Sarah and Devona and Rufus found a lot of comfort and support in their faith and church family. It had to mean a lot to them all, for Devona and Rufus's parents to spend their retirement in missionary work. Kai wished he knew how to pray and had some assurance God would listen if he did, because he couldn't think of any other way to help them out.

Things would have to get pretty serious before Eden would break her privacy rules and divulge details of whatever she was doing for Conrad. Kai never wanted things to get that bad. Conrad wasn't a good friend, but he was good company, a respected business owner, a good co-worker in Chamber of Commerce projects, and Becca Sheridan really liked him. That was a stronger testimony to what a good guy Conrad was than anything else Kai could think of.

Thursday, June 9

Eden's phone blipped when she picked it up at the eye-aching hour of 5:30am. She nearly flung it across her living room. The blip warned of at least one call during her posted non-office hours, coming from a prospective client. His inability to obey simple instructions and wait two days for her to look through the skimpy details he gave her was the entire reason she put her phone in the living room when she went to bed. She hadn't told him an irrevocable no the first time he called after office hours, and kept calling every three hours, only because Rance Harcourt had asked her to give the impatient bozo a chance. The retired FBI agent had taken her under his wing when she was in high school, just starting her quest for answers to the mystery of her and her cousins' erased identities. He had seen her potential, gave her pointers, and didn't push when she turned down the chance to follow in his footsteps. She owed him, but this headache had just tipped the scales so Rance owed her for a change.

Office hours didn't start until 9am, so she would just make Mr. Stop-the-World-For-Me wait for her answer. She had reached it at 1am, the reason she had stayed up so late working, just so she could verify her first gut reaction to his world-shaking calamity. Eden tapped the screen to see just how many times "Just call me Trip, all my best buds do," had called since she put her phone on vibrate.

She headed for her kitchen and hoped that new herbal brew Troy had stashed in her refrigerator last night was as tasty as he promised. She didn't have time to brew coffee or wait for tea to steep, and she wasn't getting out of her sleeping shorts and T until noon. She had promised herself that indulgence when she dove into bed four hours ago. So she couldn't go downstairs to Book & Mug and take whatever Kai had ordained the coffee decadence of the morning.

"Huh." She rubbed her eyes with the back of the hand not holding the phone and blinked a few times to make sure of the numbers. Trip (and she knew exactly where she'd like him to trip) had called every ninety minutes, precisely, since 9pm. The jerk had obviously programmed an alarm to remind him and do the dialing for him, until he put down his newest video game. Yes, she had found out quite a few things about him in the two days for research she had mandated before giving him her answer. Her suspicions had become solid fact, and she would turn all those facts over to Rance and let him throw several books at the bozo.

What caught her attention was the one call in the middle of the barrage of, "This is Trip, you know it's me, why won't you pick up? Call me!" An unfamiliar number, coming from Virginia, with a long voicemail attached.

A few taps activated the program patch Rufus had designed for her, to store the evidence of the barrage of calls and clear them off her screen. Then she opened her refrigerator and snatched the tall glass bottle off the top shelf. A glance at the nearly empty shelves reminded her to either go down to Green's to stock up, forage in Kai's refrigerator, or get delivery again. She nudged the door closed with her hip, settled down in her living room, and put the phone on speaker.

"Hi, Eden. It's Conrad."

A pause, long enough to let her open the bottle and take the first tentative taste. Okay, Troy was right this time. She caught lemongrass, ginger, and spearmint in a swirl around her tongue before the chill mixture washed the coating off the inside of her mouth. A second, larger mouthful was just as pleasant. He might have a winner this time.

"Sorry about all the cloak and dagger with the unfamiliar number," Conrad continued, "but I'm pretty sure my phone has been hacked. I'm setting up a new email, got this new phone. Someone has hacked me bad, and my brother is helping me dig down, try to straighten things out. Either make what I've got more secure or start completely over. I'm staying down here another week or two. Can you give me enough time to get things taken care of with Rufus, set up new accounts for me for the business? It's looking like my uncles are in some really big trouble, and they need Grandpa's company to cover up something. It's starting to look bad. I won't say national security level bad, but Steve says the less other people know about it, the easier it'll be to clean up things. So check with Rufus. I owe you a couple dozen. Thanks. You're the best."

"Okay … that's interesting." She took another swig from the bottle and grimaced as a bitter aftertaste rose up through the other flavors. If Troy put this recipe in his health food store, he should definitely sell it in small doses. Two or three swallows were fine, but something about it built up to a nasty finish after that.

Saturday, June 18

"Now I've seen it all." Rufus stopped short after making a right turn from the elevator and stared at the front of the coffee shop.

Eden nearly ran into him, coming out of the elevator behind him. She stepped up, resting one hand on the back of his wheelchair, and turned to look at what had him slowly shaking his head.

Conrad was walking out of the shop with that too-skinny Simone Radcliffe hanging on his arm like she needed him to keep her upright. That dopey grin he wore did not belong on his face. Especially focused on Simone. According to Devona, Conrad and Becca Sheridan were starting to get serious, and he was waiting for her to return from overseas.

"I didn't know he was back in town," she said, as the two walked out the front door and seemed to vanish for a few seconds, into the brilliant early afternoon sunlight.

"Neither did I," Rufus murmured. "He didn't get back to me, when I told him I finally got things cleared up with the office system. But if he figured he'd talk to me … why didn't he come upstairs?"

"Uh, looks like he has a date."

"Yeah, with a really strong dose of—" He let out a disgusted groan, but when he turned his wheelchair to look up at her, his expression was entirely mischievous. "Really, really strong mental drugs, y'know?"

"You're such a mean little boy."

"Yeah. And proud of it." Rufus let out a sigh and bent forward, giving a hard push with his arms, and slalomed his way through the incoming afternoon traffic to get to the bookstore side of the coffee shop.

Eden gnawed on his comments and what she had seen as she retrieved a mocha whip and headed back up to the office. Something just struck her as wrong, but she couldn't put her finger on it. Other than Conrad not contacting her when he got back into town. Not a word on the problems he and his brother had been dealing with. She was still facing roadblocks in obtaining the basic information on Conrad's adoption. His adopted parents had hesitated for only a day before signing release forms to make their side of the adoption accessible and open to investigation. Someone on the other side was keeping the door locked. What had Conrad's birth parents needed to hide? She wondered if Conrad's brother knew that he had asked for the investigation, and if he did, his feelings on the matter. Was he insulted, thinking his story wasn't believed?

She got to work on several requests for her assistance and waited for Conrad to make contact.

~~~~~

That evening, Kai came upstairs for a break and reported some fuss across the street for an hour or so. Heinrich, the most troublesome of the shop owners in the Windows building, had grumbled and stomped up
~~~~~

and down the sidewalk, insisting two security cameras, inside the lobby and outside by the doorway, were broken. He had online access, and nothing was visible on the screen. When the security firm that maintained the cameras came out to do repairs, they discovered someone had sprayed the motion sensors and the lenses with black paint, rendering them useless. And no one saw the vandalism being done.

Eden made note of the incident, and sent an email to the security firm, to find out if they had contracts with other businesses in Cadburn, and if any other security cameras had been attacked. Her first reaction was to blame it on more petty nastiness from someone who supported Roger Cadburn and feared Conrad would run against him in a few months. Yet how would rendering the cameras useless harm Conrad?

She was gathering more questions to ask him, the next time he could be nailed down to one place and forced to talk.

Wednesday, June 22

"Hey, Conrad?" Kai hurried over from the counter, intercepting Conrad as he hurried away from what looked like a tense, brief chat with Devona. "What's the hurry?"

"Hey yourself." The smile and shrug didn't fool Kai for a moment. "What's up?"

"That's what I want to ask you. Eden was wondering when you were going to check in."

"Don't tell me she didn't get my email. I sure hope someone hasn't hacked my new account, too." He let out a loud, gusting sigh and raked one hand through his hair. "Is Rufus working upstairs today? Need to find him."

"Hate to tell you, but you look like you've been through the wringer." Kai chose not to mention the bright yellow T-shirt Conrad was wearing. It had the same stylized fountain logo on the T-shirts Fontaine Realty gave the Little League and Peewee Soccer teams they sponsored in community sports. Usually, Conrad was a polo shirt kind of guy.

"I feel like it. Tell Eden I'll check in with her tomorrow, okay? Gotta take care of some files, and I'm trying to track down Ginny and prove to her yes, I did get ..." He gestured at the T-shirt.

Now Kai understood. Ginny Wells, who ran Pins and Needles, a sewing supplies shop and craft center, had been building up a side business designing logos and putting them on clothes and bags and other items. Now he thought he remembered hearing her grumbling about Conrad not getting back to her on something she had designed.

"And I just got a call about a leak at Windows," Conrad continued.

"Water in the lobby again, but we can't figure out where the leak came from. Nothing in the ceiling. Weirdest thing. Plus, it's been absolutely nuts lately. Grandma's been worried about me, and my phone was wonky the entire time I was in Virginia, so we didn't talk. She hates email, and right now, I don't blame her." He cast a glance over his shoulder at the bookstore. "Then there's the problem with Raymond and Devona. Has he been stopping in here?"

"Not that I know of."

"Yeah, well, he's been calling her. And I've been getting some pretty crazy calls from my so-called uncles, accusing me of encouraging them, just to get revenge. What would it hurt them if Raymond and Devona got over their problems and got together?"

"Why did they break up?"

"Grandma asked her to." Conrad shrugged. "Don't ask me why. She's not saying, and neither is Devona."

His phone blared the Darth Vader march, making him jump. Kai muffled a chuckle.

"Didn't know you were into personalized ringtones."

"I'm not." He glanced at the display and grimaced, then silenced the ringing. "Just another thing the hackers have been doing to me. Numbers programmed into my phone I never entered, ringtones I never bought, psycho twits accusing me of ghosting them and not showing up for dates I never made ..." He jammed the phone into his back pocket. "Tell Eden I'll check in later? Thanks," he said, as Kai nodded.

In moments he was dashing out the door. Kai walked up to the front window of Book & Mug and watched Conrad dash across the street without pausing more than two seconds to look for oncoming traffic. He caught a glimpse of movement in the long expanse of window on the second floor but couldn't see who was there.

Chapter Three

Tuesday, June 28

"I tell you, Becca isn't coming home soon enough," Dave Alderman grumbled, stomping through the door of Book & Mug that evening.

Kai looked around in time to see nearly a dozen people coming into the coffee shop, and more coming out of the door of the Windows building. The evening had grown to that odd half-light when the streetlights were flickering and warming up but weren't needed yet, the twilight not quite setting in. He recognized a good number of the people as members of Four Corners, the square dance club that met every Tuesday night at Windows on the River. But at 7:30, they should just be getting started, not finishing up for the night.

"What do you got that's good?" Greg Wells called out as he stomped through the door behind Dave.

"Good for cooling down some hot heads," his wife, Ginny, added.

"What happened?" Kai stepped up to the counter as Olivia moved up to handle the influx of customers.

"Got kicked out." Dave hooked his thumb over his shoulder at the building across the street.

"For what?"

"Get your facts straight," Faith Evans said. "There's some big pipe leak over there upstairs, lots of the flooring torn up. They're just angry that nobody bothered letting us know, so we could make other arrangements or just not meet tonight."

"Huh. The leak can't be too bad. Heinrich sure would have let everybody on the street know, if there was a leak at his place."

That earned a few chuckles from some of the square dancers. Heinrich had a reputation as a curmudgeon, and that was being generous. Anything that inconvenienced or irritated him was aired to everyone on the street. He didn't seem to care if he drove away customers from his coins and gems shop, or the other shops in the lobby of the Windows building. Just yesterday, he had gotten into a shouting match with Spencer Wilcox, owner of the electronics store at the end of the building. Heinrich had let everyone know the security cameras were down again. Spencer rightly pointed out that making the breakdown public knowledge just encouraged anybody who wanted to try to break in.

"Any estimate how long it'll take to get things fixed?" Olivia asked as she got to work on the first few orders.

"Doesn't matter." Tom Bedford leaned on the counter with a hangdog expression. "The sign says all clubs and meetings and events are canceled until further notice. Supposedly, they found mold when they went looking for the leak."

"Supposedly?"

"Whoever is doing the repairs isn't anybody we know. We just know what was on the sign, and what people have overheard." He shrugged. "Bottom line is, we gotta find some other place to meet. Conrad was in a lousy mood, came darn near cussing us out, just because we wanted some real answers."

"That doesn't sound like Conrad," Kai said, more to himself than anyone else.

Eden agreed with him, when he stopped by her apartment after closing up the shop for the night. She let him know that despite Conrad saying he would call her nearly a week ago, she had yet to hear from him. He wasn't answering texts or voicemails or emails. He was never available, and just when someone caught sight of him, he ran off, like he knew people were looking for him. Rufus had reported that he was always in a bad mood, he had lost weight, and he smelled like he had taken up smoking, the few times they were in the realty office at the same time. He hardly ever saw Conrad, who seemed to be avoiding everyone. It didn't matter if Rufus responded to the phone calls and emails he ignored, or if he couldn't fix any client problems without checking with Conrad, or tried to fix any problems at all, Rufus always seemed to be in the wrong.

"I'm just fed up enough, I don't care about client privacy," Eden said. "Miss Sarah asked me to try to figure out what he did when he was with his brother in Virginia. She's afraid Conrad got dragged into something, and he's cutting off everybody to protect them. Especially her."

"Well, that sounds more like the Conrad we know," he admitted.

"Maybe."

"Maybe?"

"He just never struck me as someone who would be too proud to ask for help."

"Huh." He considered that for several moments. "You could be right."

"I know I am." She smirked at him. The brief light moment faded. "She's scared for him, but until I get some answers, some information on this brother of his ... I have an awful feeling the name and information he gave me on this supposed brother Steve will prove to be false."

"Which means Conrad is in big trouble. Bigger trouble. Miss Sarah sure doesn't need that."

"Becca? When did you get back?" Jack Butler leaned into the post between booths at Book & Mug, nearly impaling his hand on one of the coat hooks, ignored it, and grinned down at her. "Gotta tell you, there's a lot of people who will be glad to see you. No question about that."

"Uh ... thanks?" Becca scooted over a few inches, so she wouldn't have to turn her neck at such a tight angle to see him.

Jack was one of the mainstays of the Four Corners dance club. Technically, she was still the leader, or would resume leadership now that she was back from her short-term missions trip. The way she felt right now, with only one day of resting and doing laundry and airing out her half of the duplex, she wasn't ready to take on any responsibilities yet. Especially with Jack grinning down at her like he expected her to save the planet with just a couple decisions.

After spending six months helping two missionary schools solve some paralyzing logistical problems and get organized, she needed more time off than she had given herself. Too bad she had declined a chance to spend a week sightseeing in England. No, she had to hop a plane Thursday night, race the sun home to Ohio, try to cure jet lag with only ten hours of sleep, then start in on notifying clients of her virtual assistant business that she was home.

Right now, she was just cranky enough to let Conrad hang for a while. What did the big jerk think he was doing, reminding her every third email about their date, making her heart skip a beat every time he used the actual word *date*, and then when he got his email back, according to Rufus, he left her hanging in silence? She tried to blame her exhaustion for the incipient headache, and not the awful feeling that Simone Radcliffe had lived up to her thinly veiled threats, and despite the juicy gossip passed on by Lisa Pascal, she had indeed "stolen" Conrad while Becca's back was turned.

No, Conrad has too much sense and good taste and honor and intelligence to let that vindictive twinkle-toes snag him.

She kept telling herself that and found it harder to believe the longer the silence had grown between herself and Conrad. He hadn't responded to her texts since she landed – five – and when she called him, his phone sent her straight to voicemail. Then she got a recording saying his voicemail box was full and wouldn't take her message. She wasn't going to embarrass herself and worry Miss Sarah by asking her what had been going on. When Conrad showed up in – she checked her watch – twenty-six minutes, she would get answers. Or ... well, she wasn't sure what she would do, besides buy a half-gallon of mint moose tracks from Goody

Two Scoops and go home to eat herself into an exhausted coma. Maybe she would throw her half of the Mizpah coin in his face? No, she couldn't do that either. The coin set had been Miss Sarah's. His grandmother had been so delighted when Conrad asked if he could have it, to give one half to Becca to wear while she was out of the country, and the other for him to wear to remember to pray for her every day.

"What was that?" She waved her hand and offered a smile that probably drooped on one side. "Sorry, Jack, I'm still jetlagged. What were you saying?"

Get your act together. You're home in Cadburn and life can get back to normal.

"Heh, yeah, should have remembered." Jack waved to someone standing by the glass block divider wall. "Look who's home at long last!"

Becca muffled a sigh and leaned forward to see Ginny and Greg Wells scurrying over with a few books in their hands. Ginny leaned in to hug her and then slid into the booth seat facing her, while Greg took up a matching position opposite Jack. For several minutes, they regaled her with news of events in town. The street fairs she had missed. The new businesses opening up. The latest complaints about the trustees arguing so much that nothing got done at the last trustee meeting. The usual smalltown gripes and silliness. Until they slid into news about Four Corners. Which was expected. Ginny was in charge of their costumes for exhibitions, and Jack and Greg took care of the sound system.

"Kicked out? What do you mean, kicked out?" Becca shook her head and fought the temptation to stick her little finger in her ear, because she couldn't have heard right. "Why would Conrad kick you out of Windows?"

Her stomach twisted around the snickerdoodle caramel freeze she had indulged in, Kai's newest decadent creation. *She did it. Simone brainwashed Conrad while I was away. How many times has she tried to change rehearsal night for her dance club so she could edge us out?*

"Be fair, honey," Greg said. "Everybody got booted. Don't know what put that bug up Conrad's ..." He coughed instead of speaking what was clearly in his expression. "There were a lot of people griping about the shut-down, and Mo at Lumber Village was ticked enough to have a coronary when Conrad went with someone else for the flooring—"

"Flooring? What happened at Windows?" Becca demanded. She half-raised out of her seat, to peer around Greg at the building across the street. What had Conrad been dealing with while she was gone? She envisioned Windows on the River, all that lovely old wooden flooring, so proudly maintained by Albert, the old-style crown molding in the vaulted ceiling, the huge windows looking down on Center on one side and Cadburn Creek on the other. Something had damaged the beautiful old meeting hall, where Four Corners had met for years?

With several necessary backtracking detours, the three eventually gave her the story about how a pipe had burst in Windows, necessitating the replacement of half the floor. Yet none of the stores on the first floor had experienced any leaks. That was odd, but everyone was grateful. Then there was the fuss with the local lumber yard. The owner was a lifelong friend of Albert Fontaine and had wavered for several weeks between insulted and afraid he had hurt Sarah's feelings, so Conrad went to another supplier for replacement flooring. Then the Macavoy brothers were in a snit when Conrad got someone from Brunswick to come in and install the new floor, instead of them. They had a gentleman's agreement since their grandfathers' time to handle all repairs and woodwork on Fontaine Realty properties. So why hadn't Conrad trusted them with Windows?

Then there was the problem with the smell that Conrad claimed was mold, the treatment to eradicate it, and the preservatives and sealers and other chemicals involved in the renovations. Heinrich had threatened to sue because the smell drove away customers, when everybody knew it was his bad attitude and lack of any idea of customer service. Then, as if in retribution for the people complaining about the inconvenience, Conrad posted a sign on the street door and the company website, declaring the meeting hall closed until further notice. All meetings were cancelled, all clubs would have to find new locations.

Becca nearly laughed at herself, over the relief she felt knowing that *everyone* had been kicked out. Including Simone and her TippyToes club.

"So where are we meeting for now?" she asked, when Jack's grumbling about Mo still being in a bad mood had run down. Ginny and Greg were just looking at her with expressions of relief that made her feel even more tired. And maybe eager to jump on the next plane back to a missionary posting. Any missionary posting. Forget about temporary.

"Overstreet's Big Barn," Greg admitted, followed by a long sigh. He refused to meet her gaze for a few seconds. "And in the park, when he overbooks or has to do repairs."

"Uh huh." She bit her tongue to keep from asking just how desperate and frustrated they had become before booking that venue.

There had been rumors for years that the Barn was on the verge of being condemned and torn down. If the roof wasn't losing shingles in every high wind, there were stories of rats bigger than barn cats living in the walls or people falling through sudden holes in the floor, when planks turned to sodden sawdust under their feet.

Becca's head hurt as she considered all the other options within decent driving distance and time, with enough room for Four Corners to spread out and practice. Three of those options were public buildings that should be available until the school year resumed, such as the high school and middle school gyms. Two were buildings owned by Simone's uncle. She wouldn't even waste the energy to think about them.

They agreed to call the rest of the leadership committee of Four Corners and ask people to think of other locations and start making calls. Becca nearly lost it at Jack's parting shot, as he followed Ginny and Greg out the door.

"Hope you can talk some sense into Conrad. He's changed. Don't know what's his problem."

"Neither do I," she muttered, and closed her eyes to lean back in the booth and take a few deep breaths.

Without thinking, she reached up and caught the half-coin between forefinger and thumb, rubbing it a few times before she was aware of it. She had been doing that an awful lot lately. It was a minor miracle she hadn't worn through the thin gold plating and erased the Bible verse engraved on it.

"The good Lord watch between us until we meet again," she whispered in the few Bosnian words she had learned, preferring that over the King James translation of the Bible verse. A sigh escaped her. "Please, Lord, I know You've been watching over Conrad while we've been apart, but what's up with him? Could You give me a clue?"

Becca glanced at her watch. Conrad should be there any minute. In fact, he should have already showed up because he always arrived early, for everything. Maybe he had seen her talking to Jack, Ginny and Greg and stayed away? But that would mean he was holding a grudge against them. That didn't sound like the Conrad she knew.

Maybe she should have chosen a different booth, where she couldn't see him coming. Was he across the street right now, looking down on Book & Mug from Windows? Maybe making up excuses for the long silence? Was he nervous? Was he irritated, wishing he hadn't insisted on this meeting? Did he still consider it a date? Just how much had he changed while she was away?

Why was she here? She should be recuperating from travel. She should be notifying all her clients that she was home, thanking the members of VA, the virtual assistant cooperative, for filling in for her. Basically, getting the rest of her life back up to speed.

Tapping her phone, she checked the list she had made in the notes app. She had thirty favorite clients she needed to contact with personalized emails. Chances were good she had lost some of them, despite protests that no matter how good the substitutes she had arranged for during her absence, they wanted to resume working with her when she returned. Some of her VA friends had let her know about clients who had proven to be headaches and might remain headaches when she took them back. Becca wouldn't mind never having to deal with them again. Those were the ups and downs of having her own business, running errands, doing research, making deliveries, handling all those pesky business details that some people just didn't want or didn't like or couldn't handle, and preferred to have someone else "pick the nits," as her grandfather used to say.

Finished with that, she checked the time. Ten minutes past the agreed-on meeting time. No Conrad. When was he ever late?

Becca shivered.

"You okay?" Rufus's voice at her elbow startled her so she nearly knocked over her half-empty glass.

"Yeah. Fine. A little tired." Her brain spun and jetlag threatened to make her weepy. That was utterly ridiculous. She picked up the tall glass. "Drank too fast."

"If you're …" He frowned, eyes narrowing. Becca turned to see him staring at a young man coming through the propped-open entryway of Book & Mug.

Odd. From that hooked nose, the thick mop of blue-black hair, blue-gray eyes and wide shoulders, she would have sworn that was Albert Fontaine. Granted, Albert from forty years ago, but Becca had seen the pictures multiple times when she had gone with Devona and Rufus to have dinner with Sarah.

"Who's that?"

For a few seconds, Rufus didn't seem to hear her, as he watched the young man stride toward them, then make a sharp right turn into the bookstore portion of the coffee shop.

"Raymond."

"That's Raymond?"

"Yep. Sorry. Pest control." He shoved hard on his wheels and sent his wheelchair zipping toward the gap in the glass block wall that separated coffee shop from bookstore.

Silence. Then the low rumble of male voices, but no distinct words. She knew she shouldn't be staring, but Rufus was a good friend, a good neighbor, and anything that bothered him concerned her. Becca exhaled slowly as Raymond came back through the bookstore entrance, shoulders slightly hunched, and stomped for the door.

Rufus didn't come out right away. She heard his voice, and the higher tones of Peggy, who took care of the bookstore when Devona was out on buying trips.

Sighing, Becca checked her watch. Still no Conrad. She glanced at the door across the street. Somehow, she couldn't see him as the kind of coward who used silence to break off a relationship that had just been starting when she went overseas.

"Gotta be a good reason," she whispered. Without thinking, she reached up to rub her Mizpah coin once more, then picked up her phone and got to work on her next email, to Charli Hall. Becca dearly hoped she would have work for her to do soon. She needed to keep busy. She had fun helping Charli research her novels. That was the kind of research work she liked, rather than the somewhat grim work that Eden Cole did as a private investigator. Although she wouldn't say no to working with Eden again, and maybe on a semi-regular basis.

"Becca?" Patty Hill stopped halfway to the door, her mouth open in a delighted grin. She scurried to the booth, arms spread wide. "Roy! Look who's here. Oh, everybody is going to be so glad to know you're back." She wrapped Becca in a fierce hug that nearly pulled her out of the booth.

Pastor Roy followed a few steps behind his sister, carrying a bag bulging with books. The three of them chatted until the pair's order of drinks was ready. When they left, Patty urged Becca to join them for dinner that evening. She only hesitated a moment before agreeing, then regretted it as soon as they had vanished out the door. Why had she agreed to go out for the evening, when she was so tired?

What was she doing sitting here and waiting for Conrad to show up when it was pretty obvious? He wasn't coming.

Despite knowing she should get up and go home, Becca stayed sitting and staring across the street. She didn't know what she was waiting for, until a woman flounced down the sidewalk to the door of the Windows building. A spear of afternoon sunlight sparkled on dozens of thin bracelets and chandelier earrings and multiple glittery beads hanging around her neck. Becca caught her breath, seeing the picnic basket swinging from Simone Radcliffe's hand and the extra-wide, "so there" swing of her hips.

She knew better, but Becca got up anyway, slipped her tall glass into the nearby bus pan, waved to someone who called out goodbye behind her, and headed out the door. She tipped her head back to look up at Windows as she waited for several cars to pass. No movement. When she had crossed the street and stepped into the lobby, she looked for movement, listened for voices. Nothing. Common sense told her to turn around and leave, but she was too tired and cranky to listen. The door to the stairs was open, and the sign announcing the closing until further notice hung next to the door. She went up the stairs, pressing against the wall on the eighth, ninth, and twelfth steps to avoid creaks.

"Hey, that looks good. Thanks," a man said. For a few seconds, she didn't know who was talking. That raspy voice couldn't be Conrad.

Two more steps and Becca's head came above the half-wall that separated the stairwell from the rest of the long meeting room. She paused and turned to follow the sound of the voice. Funny, but she didn't really feel anything. Not relief or anger or betrayal, which she should have felt, as she watched Simone go up on the toes of her stiletto shoes – how did anyone dance in shoes like that, anyway? – and brush a kiss across Conrad's cheek.

"Anything for you. You know that, don't you?" she cooed, and wriggled a little, like an eager puppy.

Becca swallowed down the entirely catty reply, *Yeah, that's what everybody says about you.* That wasn't nice of her, that wasn't the kind of woman she was. At least, she hoped so. All bets were off when she was this tired and irritated and feeling sort of empty inside. Bottom line: no matter what grudges Simone carried against her, she shouldn't give in. And yet …

"There you are." Becca didn't even smile when Simone turned sharply enough to wobble on her stilettos and Conrad jerked back out of her reach. He frowned at her with a "Do I know you?" expression, not the "Oh, heck, now I remember" look she expected. Simone giggled and muttered something to him as she stepped around him, dragging her other hand across his chest.

"Oh, hi, Becks," Conrad said.

Becks? Since when did he call her *Becks*? That nickname was Simone's snarkiness. How many times had Conrad told her to stop using it? Obviously not enough.

How many times had Simone used that unwanted nickname until Conrad picked it up?

"Hi." Becca knew how to keep her voice and face calm, impervious. She would treat him like a demanding, not-worth-the-hassle prospective client who had to be persuaded that, despite his stop-the-world-for-me emergency, he really didn't want her to work for him. "Just making sure you forgot about our appointment. I'm not someone who cancels out on a business appointment without proper notification."

"Oh, yeah, business." He nodded. The big oblivious idiot hadn't caught on, obviously, that she was referring to him. "Sorry, kind of busy this week. What were we working on?"

"Getting your business organized, fixing a lot of problems, sabotage from your nasty uncles, filling out lots of legal documents. That sort of thing."

"Oh, that's great. Becks is such a big help, she's so good with all that office-type stuff," Simone said. "But Connie really doesn't need your help. He's got it all handled."

"Yeah, all handled." Conrad nodded. "Sorry to have wasted your time."

"You'll send a bill, won't you?" Simone added.

"Hmm, no, I don't think so. I was helping more as a friend, but …"

Becca shrugged and inhaled slowly, fighting the squeezing sensation around her ribs. "Enjoy your dinner."

You win, she thought, but refused to say it aloud, as she headed down the stairs. Yes, she knew pride was yanking on her internal steering wheel, but she was just too tired to fight. *He's all yours. I really, really hope you suffer buyer's remorse big-time, Simone. You two deserve each other.*

Chapter Four

Sunday, July 3

Becca thought the morning sun shone too brightly as she stepped out of the back door of the duplex to go to her car and head to church. She paused and raised a hand to shield her eyes and considered turning around and going back inside. No one would blame her if she didn't come to church that morning. Patty and Roy had both expressed concern last night that she had worn herself out, trying to get back up to speed so soon after returning home.

The other back door opened. Rufus slid out onto the porch, followed by Devona. The siblings paused. If Devona could get herself up for church, after returning from her business trip at 2am, Becca decided she could make the effort too. When Rufus suggested they ride in together, she was glad to accept.

Until she saw who was getting out of a car in the handicapped parking space next to the one where Rufus parked his van. Silver-haired, frail, elegant Sarah Fontaine was the last person she wanted to see.

Especially with a curl of guilt dropping into her stomach to stab her. She wasn't wearing the Mizpah coin. She wasn't sure where she had dropped it yesterday when she got home from Book & Mug.

And yet ... if anyone would understand what was going on with Conrad, that would be his grandmother.

Becca wasn't in the mood to even try to play act, to pretend she didn't see Sarah until she opened the van door to climb out. She waved as soon as she saw the older woman's head turn in their direction. Her smile froze when Sarah covered her mouth and turned her head. Becca climbed out of the van and nearly stumbled.

This had to be very bad. Becca wished Sarah hadn't played matchmaker. They could still be friends, Sarah could still be her mentor and role model, with no awkwardness between them. If the shadow of Conrad wasn't there, hovering over them right that moment.

Conrad was a jerk. He and Simone certainly deserved each other. Becca couldn't think of a single thing she had done to make him look at her like he had no idea who she was yesterday. She would have thought, from seeing him in business and trustee meetings, and at church and community events, he was the kind of man who would let someone know if they had offended or irritated him, and do it privately, politely, calmly.

Not act like a brat. Was he punishing her because she followed through on her commitment to six months of missions work, a promise she had made before they started getting serious?

Definitely, he and Simone deserved each other.

"Oh, my dear." Sarah reached out a thin, elegantly long hand to clasp Becca's. "That big nincompoop did something wrong, didn't he?"

She wanted to laugh, lightheaded with relief that Sarah wasn't blaming her. If she had to lose anybody when this relationship with Conrad went south, she didn't want that person to be Sarah.

"Well, he called me Becks, for one thing. And Simone was hanging on him, and they were getting ready for a picnic supper at Windows." She shrugged. No way was she going to admit that Conrad played the "Oh, hello, stranger, what do you want?" card on her. So juvenile.

"I honestly don't know what's happened with that boy. He's avoiding everybody, irritating clients, changing everything around at the office." Sarah held out her bent arm for Becca to loop with hers, and they turned to head across the parking lot to the back door of the church. "Between those mules I call sons and that brother appearing out of the blue ..." She sighed and patted Becca's hand. "It's like he's had a nervous breakdown. But of course, big, strong men don't admit they've got nerves, so he has to push away everybody who cares about him."

"And then some," Rufus said, catching up with them and passing them with a few pushes on his wheels. "Guy's ticked every time I try to fix the newest thing he messed up with the office computers." He shook his head, then sped up, zipping to the left to the wheelchair ramp into Cadburn Bible Chapel.

"I hope you don't mind," Becca said, when Devona had gone ahead of them, and they slowed down to take the four steps. "I'm just too tired to ... to fight for him."

"Oh, my dear girl." Sarah squeezed her hand. "I don't blame you in the least. I don't much like Conrad right now, myself. He calls me 'Granny.' When did he pick that up?" She shook her head. "Until that boy gets his head out of his backside, I wouldn't inflict him on anyone. Let's give him a few weeks to straighten out and realize that sparkly, jangly little two-stepper isn't right for him." She winked when her words got a snort of laughter from Becca. "Then we'll make him work a little while for our forgiveness. If he doesn't straighten out ... well, I'm still of sound mind and body, and nobody has a legal leg to stand on if I decide to give the company to someone else. Ever considered becoming a landlord?"

"Me?" She caught her breath, forcing a laugh when the words actually brought a stab under her breastbone.

Becca most certainly had considered going into the landlord business. When she thought she and Conrad would become business partners, then partners in a much deeper, more personal aspect. She shrugged, helped Sarah up the stairs, and fought not to let a different image fill her mind: Simone working alongside Conrad, changing policies at Fontaine Realty, offending clients, giving management jobs to her relatives, and ruining the reputation that Albert and Sarah had worked so hard to establish.

For Sarah's sake, she might just consider it.

Wednesday, July 6

The door opened behind Becca, letting mid-afternoon sunshine stream into the cool, shadowy interior of Frenchy's restaurant. She glanced at the wide-shouldered, pale-haired figure that stepped inside, but the light was at the right angle to hide all other features.

"Becca?" Andre Pool stepped up to the takeout counter, holding out the bag with her order. "Good to see you back."

"Thanks." She inhaled deeply, mouth watering at the aromas of potato and onion pierogis, smoked sausage, and fried sauerkraut leaking from the container. "Oh, definitely, this is what brought me home."

"Put it in writing, honey."

"Next time you have me write ad copy, I will!" She turned, laughing with Andre, and nearly ran into the man, who had stepped up too close behind her. "Oh. Conrad."

"Hey ... Becca ..." Conrad nodded slowly, a smile just as slow spreading across his face. He looked her over. "How's it going?"

"Fine." Her stomach twisted, remembering instantly the last time she had run into Conrad at Frenchy's, picking up one of their "Ethnic Specialty Surprise Meals." That day had also been pierogis, sausage, and sauerkraut. Conrad hadn't had to do more than smile and sniff deeply and pretend he would steal the bag from her, and she had offered to share with him. She always ordered enough for a full meal later. Becca swallowed hard, quelling the urge to snap, "Don't expect me to share this with you."

"Anybody ever tell you ..." He shook his head. "We've got a lot to catch up on, y'know?"

"Uh ... no. No, I don't know." She headed for the door, cringing at the chance that Andre was watching right that moment. He wouldn't gossip, but he would care enough to ask what was wrong between her and Conrad. "Excuse me, got some things to do before I can go home."

"Yeah, you're one busy lady. That's what I've been hearing." He chuckled and stepped aside, to let her go to the door.

Conrad from eight months ago would have hurried to open the door for her, then teased and hinted until she invited him to share her dinner.

Becca tried to ignore the tight sharpness in the pit of her stomach. She was just hungry, that was all. Even though her meal didn't smell all that wonderful anymore.

"Hey, babe," Conrad said, following her outside.

Since when did Conrad call her, or anyone, *babe*?

"Could we meet up, talk, get some things straightened out?" He grinned and shrugged and jammed his hands into his back pockets.

"Sure," she said without thinking. She flinched, hating how easily she gave in. Usually, she adored that shy little boy gesture Conrad always used on her and his grandmother, when he teased to get his way.

"Great!" He grinned and pulled out his phone in a camouflage pattern case. What happened to the ribbed, clear plastic case with the pocket for business cards? He had nearly kissed her in gratitude when she found it for him last year. "Tomorrow? Dinner? Give me your—" He shook his head. "Give me your number, okay?"

"You've got my number." She shivered, despite the heat beating down on her shoulders, the dry air reaching down her throat.

"New phone. New email. Got hacked bad, had to trash everything, start over. Nothing transferred, the hacking was that bad."

"Oh." That made sense. She almost asked him if that was why he hadn't responded to her texts when she was on her way back to the States. But Conrad could have gotten her email and phone from Devona and Rufus as soon as he replaced his phone.

Plus, there was that look on Saturday, like he didn't know who she was. When she caught him with Simone, getting ready to have a picnic.

She gave him her number, and he promised when he had checked his calendar, he'd call her that evening to make arrangements. Becca thought about asking him if he had had a cold on Saturday, because the rasp was gone, although his voice did seem a few notes deeper. She considered teasing him that he had probably forgotten where she lived, but some shiver of instinct stopped her.

Conrad leaned against the black pickup that was the only other car in the customer parking at Frenchy's, watching her as she pulled out of the lot and headed down Ivy to Longview. What had happened to the dark green SUV with the Fontaine Realty sign on the doors?

So many changes and questions. She wavered between wanting answers and wanting to just wash Conrad out of her life. Had too much time passed? Had he changed too much while she was out of the country for them to go back to what they had started to build? What about what Sarah had said on Sunday? What about the long silence? What about Simone, hanging on him like he had surrendered and was the prize in the war Becca had never declared?

When Conrad called at nearly 10:30 that evening, Becca was tired.

She blamed that for how easily she agreed to meet him for dinner at Bluebird Café in Medina, on Thursday, at 7:00. He would be out of town all day running errands but planned to be back as far as Medina by then. Becca regretted agreeing as soon as she put down her phone. She had spent too much time remembering all the good times she and Conrad had enjoyed together and thinking how happy Sarah would be if they fixed this somewhat large pothole in their relationship. Conrad had a lot of explaining to do before she could move forward with him. She couldn't pick up where they had left off. That was lost for good.

Thursday, July 7

"Well, Miss Sheridan ..." Roger Cadburn's lip started to curl up in his usual superior sneer, but he stopped himself.

Becca mentally slapped herself for explaining his better-than-usual manners on the fact that this was an election year.

"To what do we owe the honor?" He stepped up on the other side of the bin of scratch-and-dent sale items at the front of The Office.

Becca always checked there, even if she didn't need to replenish any office supplies. There was always some gadget or paper good that she wanted to try, but not at full price.

"Excuse me?" She knew better than to look around, to see which audience Roger was playing to today.

"Back in town." He huffed. "No longer out trying to make the world a better place."

"I always try to do that, no matter which side of the world I'm on." Two could play the fake smile game. "Is there something I can help you with, Mr. Cadburn?"

Doggone if she was going to address him as *Trustee*.

"Looking for steady employment?"

Becca felt like her face was going to crack, but she held onto her smile. "I have more than enough to do right now. Thanks. Back at you: to what do I owe the honor?"

"Now that you mention it, I can do you a favor. I hear your dancing friends are looking for a new meeting place. I happen to have three suitable locations."

"Thank you for offering. We won't be deciding on a new location until probably September. If we need a new location. Plenty of time."

Nothing in the world could persuade her to remark that his "suitable" locations were not suitable for the simple fact that he had already quoted Jack Butler a monthly fee three times what they had been paying at Windows on the River.

"Really?" Cadburn raised his eyebrows in totally unbelievable surprise. "That's not what I've heard. Oh, but then, you don't have access to the county inspector's files, do you?"

She wouldn't put it past Roger Cadburn to bribe or threaten someone to ensure that Windows never passed inspections, once the repairs had been completed, so Conrad could never re-open the meeting room for use.

"If you need help, you know where to find me," he added, and turned to head up the aisle toward the checkout.

Becca pretended to rummage through the bin for a few minutes more, though she honestly couldn't remember what she looked at, or any of the prices or damage she saw. She knew exactly where to find Roger Cadburn, but she had learned in third grade not to pick up stones to see what slimy creatures lived under them. Finally, when she couldn't think of anything else to check out in the store, she made her way to the front of the store. She waved to Megan at the counter and headed out the door. The sudden change from cool and dry to steamy-hot made her pause and catch her breath. Could she justify a stop at Book & Mug for something frozen and highly caffeinated before –

"Ooh. Watch where you're going!"

Becca took a step back, about to retort that she was the one standing still and the overly perfumed, jangly woman had almost run into her. Conrad stopped short, wrapping his arm around Simone as she wobbled on her stilettos. She glared at Becca, and several drops of sweat knocked loose along her hairline to race down into her eyes. Another squeal, and she swiped at her face, dislodging a layer of blue makeup on her left eye.

"What are you doing here?" Becca blurted.

"Oh, that takes a lot of nerve," Simone squealed.

"Conrad, I thought you were running errands in Akron all day today," she continued, raising her voice before Simone launched into her usual diatribe, listing all her complaints for the day.

"I was – I mean, I am – I mean I was planning on it, but ..." Conrad shrugged.

"He got a better offer," Simone said, and leaned into him further.

In this heat, how could they stand being so close? Becca supposed Simone did it to ensure Conrad couldn't run away at the drop of a hat.

Oh, I am so nasty ...

She didn't feel particularly repentant. Not after that run-in with Roger Cadburn, and now Simone with her overpowering perfume that made Becca's nose burn. How did Conrad manage to keep breathing, enveloped in the cloud like that?

"Okay ... then do you want to change our arrangements for tonight?"

"Tonight?" Conrad blinked.

His voice had that rasp again. Maybe that overdose of perfume affected his sinuses or his tonsils or whatever.

"Connie and I have plans for tonight," Simone said. "Whatever you're thinking about, you've got it wrong. Right, Connie?"

"Yeah. Absolutely. Messed up communication." He nodded. "Don't know where you got the idea we had plans."

That wrinkle between his eyes told her he was confused, and panicking. Something inside her rose up, with claws.

"Okay, then are you going to tell Miss Sarah we're not coming over to sign that paperwork and transfer those funds?" she said, and nearly laughed aloud at how easy that lie spilled from her lips. "Too bad, I was really looking forward to trying that new recipe for coffee cheesecake she was talking about." Becca shrugged. "So, cancel tonight, right?"

"Yeah, right."

"Good to know." She offered them the smile reserved for clients she hoped never to work with again and turned to leave. "Later!"

"Uh, hey, Becks?"

So he was back to calling her Becks?

"Yes?" She paused but didn't turn around to look at him.

"Could you call Granny and cancel?"

"You were the one who wanted the meeting, so you can cancel it." Becca resumed walking and heard frantic whispering between the two of them. She couldn't make out the words, just the argument tones. *Yeah, I really am nasty. And I am not sorry at all. Those two deserve each other.*

~~~~~

Becca's phone rang at 7 that evening. She ignored it and put it on vibrate. The sacred hour was from 7 to 8, first *Wheel of Fortune*, then *Jeopardy*. Everyone who knew her knew not to call.

At 7:15 her phone lit up and vibrated, displaying a number she didn't recognize. While she was looking at it, a text came through.

Are you coming? Conrad.

"The man is a nutcase," she said on a sigh, and put her phone down.

Seconds later, she changed it to screen side down, so she could concentrate on the scared-witless contestant who forgot the rules and put "and" between each word when he tried to solve the crossword portion of the game. The sad thing was, he got all the words right, he just added "and," and lost. Meaning he handed the game to the next person in line.

Her phone hummed at her again just before the commercial break before the bonus round. Just once, Becca wished someone would mess up and agree with Pat Sajak when he jokingly offered them the choice to skip the bonus round. To be fair, she sympathized totally with the contestants. She might make just as many ridiculous mistakes if she were playing, with cameras on her and knowing in a few months the entire English-speaking world could be watching her messing up.
~~~~~

"Leave me alone, or at least make up your mind," she said, reaching for her phone. Another query from Conrad. What was his problem? This one, she had to answer.

??? You canceled tonight. 10:45 today, in front of The Office. Simone was there.

She considered blocking Conrad's number, then tucked her phone under the seat cushion. Nothing was going to stop her watching tonight's *Jeopardy*. Would the current champion make it ten games in a row, or go down in defeat?

The closing credits and music for *Wheel* were playing when Devona tapped on her back door. She and Rufus had just gotten home. Did she want to join them to watch *Jeopardy*? Had she had dinner? They had the party pack from Seaver's Cleaver. A bowl of cereal did not count as dinner, and she didn't want to be alone with her TV, especially if her phone rang again. Becca accepted gladly.

Dinner and *Jeopardy* turned into several rounds of Skip-Bo and talking about the missionary schools and catching up on what had been going on in the Singles group at church. When Becca went back to her side of the duplex to get her phone and share photos, she noted that Conrad hadn't called or texted back.

Friday, July 8

Becca was in the library that morning, trying very hard to ignore the hissing whispers of Twila and Officer Carruthers. She had pages in several books she needed to photocopy and get out of there before Twila noticed she was there. The front desk librarian had finally caught on that Becca worked for Charli Hall, whom she had an unreasonable grudge against.

Ashley Cadburn came dancing through the door as Becca reached for the second of four books. Always color-coordinated, jewelry and nail polish and clothes, today she was in lime green. She released the hand of her stepdaughter, Daphne, bent to kiss the top of the little girl's curly head, and gave her a nudge toward the corner of the library with the floor pillows and all sorts of plush toys. For all her flaws, Ashley truly did love Daphne. Too bad she had the bad taste to fall for Roger Cadburn. Yet what did that say about Roger's first wife, Deirdre?

Becca didn't want to think about that. It would make her head hurt.

"You'll never guess what I saw just now," Ashley hiss-whispered, joining Carruthers and Twila at the front desk.

Becca slowed down what had become a smooth, efficient routine of taking the marker paper out of the book, putting the book face-down on the copier, inserting the dime for her copy, and pressing the button. She would have to walk past the front desk on her way out. With Ashley joining the gossip circle, Carruthers would linger, probably until someone noticed the patrol car parked in front of the library and called the police station to ask what emergency had a police officer in the library so long.

"Conrad Price with a black eye and a fat lip," Ashley continued, wriggling slightly in glee. "Somebody finally gave that crook what he deserves."

Becca pressed the copier button and let the hum of the old mechanism drown out their voices for five seconds. She sped up now, because she did not want to linger and hear them gloating or speculating on which of Roger Cadburn's yes-men had done the deed.

Still, curiosity got the better of her. She went into Book & Mug, making a slight detour before dropping the copies off at Charli's townhouse. She had earned an iced drink, and it really was hot today. The question was whether she could justify lingering until she heard someone gossiping and Conrad's name came up. Or maybe she should bring the subject up herself and get it over with.

Her phone chimed with a text just as she was reaching for her frozen limeade. Becca stepped aside, put the drink down on a conveniently empty table, and pulled out her phone.

Sorry about last night. Make-up? Tonight? Conrad

She didn't have to think more than a few seconds for her answer.

Can't. Obligations. Going out of town. Thanks.

She didn't owe him anything, such as clarifying that she wasn't leaving until very early tomorrow morning to drive up to the lake and spend a week on Old Man Island with Charli and her writing friends, Rita, Megan, and Tamera. Megan's family owned the island that used to be a fashionable resort around the turn of the last century. Her very large family shared it among four generations, numbering over sixty people now. The main house was a forty-bedroom hotel, so no matter how many people showed up for a week or weekend or a month, there was always plenty of room. Such were the perks of being a virtual assistant and good friends with the people she worked for. Inexpensive vacations and sneak previews of fascinating new books.

Becca took her time wandering around the bookstore, sipping her limeade and waiting for the phone to chime at her. Silence. No argument from Conrad, no offer to get together another night. That wasn't like him.

She finally gave up on finding a book that caught her interest. To be honest, she really hadn't been looking. With a nod to Peggy at the register, and then a wave to Mike behind the counter, she headed for the door.

And nearly collided with Conrad, coming in, sweating, and looking harassed.

With a slightly swollen, very purple eye, just starting to brown around the edges, and a swollen lip. His eyes widened when he saw her, and he winced. She was about to open her mouth to ask if he was stalking her, and how did he know where she was, anyway?

"Hi. Sorry. Can't stick around and talk." Conrad turned and hurried down the sidewalk.

Was that fear she saw in his face, heard in that wobble in his voice? That didn't make any sense.

Conrad Price just flat out didn't make any sense lately.

Chapter Five

Monday, July 18

Eden went down to the first floor of Book & Mug in the brass cage elevator. Devona and Sarah were waiting, looking far too pale and somber for so early on a bright summer morning. Silently, she pushed the gate aside and stepped out, to let them get in. Rufus was waiting in the office for them to join him, and he had the same expression, as if they had all received grave news.

"Anybody see you?" he greeted them. One side of his mouth crooked up in response to Eden's frowning glance. "Maybe you haven't noticed, but things are getting kind of weird around here."

"You mean besides Raymond showing up every couple weeks and you running interference like you've got an ankle monitor on him?" Eden shook her head and led the way to the conference table. "Nope, not a thing."

"You're a dear," Sarah said with a sigh. Devona pulled out a seat for her. "We need your help pulling off a … a nasty little trick, I suppose. Or rather, what we hope will just be a nasty trick, and jolt some sense into people who should know better."

"If anybody can handle the sneaky stuff," Rufus said, before Eden could ask, "we figure you have the connections. We need you to persuade the Worters to help us. The thing is, when I was handling all those computer problems for Conrad and looking for hackers, back in the spring, I kind of left some back doors open."

"On my request," Sarah hurried to add. "Something strange is going on with the company funds, and I truly fear that all Conrad's oddness the last month or so is related to something nasty, using the business to cover it up or make it seem legitimate. If I'm right – I pray the good Lord I'm right – he's been protecting me, keeping me in the dark. If I'm wrong …" She shrugged.

"Mama Sarah's in danger," Devona said. "We need your help making sure she gets out of danger and stays safe."

"Sure." Eden settled in the seat next to Sarah and took hold of her hand. "Whatever you need. I'm here for you."

Saturday, July 30

This was wrong. So very, very wrong.

Becca stood in the back of the sanctuary at Cadburn Bible Chapel, watching as Conrad settled into the left side of the center front pew all by himself. He had been moving like a sleepwalker for the last three days, ever since word came that Sarah had died on a trip with Devona and Rufus.

He shouldn't be alone, but his parents were out of the country and couldn't get back to Ohio for two weeks. Why they couldn't wait for Julia to attend her mother's funeral, Conrad hadn't been willing to explain. Becca didn't have the right to sit with him, although she knew Sarah would have wanted her there. Rufus and Devona sat on the far right of the pew, with lots of distance between them and Conrad. Sarah's sons and their wives and the grandsons hadn't showed up yet. Becca had the awful feeling Conrad hadn't notified them yet. If he had, maybe they had the tact not to show up, after the ugly scene they created when Albert died. And that thought led to another awful suspicion she kept trying to avoid: what if he hadn't notified his parents? But why would Conrad lie about something like that? Why had he done any of the uncharacteristic things he had done lately?

Simone was nowhere in sight. How could she not know Sarah had died? Maybe she had the courtesy not to show up because she didn't have anything appropriate to wear in church to a funeral? Becca knew she was being catty, but chances were good Simone had black sequins among all her flashy, glittery clothes. Where was she? Didn't she care about Conrad? Why wasn't she at the funeral, playing devoted, supportive girlfriend?

Yet what kind of funeral was this? There was no body. Sarah had left instructions donating her body to medical science at Case Western Reserve University. Pastor Roy and Patty had been chosen to carry out the funeral arrangements for her, taking everything out of Conrad's hands. And the hands of her estranged sons. Rumors were already flying that Sarah had left a drawn-out timetable for handling the disbursal of her estate and control of the family trust and the business. Simone's cousin, Angelica, worked for Worter, Worter & McIntosh, the Fontaine family lawyers, so maybe she was the source of the rumors. Maybe Simone wasn't here because she already knew Conrad was getting nothing?

Which begged the question: What had happened between Sarah and Conrad before she died, that she would change the family trust? Maybe that plan to work with his cousin Raymond and mend the family rift had worked after all? Maybe too well? Maybe the three estranged sons were getting everything after all?

"Full house?" Moira Usher whispered, stepping up to the doorway beside Becca.

"And getting fuller," she whispered back.

Becca offered a smile for the older woman and resumed counting the people still walking up the aisles and filling the pews. She had agreed to do the preliminary head count at the start of the service, to make sure there was enough food for the funeral luncheon. The other ladies on the hospitality committee were very kind to give her the task, as the new member. Someone had to step in now that Sarah, the mainstay of the committee, was gone. More experienced hands were busy decorating tables and arranging the buffet line and making sure there were enough urns of coffee, tea, and punch, plates and napkins and utensils. Becca couldn't seem to wrap her mind around the calculations needed to translate dozens of casseroles and plates of baked goods and bowls of potato salad and trays of lunchmeat and cheese into the amounts necessary to feed the mourners. She would learn. If only to make Sarah proud of her.

"Please, God, help Conrad through this? And let this service go off in peace? No nastiness?" she whispered. Time to take her estimated count to the ladies at the other end of the church in the fellowship hall. The organ music was changing key, a clear sign the service was about to begin.

A muffled clatter of metal behind her made her flinch. Ushers pulled a long cart of folding chairs through the doors into the narthex. At least twenty people waited to find seats. A standing-room-only crowd was more than fitting for Sarah Fontaine's farewell.

Monday, August 29

"What do you think?" Ginny spread the turquoise and lavender gingham swatches across the picnic table on the north side of Cadburn Township municipal park.

"I like them … " Becca held onto her pleasant smile. The women in Four Corners would love those colors for their new shirts, but a new problem had popped into her head. "Um, Ginny … is that as far as you've gotten? The parade is in one week. Rehearsal is Friday, dress rehearsal is Saturday."

"Don't you worry." Ginny swept the swatches into her enormous square-bottom tote bag that sometimes matched the capacity of Mary Poppins's carpet bag. "I have a middlers sewing class who can get these shirts cut out and basted together tomorrow, and have everything finished off, buttons and buttonholes and all the ricrac by Thursday."

"Okay." She tried to take a couple discreet but deep breaths.

"We're gonna put those dippy-tippies back in their place, just on dignity points. Maureen was having hysterics last week over the costumes

Madame Hitler insists they have to wear. There's more sequins and neon green marabou than anything else. I spied in her project basket." Ginny snickered and looked around, to make sure she had swept up all the bits and pieces she had been showing the other leaders of the club.

"I heard some of them are ready to go on strike." Will Hanks stepped up to lean against the support pillar for the picnic pavilion. "Some of them are saying they'd feel less exposed if they were wearing string bikinis."

Becca sighed and swallowed down a half-dozen responses. She was trying to be a better Christian, and that meant not adding to the popular sport of trash-talking Simone. But those costumes certainly sounded right for her taste and style. Glitz meant more to her than comfort. Simone had also clearly forgotten what it was like to dance down the street on a hot Labor Day afternoon.

Greg snapped out several muffled curses and raised his cell phone like he was about to slam it to the ground. His face reddened as everybody gathered around the picnic table turned to look at him.

"Sorry, ladies. Gents." He nodded in apology. "That lying moron over at the Barn suckered us again."

"Now what?" Becca half-whispered.

It seemed like every other meeting of Four Corners had to be held here in the park, because of some structural problem at the Barn. Becca tried to be grateful for a roof over their heads, but was it too much to ask to have floors that didn't shake, with a chance of being dive-bombed by the occasional stray pigeon or cats walking far above them and knocking down thirty years of dirt? On the plus side, whenever they met and practiced in the township park, they had picked up a couple new members, but this was the end of August and the weather would start turning. They needed a regular, reliable indoor meeting place, and soon. The school gyms were out once the school year started. None of the nearby churches had gyms to borrow.

"According to the county inspectors ..." Greg shook his head and bent over to dip two fingers into Ginny's bag and pull out the gingham swatches again. His lips puckered up like he had bitten into a dill pickle filled with horseradish. Ginny slapped at him, and he stepped back snickering. "There's no way for the Barn to meet safety code standards by our next meeting, or the next ten."

"I'm sorry," Becca said.

"Oh, honey, it's not your fault." Ginny reached over to pat her hand. "Roger is a vindictive little snot who's still punishing boys who beat him in the spelling bee in third grade."

Becca appreciated Ginny's support, but she still felt guilty. When she turned down Roger Cadburn's offer to rent space in one of his buildings, he had alerted county officials about the sad conditions at the Barn.

Inspections that had been neglected for years were now overdue.

"Thanks, but it's my responsibility to get us a meeting space." Becca shrugged. "I'll get to work on that. Hopefully not in another county."

Please, God ... have Conrad in a good mood when I approach him?

Rumors said Windows on the River was open for rentals again. Several groups with fundraising dinners had talked him into letting them use the room. The stories of loose flooring and odd smells had dissipated in the last few weeks. However, the stories of Conrad being even more irritable had increased. Along with complaints about being hard to reach, and the door of the stairs to Windows staying locked. Becca feared securing that big, beautiful room was as likely as Cadburn Creek flooding its banks during this dry, hot summer.

If only Sarah had come through on her threat to have a "come to Jesus moment" with Conrad, whack him good with her knitting bag if necessary, and straighten out his head before she went on that little trip and died of the euphemistic "natural causes."

Time to take a deep breath, practice those mental calming exercises she used for her most difficult clients, and hunt down Conrad Price. The Four Corners were depending on her.

"It'd be great if we got Windows back. Maybe don't go straight to Conrad?" Will said. "That one cousin keeps showing up every few weeks." A horn sounded in the parking lot south of them. He turned and waved. Becca didn't even try to identify which of his many grandchildren had come to pick him up this afternoon. "Rumors say the sons are contesting the conditions of the family trust. If Becca makes friends with this Raymond guy, maybe he can put in a good word for her when the Fontaines yank everything out of Conrad's hands. Sorry to say, but there ain't many who would feel sorry for him if he lost everything. The guy's had a complete personality transplant. I'm talking brain tumor, of the soap opera variety."

"What makes you think they'd want to come back, with everybody knowing how they treated Albert and Sarah?" Brad West said, punctuated with a snort. "With our luck, they'll sell everything at a discount."

"Well, look on the bright side. Cadburn can't afford to get his hands on the property," Melanie Jones commented in her dry-as-dust voice. "I'd love to see him squirm and scramble to find someone stupid enough to loan him the money. You know that's what he lives for, why he keeps running for trustee. If his family can't own the whole town, then he needs to have political power over everybody and everything."

"He can *think* he has that power all he wants," Will said. "Doesn't mean he has it. Come November, he's out on his arrogant backside."

That comment earned chuckles from the rest of the group gathered around the picnic table. Everyone agreed they'd start asking questions --

discreetly, to keep the TippyToes club from learning they were again hunting for a meeting space.

The group gathered up the paperwork and footwork diagrams they had been conferring over. Sunset colors were just starting to streak the sky as their group reached the street running along the western edge of the park and paused to check traffic before crossing.

Becca mulled the challenge ahead of her as she headed west down Center. She didn't mean to, but her gaze crossed the street, to the long expanse of windows in the second story that gave Windows on the River its name.

Movement in the doorway into the lobby had her turning away. With her luck, that white-blond head and forest green shirt would be Conrad.

She focused on the door of Book & Mug. After all the hard work she had done today, for Four Corners and three new clients, she had earned a mocha chip frozen whip. And maybe she would check out the new arrivals shelf in the bookstore. That was always a good place to lose herself and enjoy the air conditioning.

~~~~~

Kai spotted Becca, sitting in a booth and scribbling in one of her ever-present notepads as she sipped a frozen drink. He pulled out his phone and texted Eden.

Becca here. Keep her?

She responded in less than a minute.

Yes! Finishing a call. Down in five.

Kai kept an eye on Becca, not hard with so few people in Book & Mug at this time of day. Eden had been talking about taking on Becca part-time to help her with some of the research chores that required hands-on digging through records and documents that weren't digitally stored. Becca had a good reputation as a virtual assistant and researcher, which dovetailed perfectly with Eden's investigative business.

He looked up a few minutes later to see her close her notepad. Eden hadn't come downstairs yet. That phone call was taking longer than she estimated. Kai was about to step from behind the counter and cross over to the booth to ask her to wait when the door thudded open. Raymond Fontaine stomped in. Kai smiled, relieved that Devona had left to drive up to an estate sale in Toledo.

Olivia stepped up to the counter to meet Raymond. "What'll it be?" she said, offering her most cheerful smile. Kai silently ordered the man to be there for coffee, not harassment.

The door banged open, startling Raymond's scowl off his face for a few seconds. Conrad stomped into the coffee shop.

"I told you to leave them alone," he barked.

"Who put you in charge?" Raymond shot back. He sounded more
~~~~~

tired than angry. "Not Granny."

"You've got no right to call her that." Conrad stepped up, reaching out like he would shove Raymond back against the counter. "You never even talked to her until Grandad died. And anyway, I'm just backing up what Devona has been saying all along. Leave her alone."

"Not until she tells me why. Is that too much to ask?" He turned and looked around the coffee shop. Everyone was either watching them or making a visible effort to ignore the confrontation. "The things I've been hearing make me wonder if you've got a vested interest in keeping us all locked out, and in control of Devona."

"Oooh," he sneered, "get all mysterious, why don't you? I'm not going to ask. Oldest trick in the book. I don't play games like that."

"No, you just play games that make our grandmother lock up the family estate and put in all sorts of conditions and make sure you can't do anything, can't sell anything, until this big family meeting next month. Why the wait? Why aren't you in charge, like you expected?"

"None of your business."

"Yeah, real mature answer."

Kai figured he was about three minutes late intervening. Then again, Conrad used to be someone he liked to see come into Book & Mug. They hadn't talked much lately. Most of their interactions had been a nod, a raised eyebrow, a shared glance of disgust during trustee meetings when a Cadburn supporter strayed too far from reality.

"Sorry about the scene," Raymond said, turning to him. "Is Devona here? I just want to talk to her."

"Yeah, and get her to let you read Granny's letter," Conrad spat.

"What letter?"

Conrad's eyes shifted right and left, then he raised his hands in apparent surrender and exhaled a ragged chuckle.

"No, Devona's out of town on business," Kai said. "I'll tell her you stopped by. Again."

"Thanks." Raymond nodded to him and made a wide detour around Conrad to head to the door.

Conrad looked around, his face taking on that sharp, calculating look that always made Kai think he didn't know the man standing there. Several customers finished up their drinks or took their to-go orders and detoured around him on their way to the door. Becca sat still, looking down into her empty mug. From where he was standing, Kai couldn't tell if she was breathing or not. He wondered if she was doing what he had done when he was a child in uncomfortable situations like this, wishing herself invisible and silently begging Conrad to just turn and walk out.

The only thing that could make this moment more uncomfortable was if Simone pranced into Book & Mug and gave Conrad a big effusive greeting. Rubbing it in once again that she had won the rivalry that, according to town gossip, had existed since middle school. Kai didn't believe it. He thought Becca was too smart, had too much good sense, to compete with Simone Radcliffe over anything.

"Wager on how fast he gets out of here?" Olivia murmured, sidling up next to Kai. "And if he creates a sonic boom as he leaves?"

He muffled a chuckle and gestured for her to be quiet. Kai added a few silent repetitions of, "Go on, get," to whatever Becca might be thinking. Instead of leaving, like he usually did when he encountered Becca in public, Conrad just stood there, watching her. She raised her head. Her expression didn't change as she met his gaze.

Good for her. Don't give him any satisfaction. Make him make the first move.

Kai wondered what was taking Eden so long. She might want to see this, whatever happened next, just because she was irked with Conrad too.

"Hey, Becks," Conrad said, gesturing to her.

"Uh oh," Olivia murmured. She took a step back from the counter and crossed her arms. "This is gonna be good. At least, I hope so."

"What?" Kai stepped closer, to hear her, and get a better view as Conrad approached Becca's booth.

"For one thing, Becca hates the nickname Becks. Simone always uses it for her," Olivia said. "For another—"

"Hi, Conrad," Becca said, her voice clear, sounding tired. Maybe wary, or did Kai just imagine that? "Could we talk?"

"Uh … yeah. That'd be good. I need to talk to you about a few things. Granny asked me to … Not here, though." Conrad looked around the shop again. Kai didn't even bother turning his head to make it look like he hadn't been watching.

"I want to talk to you about Windows—"

"Why? What have you heard?" He took two steps back.

"Nothing."

"Then why do you want to talk about it?"

"Just business." Becca held onto that pleasantly neutral expression.

"What kind? I don't know what they've been telling you about Granny's will, but I'd bet it's all wrong. The lawyer isn't meeting with us until a whole bunch of stupid conditions are taken care of, and that could be another month, maybe two."

She shook her head. "Nobody has said anything to me about it, but I do know Miss Sarah set up a trust, not a will."

"Yeah? And what else do you think you know?"

"Conrad, I'm trying to discuss business, having to do with Windows. Can we leave personal things out of this?"

"Yeah, fine, whatever." A pinging sound came from his pocket. He pulled out his phone and scowled at the screen. "Just not now."

"When?" She stood up as he took a step backward toward the door.

"I'll call you. Or come by the office."

"Windows?" She hooked her thumb over her shoulder, across the street at the building.

"No!" Conrad's voice rang off the ceiling and tile floor. He hunched his shoulders. "I'm consolidating things. Should have done it years ago."

"Really? You mean, you're finally using all the plans we were making for consolidating?" She flinched as her voice threatened to crack.

"We did?" Conrad flinched. "Oh, yeah, right, those plans." He shrugged, offering a grin that just didn't fit with the guy Kai used to know. "Forgot. Too much going on lately."

"You're telling me," Olivia muttered. She wrinkled up her nose at Kai, as if she expected him to scold her to be quiet.

"Whatever." He backed toward the door. "I'll call you, okay?"

Before Becca could respond, he slammed out through the door. She got up and brought her mug to the bus pan on the counter.

"Funny," Eden said, startling Kai as she stepped into the edge of his vision. "I remember you two sitting here at the counter, talking about that, and him teasing you that you couldn't leave the country until all that work was done. How could he forget that?"

"The big bozo's been brainwashed, that's what," Olivia said. "All that perfume of Simone's kills brain cells." She swept up the full bus pan and headed for the kitchen.

Bekka managed a half-hearted chuckle. She adjusted the strap of her tote on her shoulder and nodded to Kai and Eden as she turned to leave.

"Hold on," Eden said. "Are you in a hurry to get anywhere?"

"Home. Put my feet up. Figure out how to talk Conrad into staying in one place long enough to conduct business." She shrugged.

"I want to talk with you about coming on part-time, helping me with research projects. Interested?"

"Always." Becca's face brightened.

"Got time right now?" Eden gestured toward the door at the back of the shop, into the stairwell.

Kai wasn't sure why he was holding his breath. He let it out in a rush when Eden and Becca vanished through the door, heading upstairs. Then the handbell choir from Living Word Baptist came in for their weekly after-practice coffee-and-brainstorming session, closely followed by the historical fiction book club, and he didn't have time to consider the question for a good twenty minutes.

Lisa Pascal came in about the time the book club had settled into the seating area behind the bookstore portion. She let the strap of her overloaded tote slide off her shoulder and down to the floor and flexed her newly freed joint a few times before responding to Kai's greeting.

"Is it quitting time yet?" she added, after placing her order.

"Uh, depends what time zone you're in. Rough day?"

Lisa always ordered the frozen special of the day. He had four blender carafes sitting in the cooler, waiting to be whipped a second time. Kai pulled out the front one and put it in the blender dock.

"Month. And getting rougher. On top of a bunch of idiots contesting estates they have no legitimate claim to, now we're dealing with a twit-who-shall-not-be-named, suing us for unlawful termination because we caught her taking pictures of sealed documents. She insists since she didn't send them to anyone, and the pictures were removed from her phone, she didn't actually do anything wrong. As if working as a secretary at a law firm confers a law degree?"

"My brain catches on the word 'sealed,'" he offered, and pressed the button for punctuation.

"Exactly!" She raised her voice to be heard over the blender whirring. "Oh, baby, come to mama," she whimpered as he poured the frosty, dark chocolate and espresso concoction into the largest hurricane glass Book & Mug owned. "Plus the fact it was in a senior partner's filing cabinet, inside a pocket folder. She had three of those gold seals waiting to replace the ones she was very careful to peel off the file. Kind of makes a lie of her claim that she was just curious, the seals were loose and came open before she realized they were there. And oh, yeah, she was just checking something for a friend, no harm no foul."

"Who's the friend?" Kai expected her to say she couldn't say, because that would give away the legal case and parties involved. Lisa loved to grumble and chatter, but she had a sharp mind and knew just where to stop, so she could never violate confidentiality.

"She refuses to say, and she was using a burner phone, with no addresses or phone numbers on it." She snagged a straw from the holder studded with cat's eye marbles, peeled it, and stabbed it into her drink.

"Y'know, that kind of sounds like premeditation to me."

"And the fact she's supposed to be at the other end of the building, nowhere near any of the senior offices." She took a long pull on her drink and sagged dramatically against the counter. "You have saved my life once again. Remind me to name my firstborn after you."

Kai just laughed. Now they were edging into their normal routine. At least three nights a week, Lisa worked long past closing hours, and came into Book & Mug for something to fortify her for the long, exhausting, ten-minute walk to her loft apartment on Shackle Avenue. She had worked her way up from clerking in high school to becoming office manager and executive assistant to both Worter brothers. The firm of Worter, Worter & McIntosh had supposedly been a fixture in Cadburn Township since Edward Worter followed Matilda Cadburn home from

Boston, begging her to marry him.

"Eden in?" Lisa asked, after a third pull and wincing, as she always did, from drinking frozen whip too fast.

"Upstairs. Is she expecting you?"

"Not officially. Would it be okay if I just went on up?"

The mischief had died from Lisa's eyes. Despite her smile and careless shrug, this was important. Kai didn't have to think for more than a few seconds. Whatever Eden was discussing with Becca, it wouldn't be classified or confidential. Not this soon.

Conrad stomped through the door. "Just what I thought," he spat. "You keep dodging me, Lisa, and I'm sick of it."

"I'm not dodging you." She took two steps forward and glared up at him. "You don't answer any of my calls."

"What calls?" He dug into his back pocket, whipped out his phone, and tapped hard enough his nails clicked on the screen. "Here. See?" He scrolled down. "All my calls the last few days. None of them from you."

"So we're gonna play that game?" Her cheeks flared hot pink and she gave Kai a sideways, clearly apologetic glance. She dug her phone out of her purse and went through the same motions as Conrad. "I called you six times just today. If you'd answer your phone—"

"No calls." He waved the phone screen in front of her.

Lisa's jaw muscles visibly clenched. She glared at him, with enough force to stop whatever he had been about to say next. Kai managed not to cheer. She tapped her phone, apparently putting it on speaker, because the sound of ringing followed her final tap.

Silence. Her glare cooled down several degrees. Conrad smirked and held his phone even closer to her.

"Notice it's not ringing?"

Kai shook his head and didn't care if Conrad saw or not. He hadn't needed to say that.

"Hey, this is Conrad Price," said a pleasant voice Conrad no longer seemed to use. "I'm busy somewhere, doing something. Leave your name and number and what you want to talk about, and I'll get back to you."

Lisa hit the red phone icon and lowered the phone. "That's the number I've been calling. For the last two weeks. Don't tell me I've been dodging you."

"Must have picked up the wrong phone," Conrad muttered.

"Just how many phones do you have?"

"One for each face?" Olivia muttered. Fortunately, Conrad didn't seem to hear.

"This is the number you gave me, when the mess started with the Fontaines last winter," Lisa said, punctuated by jamming her phone back into her purse. "If you've got a new number, you should have given it to me. Especially since you seem anxious to talk to me."

"Try moving from anxious to frantic and pretty much pissed off! News flash. I'm responsible for protecting Granny's interests. There's something really nuts about all the errands everybody has to run, the letters different people are entrusted with, all the secrecy. What's the matter? Didn't Granny trust her own lawyers, she has to ask other people to protect her instructions about the family estate?"

"Where did you hear that?" Lisa went utterly still. Kai felt the chill emanating off her from five feet away, with the counter between them.

"What do you mean, where did I hear it?" Conrad flushed and looked around. "It's common knowledge."

"Uh, no, it's not. The only people who know about the letters and lists are Bill Worter and me. We took care of everything when Miss Sarah made all her changes the week before she died." She took a step forward, and despite being nearly two feet shorter than Conrad, she made him back up. "Oh, yeah, and the idiot who broke into the locked filing cabinet to read the cover sheet with the list of names."

"I don't know what you're talking about." His voice wobbled with an effort to laugh.

"I sure hope you paid enough money to cover her legal fees."

"Why would I have to pay anyone to see my grandmother's —"

"Because she's Simone's cousin with a single-digit IQ, that's why!" Lisa's voice bounced off the racks of glass mugs on the counter to her right.

"You're kidding me, right? How would I know Simone's cousin works for you guys?"

"Worked. Past tense." She glanced away from Conrad to her glass.

"To-go cup?" Kai asked.

"You are my hero." She fluttered her eyelashes at him and bent to pick up her tote and sling it over her shoulder. "If you've got questions about everybody's chores to prepare for the estate meeting, then you need to talk to Bill. In the office. Not me. Not in a public place. He's probably still there, if you want to check." She gave Kai a smile that only partially revealed the strain she had to be feeling, took her tall paper cup, and turned to the front doors. "Tell Eden I'll stop by tomorrow on my way in?"

"You got it." Kai nodded.

The few people who had been watching the exchange stayed still and silent. Conrad bowed his head, glowering, and if Kai wasn't mistaken, muttering under his breath. When had he started doing that? The man was definitely falling apart.

Lisa paused with one hand out to push the door open. "Coming?"

"Got some meetings tonight." Conrad hunched his shoulders and wouldn't look at her.

"Is one of them with Becca Sheridan?"

"Why?"

"Miss Sarah put that on the list of things she wanted you to do."

His shoulders twitched, like a partial shrug.

"She wanted you two to get back together. Why you broke up with Becca is a total mystery to anybody who knows both of you."

"Come on. If Becks wanted us together, she could have said something." He tried to smile.

"So, so wrong," Olivia whispered. She snorted when Kai widened his eyes and gave a slight shake of his head. Now was not the time to attract Conrad's attention and ire. She grinned and stepped from behind the counter, to vanish around the corner.

"Why should she try? For one thing, her name is Becca," Lisa said, voice cool. "Not Becks. And you used up your seventy times seven a long time ago." She turned, nudged the door open with her hip, and was gone.

"What is her problem?" Conrad asked the ringing silence that dominated Book & Mug after the door closed behind Lisa. He sauntered up to the counter and leaned on it with a loud sigh. "Women. The man who finally figures them out should get the Pulitzer."

Kai nearly choked on the need to tell Conrad the Pulitzer was for the arts. He was pretty sure the other man meant the Nobel Prize. And he wasn't going to admit that he agreed sometimes with that assessment.

"Did you understand that craziness she was spouting?"

Kai figured claiming he didn't listen to private conversations probably would go right over Conrad's head.

Heck with it … "She was probably referring to the Bible, where Jesus said to forgive someone seventy times seven."

"Yeah?" Conrad frowned. "Seventy times … that's nearly five hundred times she's forgiven me?" He scratched the back of his head. "Forgive me for what?"

"You call her Becks every time you see her, and she keeps telling you that's not her name."

"Yeah, but don't girls love when you give them nicknames?"

"What manual did you get that from?" Kai leaned against the counter and mentally urged Conrad to get out of there.

"I don't know why she's ticked. I honestly don't."

"That's pretty obvious," Eden said, stepping out of the shadows on the other side of the counter.

Kai looked. Becca wasn't with her. Most likely, Eden had let her leave by the side door on Apple, to avoid the scene between Conrad and Lisa.

"Common sense says to ask," Eden continued. "And just for a hint: those stupid, sideways apologies you guys use all the time, 'oh, hey, if I made you mad, I'm sorry,' nope, they don't count."

Conrad shook his head, muttering about "women all stick together."

He watched Eden step behind the counter and scoop up a tall glass and a straw and walk to one of the coolers to lift out a frosty pitcher. With a smirk and a salute of two fingers tipped off the end of his eyebrow, he turned and headed out the door.

Kai watched Conrad through the growing shadows of evening. He jaywalked, as usual, and didn't bother looking for oncoming traffic as he crossed to the Windows building.

"Are we really that bad about apologizing?" he asked Eden, once she finished blending the drink and poured it into her glass.

"Hmm, most guys. But you and Troy learned your lessons early. Survival skills." She leaned on the counter and took a sip as she watched Conrad enter his building. "That man needs a keeper, but I wouldn't inflict him on Becca. She deserves better."

"Do I need a keeper?" Kai grinned. "Besides you?"

"Nah." She patted his cheek and stepped away, to duck under the pass-through of the counter. "I raised you and Troy right. You're both almost ready for whatever lucky girl snatches you up."

She walked away, vanishing back into the shadows of the back of the shop. The door to the stairwell clicked open, then sighed closed, and still Eden didn't call back the expected words: "Like Saundra."

Life had certainly become more interesting since Saundra Bailey came to town. Smart and fun and a good sense of humor, she fit in with the Guzzlers and got along with everyone she met. Well, almost everyone. The fact that she didn't let Trustee Cadburn and his supporters harass her just showed how smart she was.

Yeah, he could see himself and Saundra a year from now, laughing together about the recent crazy events. He liked that mental image. It almost made him feel sorry for Conrad.

Chapter Six

Tuesday, August 30

That morning, Becca stopped at Windows. The door was locked, the faded "temporarily closed" sign replaced with a new one. At the other end of the lobby, grumpy old Heinrich was complaining.

"Can't nobody build a security camera that can't be broken? What's it gonna take to feel safe in this town?"

What real danger was there in Cadburn? Other than that man who essentially killed himself breaking into the Mug building in the middle of the night, what sort of violent crime had there ever been in Cadburn? Yes, some of the trustee meetings got loud, so she feared violence would break out, but she knew more than half the audience wouldn't be upset if Roger Cadburn was on the receiving end.

Sighing, she leaned back against the wall, closed her eyes, and tried to think of her next step. She had a few free hours today, in between client appointments. Should she play what Rufus had started calling "frustration roulette" and try to catch Conrad at one of the Fontaine properties? He was never at his office. He was never home. She didn't even have the option of calling Sarah to find out if she knew what Conrad was working on that day and where he could be found.

Supposedly, there was a way to set up a homemade GPS by making a call to someone and creating a link between the two phones. She considered trying that if she couldn't catch up with Conrad in the next few days. Why didn't the man answer his phone?

Skimming through the contacts list on her phone with her thumb, she crossed the lobby and pushed the door open with the other hand. A tap on Conrad's name. She raised the phone to her ear as she listened to it ringing on the other end. "Figures," she muttered, getting the same voicemail message.

"Becca."

Had Conrad picked up the phone before the outgoing message finished? Flustered, she nearly ran into Conrad, who just smiled at her. A real smile, not that smirk or that crooked, almost placating smile like he expected her to wallop him without warning. Becca ended the call and slid the phone into her pocket.

"Hey, Conrad. I was just calling you."

"What a coincidence." He crossed his arms over his chest and tipped his head to the left, and his smile grew a little wider. "Did I scare you?"

"Startled. For the first time in weeks, I'm looking for you and you actually show up."

"Yeah, I heard you wanted to talk. About what?"

She blinked, wondering why he used that phrasing. She had told him she needed to talk to him, so how could he say he had *heard*, like other people told him?

"Windows." A growl threatened at the back of her throat when he shook his head, like he had no idea what she was talking about. She hooked her thumb upward, pointing to the second floor. "Renting—"

"We're still closed for repairs. Problems with the glue for the flooring. City inspectors. That sort of crap. And somebody's going around telling people I'm not going to be in charge, so people don't want to do business." He groaned and raked one hand through his hair. "Ever feel like just taking off? Put this one-horse town in the rearview mirror?"

"Uh … depends on where you're going when you take off." Becca's attention snagged on the rasp that touched his voice. She couldn't tell what emotion lay behind it, but it was strong, and not exactly pleasant.

"We could have some fun. Just think about it. Put all this behind …" His mouth flattened into a hard line and his eyes narrowed as his gaze went over her head, looking down the street. "One of these days, somebody needs to put that arrogant old … yeah, put him out of everybody's misery." He shook his head. "Look, I gotta take care of some things, but you and me, we do need to talk. Things got messed up, and I'm gonna make that moron pay. Just not now. Okay?"

"I have no idea what you're talking about, Conrad."

"No, you don't." He glanced past her again, then muttered something and turned and dashed across the street. Fortunately, there was no oncoming traffic in either direction. Becca watched him trot west down Center and turn north on Sackley.

Well, at least she had a partial answer. Windows was closed. How long did it take to get a wooden floor replaced and pass inspections? How much influence did Roger Cadburn have with all the county officials, that he could hold up inspections and approvals?

"Hey, you." A baritone voice startled her out of her musing. A hard, gnarled hand landed heavily on her shoulder. "Was that Conrad Price you were talking to?"

"Yes." She turned around and lost her breath. For a moment, she was looking at Albert Fontaine. But Albert from twenty years ago.

However, the Albert she had adored as Sunday school teacher and community leader and sponsor of Kiddie Safety Town had never worn that bitter, frustrated expression. She had never seen that anger simmering at the backs of his gray-blue eyes, or digging those deep crevices in his olive-toned skin.

"What's he doing? You know where he's going?"

"No." She twisted her shoulder out from under his grip.

His mouth curled up in a scowl. Then he stepped back, dropping his arm to his side.

"Nobody's able to get hold of Conrad lately," she said, when there was no apology forthcoming. "I've been trying to get hold of him to do business. Good luck catching up with him." She turned to leave.

"You know who I am?" He raised his hand like he would grab her shoulder again, then gave up.

"I'm guessing you're one of Sarah's sons who broke her heart." She braced herself for the cursing that churned behind those eyes.

"You don't know the whole story," he said, his voice softening. The heat in his gaze faded and he looked away.

"I know that everybody in this town loved Albert and Miss Sarah, and you won't get much sympathy if you go around snarling at everybody like you just did."

"I don't give a—" He muttered something and spat into the street. "All I want is for that boy to sit still and listen to me. His mother is listening to me. 'Frankie,' she says, 'you gotta help me. You're my big brother. My boy, something's wrong with him. Mama was scared of him right before she died. He's cutting everybody off and cutting everybody out.' How am I supposed to protect the family when the only one who knows what's going on won't talk?"

"Did you give him a chance to talk when you waltzed into town after Albert's funeral and demanded everything be handed over to you?" At least she knew his name now. What rude jerk didn't introduce himself?

"That ain't how it happened!" Frank Fontaine stomped over so close she had to lean back or his nose would be touching her forehead.

Becca put out one hand and planted it flat against his chest, pushing slightly as she backed up one step. Two steps. Her hand shook slightly when she lost contact with his hard, heaving chest, and she dropped her arm to her side so he wouldn't see her shaking.

"That's not up to me," she said.

"Becca, you okay?" Allen Kenward pulled up to the curb in a Cadburn patrol car. "Got a problem here?"

"No problem, officer." Frank seemed to deflate as he took a step back. "I apologize, young lady. I'm an old man with a lot on my mind and can't get nowhere, with nobody. I'm gonna go now." He nodded to Allen and to Becca and headed down the street.

She could almost feel sorry for him. At least, Becca thought so. She wasn't sure what she felt.

"You sure you're okay?" Allen asked.

"Yeah."

"Offer you a ride wherever you need to get to?"

She considered it, but that would probably mean answering some questions. Right now, Becca needed to be alone to try to coax some order out of her tangled thoughts. There truly was something weird going on here.

The only thing not weird? Conrad had seen his uncle coming, and he ran. That made perfect sense.

She thanked Allen and waved as he drove off, then crossed the street. She needed to get to her car and drive down to Bedford for a meeting. Too much to do today before the Four Corners meeting.

~~~~~

The park lights had stopped their stuttering and flashed twice before coming on to full strength, turning the twilight between the gazebo and the baseball diamond to full daylight brilliance. Four Corners' rehearsal was done for the night. Becca turned, as discretely as possible, to see if some unwanted watchers were still sitting in the shade of the picnic pavilion, watching them.

No. Worse. Now they were crossing the lawn. Other members of Four Corners were turning to look. She silently begged them not to make eye contact. She had recognized at least two of them as members of TippyToes. Looking would just encourage stupid remarks.

"What's the matter?" a crackling tenor voice called from the group as they crossed the lawn to the sidewalk. "Didn't your fiddler show up?"

Yep, right on cue. Didn't Simone have anything better to do than sic her followers on Four Corners? Didn't they have anything better to do with their evenings?

"Fiddler?" Greg muttered. He turned to pick up the metronome sitting on the water pump that had been dry for at least twenty years.

"It's so sad that they need music to keep themselves together," Melanie said. "What are they going to do if their tippy-dippy soundtrack fails them during the parade? Like ... say ... some certain mischievous high school boys steal the batteries from their boom-of-doom box?"

"You wouldn't." Becca tried not to laugh.

Other members of the Four Corners did. Some muffled responses came from the tap dancers, who were now even with them on the sidewalk. Fortunately, most of them kept moving and didn't stop to heckle further.

"Hey." Ellen Tanner trotted across the lawn as the other tap dancers continued up the sidewalk. "Don't mind them. Simone was in a snit tonight."

"You don't usually have practice on Tuesdays," Becca said. Which was more than she really wanted to know about Simone and her followers.
~~~~~

She tried to practice quantum physics when it came to irritating, frustrating people. One theory of quantum physics postulated that paying attention to things affected them. So in theory, ignoring things, and people, would eventually make them fade away.

"Yeah, well, she called a meeting." Ellen shrugged and looked around, like she was worried about being overheard. Few people were left in the park. "Did you hear that her uncle sold his properties to Jacobs & Visconsi about five months ago?"

"No." What did that have to do with Simone's bad mood this week?

"Well, they're all being developed, including dividing up the studio we were using into separate shops. It's really a clever concept, a formal wear shop, a beauty salon, and a catering business. One-stop shopping for big events. Anyway, Simone got us practice space at St. Theo's for the summer, but now we're hunting for a new place to practice because they need their gym every night, with the school year starting up."

"And she waited until the last minute to find other options." Becca held back a sigh. That was typical Simone. She had gone through their high school and college years expecting the universe to know what she wanted and just drop it in her lap.

"She's been trying to convince Conrad to let her have Windows. Turns out he's avoiding everyone lately. Like that's our fault?" Ellen rolled her eyes. "Anyway, I thought I should warn you, she's out to take whatever you find now that the Barn is condemned." She sighed. "And yeah, she was crowing about that."

"Right." Becca held back a groan. "Thanks, El. I hope you don't get in trouble for helping the enemy."

"Hey, I don't see you guys as the enemy. It's dancers against the non-dancing world, as far as I'm concerned. But you might want to step on it. And if you inconvenience Madame Hitler … some of us might be cheering you on. Very quietly." She winked and turned to hurry away.

"Thanks. Good luck to you guys, too." Becca felt very tired.

She took no comfort in knowing that everyone else was having as hard a time catching up with Conrad as she was. Why couldn't the man answer his phone? She needed to officially renew the lease on Windows for Tuesday nights. Yesterday, if not sooner. No matter how awkward the whole meeting might be, and no matter how long it would take before they could start using the room. Either that or resign herself to taking My Four Corners out to Medina. The fairgrounds had several barns that were always open for rental, but not at the same time as the club's usual meetings. Rescheduling might mean losing members.

There just weren't that many locations that wouldn't require either a half-hour to forty-five-minute drive, or a major increase in the rental fees for the space. She knew, thanks to fourteen calls she had placed during the day, in between research phone calls for Charli Hall. Being a virtual assistant did have its benefits when it came to flexibility. She just hoped it worked out for her when it came to finding a new venue for rehearsals.

Wednesday, August 31

Lisa Pascal texted Becca when she was at the library Wednesday afternoon. She wanted to know if she could stop by Becca's house while she was out running errands, and promised it was a short matter, two minutes at the most.

At the library. Should be done in ten more minutes. I'll let you know when I leave.

Perfect, Lisa responded.

Becca wasn't surprised when she stepped out of the library and found Lisa waiting for her, sitting on one of the park benches spaced along the front sidewalk.

"Is this bad news?" She immediately thought of the Labor Day parade, and the two rehearsals coming up. Lisa was on the parade committee, representing Worter, Worter & McIntosh. Had the order of the participating clubs and civic groups been redone? For the fifth time since the July 4th parade?

"Shouldn't be. I just thought, and Bill agrees with me, although it took him long enough, that you should be given a heads up." Lisa got up from the bench before Becca could sit down. She gestured toward the parking lot, where her forest green Cavalier sat next to Becca's Jeep.

"About?"

"You're involved in the Fontaine estate mess."

"How?" Becca stumbled at the mere thought that Sarah had done some finagling to fix things between her and Conrad.

"Not really sure." Lisa held up her hand to stop the questions catching in Becca's throat. "There's all this hush-hush going on, and lots of people have different tasks to take care of before the big estate meeting. You just need to be warned. There have been some leaks, and spying. Information has gotten out that shouldn't have been released until the meeting. You need to be prepared for some pressure from the Columbus Fontaines, if they're the ones behind the leaks. Miss Sarah has given you authority to make decisions. She left a lot of things in writing, and Bill refuses to open those sealed letters until the right time. All I can say is that she wanted you involved in something, to fulfill conditions of the trust."

Becca muffled a groan. This wasn't going to be the two minutes Lisa had promised in her text. How long would this take? She was on several deadlines, with her errands carefully mapped out. Starting with getting to

Charli's condo in half an hour to give her the new batch of photocopied pages.

"Maybe Miss Sarah chose you as a tie-breaker or mediator or something. Of course, on that last visit to the office before she died, she did mention how badly Conrad treated you when you came back from Europe." Lisa's expression turned somber as they reached their cars and stopped. "I wouldn't be surprised if this wasn't a last-ditch effort, reaching out from Heaven, to get you two to talk and fix things."

"Knowing her, I wouldn't be surprised. That probably explains ..." Becca muffled a groan. Maybe that was behind that awkward scene at Book & Mug the other day? And Tuesday, before his uncle Frank showed up and sent him running? Conrad was feeling guilty from lingering pressure Sarah had put on him to make up with her?

Becca went on automatic pilot as she thanked Lisa for the warning, and they made their farewells. At least the Labor Day parade hadn't been sabotaged. She watched Lisa get in her car and pull out of the library parking lot, but she couldn't make herself put the key in the ignition. She knew what she had to do right now while she had time before her meeting with Charlie. She just didn't want to do it.

The possibility of constantly having to make peace between the Fontaines made her tired. She needed to focus all her energy on one thing: finding a rehearsal space for Four Corners. Why couldn't Conrad be reasonable and let her have the rehearsal space and time at Windows that Four Corners had been using since she was in high school?

"Please, God ... help me catch up with him, and put him in a good mood. And please keep his uncles away from me? I so don't need the pressure right now." Becca shuddered as she unlocked her car, deposited the papers she had just picked up, locked it again, and started up Apple toward Center. And Windows on the River.

On the short walk, she considered several tactics for when she confronted Conrad. Far too soon, she was across Center and at the door of the Windows building. And she still wasn't sure what to say.

"Okay, God ... help?" she whispered, as she reached for the door handle and pulled it open to step inside. She wondered if maybe she should call in the big guns. Meaning calling Pastor Roy and asking for some prayers on her behalf.

No, she couldn't make a phone call here in the lobby. The acoustics were awful, and conversations carried too clearly up the stairs, even with the door closed. Warning Conrad that she was asking for prayers to help deal with him would just put him on the attack.

The stairs door was open, for the first time in weeks. A good sign?

Still ... looking up the tall flight of stairs, she considered turning around and leaving this conversation for another time. Maybe after a few more messages left on Conrad's phone.

No. She couldn't delay any longer. If nothing else, she could find out if the regular rehearsal time was still open, or Simone had changed TippyToes rehearsals from Wednesday to Tuesday just to lock out Four Corners. That was a typical Simone move, going back to middle school.

A thud echoed down the stairs to her. Followed by a clatter, like wooden planks falling against each other. Becca froze on the third step with one foot raised. No other sound followed. The stairs were shadowed, but light filled the space where they opened into the long room.

Nothing.

She resumed climbing, automatically avoiding the creaky steps, and trying not to remember the last time she had been here.

Another clatter of wood-on-wood. Then a couple echoing footsteps. They sounded like heavy boots. Then a man's muffled voice. No one answered.

"Hello?" she called, in case Conrad was on the phone. She didn't need him to be startled, maybe even irritated.

More footsteps. A gush of warm air brushed past her. Silence. She paused before her head cleared the half-wall that framed the stairs opening. Becca leaned forward, trying to peer around it, as she came up the last four steps.

The long, sunlit room was empty. Well, empty of people. Four rolling racks of chairs sat at one end, and the double doors of the storage room were open, revealing the piles of tables. The kitchen door at the opposite end of the long room was closed. A small nook next to the kitchen looked like it was being framed in, to create a room. Maybe the carpenter had left for the day down the outside stairs? But why leave the door open?

Several boards lay on the floor, across a place that looked like a couple planks had been pried up. That explained the clattering she heard.

She sniffed. No odd smells. Nothing sour or wrong, to indicate another pipe leak or that black mold that Conrad blamed every time someone asked when Windows would be open again for rentals. Why had the boards been pried up?

What was the room for? Maybe storage for those cardboard bankers boxes sitting in the corner? A bathroom would be nice, instead of making people traipse downstairs to the public restrooms in the lobby.

"Hello?"

No response. No footsteps. No voice in a phone conversation. She crossed the room to the half-open sliding door to the long balcony on the creek side of the building. Warm air slipped past her. She cautiously peered out, looking both directions. Nothing and no one moved except the leaves on the trees lining both sides of Cadburn Creek.

She called again, just in case someone was sitting around the corner, trying to have a private conversation. No voices. No sounds of footsteps on the balcony.

Becca walked around the room three times. No one came back. That seemed odd. Why would Conrad leave the room alone for so long?

She called the realty office. The outgoing message still had Miss Sarah's voice. Becca almost hung up, unwilling to listen long enough to stir hurt, and maybe some resentment. She decided to leave a message, but the mechanical voice at the end said the mailbox was full.

"Typical."

Why did it feel like Conrad had forgotten how to do business? Like he didn't care about the business his grandfather had worked so long and hard to build into something admirable and reliable?

She refused to call the number Conrad had given her at Frenchy's. Maybe that was stupidly proud, but she didn't want to use it. She wanted to avoid the oddness of those couple of days, the date that had been mangled before it began, the feeling that she had been dealing with two different Conrads, and Simone was at the center of the differences.

Sighing, she called the number that was, in theory, supposed to take her to the booking system for Windows on the River. She had never used it before because she had never needed to.

No phone rang in the building, even though she heard the ringing on her phone. That was odd. Did Conrad have an office and the phone for this location downstairs?

"Don't have time for this," she said, even before she checked her watch again. Time to go meet with Charli.

When she got to the lobby, she took the time to check each shop door. None of them were the leasing office. The mailbox slots in the lobby clearly showed Windows on the River on the second floor.

What was going on?

Sighing, she put this errand to another day. She could chase Conrad from the comfort of her duplex, with her shoes off. After she delivered those photocopies to Charli. She did have a business to run, after all.

Becca was halfway down Apple to return to the parking lot, when she got that prickly shiver that meant someone was watching her. Or maybe she was just feeling paranoid. She fought the urge to turn around. If someone watched her, she wasn't going to give them the satisfaction of letting them know it bothered her. Becca kept walking dand was glad to put another block, and the buildings on it, between her and her watcher. And even more glad to get back into her car.

<center>~~~~~</center>

She ended the day on a high note, having dinner with Charli and her writing friends, at Charli's townhouse. Becca needed the laughter and mild guy-bashing, which naturally shifted to Twila-bashing for a few minutes. All of them had run afoul of the temperamental librarian. When she mentioned she felt sorry for Saundra Bailey, the new children's librarian, she learned all of them knew Saundra and adored her. They made plans for Becca to join them the next time they met at the Cadburn Library and have lunch afterward with Saundra. They assured her that her first impressions of Saundra were spot-on, and she would be a good friend.

Becca was tired, but smiling, as she pulled into the driveway of the duplex. The lack of lights on Rufus and Devona's side meant the siblings weren't home yet. Movement in the shadows of the back porch startled her. She turned in time to see a man jump off the porch and run up the driveway, to the dark green sedan she had seen parked in front of the house next door. She hesitated for a few crucial seconds, then put the car in park, and turned off the ignition. She ran a few steps down the driveway just in time to see the mystery man drive away.

"Huh?" For a second, as he passed under the streetlight, she thought she had seen Conrad in the driver's seat.

But what would Conrad be doing here so late, and why wouldn't he wait and talk to her when he knew she wanted to talk to him?

Maybe he had left a note. Of course, if he was visiting Devona and Rufus, it was none of her business. Common sense said he would have called them before coming over. So, if that was Conrad, he hadn't been here to see her, either.

"Stop giving yourself a headache," she whispered, as she climbed the steps to the porch shared by the duplex. No sense in making the neighbors fear she was either nuts or paranoid. She opened her back door and turned on the porch light. No note. No sign anyone had been there.

If that wasn't Conrad, who was it, and what had he wanted?

Chapter Seven

Saturday, September 3

Becca stepped into her kitchen, headed for the refrigerator and contemplated yet again the idea of getting a dog. Something small, fluffy, quiet, and snuggly, content to sit beside her and snooze while she did online research, but ready to take long walks whenever she needed to get the blood pumping. She snorted at her thinking, the irony and contradiction of thinking about getting regular exercise when she had slept in until the utterly decadent hour of 9:30 on a Saturday morning.

A scraping sound made her pause with her hand on the door handle. A board creaked like a gunshot, right in that telltale spot on Rufus and Devona's side of the porch. Somebody was out there, and Becca knew both siblings were already gone for the day. She hurried to the back door, reached for the knob, and had it open before she thought it might be smart to arm herself. Just in case. A knife. Or at least her phone, to call 911.

"Conrad?"

He jumped back, letting the screen door to the other side of the duplex bang closed, and dropped into a crouch. For a moment, she didn't recognize him. The lines of his face turned sharp, fierce, and she instinctively checked the lock on her own screen door.

"Oh, hey … Becca." Conrad's voice rumbled out low and smooth and that crooked, confident, unfamiliar smile brightened his face. He straightened up. "What are you doing here?"

"Uh, hello? I live here?" She shivered and seriously considered slamming the door and racing to her phone. How could Conrad forget that? While she paid her rent to Devona and Rufus, Fontaine Realty handled the maintenance. Conrad had been here dozens of times with Miss Sarah, or for Singles backyard cookouts. He had often knocked on the door to check on her, see if everything was all right with the house.

"Yeah … I knew that." He shrugged. "I meant, why aren't you out and running already? You're so hard to catch up with."

"Me? Look, Conrad, we need to talk."

"Yeah, babe, we really do, but I've got stuff that kind of has a higher priority, know what I mean?"

Again with *babe*? At least he didn't call her *Becks* this time.

"Like breaking into Devona's place?"

"What?" He shook his head, his grin going wider. "Nope, got a call from the neighbor. Saw someone sneaking around, testing the windows. Figured I'd check the windows, the doors, make sure everything was okay before I told Devona. Didn't want to scare her without need, y'know?"

"Yeah. Makes sense." Somehow, she was angry that his explanation did make sense. "How do the windows look?"

"Frames are solid, what I've checked out. Locks are good. I was hoping I remembered where she hid the spare key, so I could get in and check things out from the inside." He gestured up at the top of the wide, old-fashioned frame around the door. "No luck."

"That's because Devona knows that's the first place some crook trying to break in would look." She snorted. "Remember when we had that *Benson* marathon, and the one episode where that ditzy girl married to the press secretary hid money in a fake cabbage?"

Conrad shrugged. He looked like he was going to agree with her, then something sharpened in his expression. "No, sorry. Don't remember. What does that have to do with …" He gestured at the door.

"There are lots of places to hide keys. Some of them are pretty obvious. Like plastic rocks that don't look real enough. Or potted plants."

"Yeah." He took another step back, making that board pop-bang again, and surveyed the porch. Stacking chairs under a plastic cover, picnic table that folded up against the wall. Waist-high heavy-duty plastic storage box. "No luck. You don't happen to have any idea where they put the spare key?"

Becca spread her hands and shook her head. "How about instead of sneaking around, you just tell them what you want to do? Or if you're trying to avoid scaring Devona, ask Rufus to let you in."

"Yeah, might have to do that. Thanks." His gaze slid down her, and his smile flattened a little, in a way that made her feel like she was standing there in skimpy underwear instead of a long T-shirt to her knees, with cotton lounging pants. "Got any plans for breakfast?"

"Sorry, yes, I do." From far away, she heard the chime of her phone, getting a text. That was probably the newest demanding prospective client. "And that's my first phone meeting of the day. We can talk later?"

"Yeah. Sure. Check you out later, babe." Conrad stepped backward toward the porch steps, watching her.

It took all her self-control not to slam the door and slide the deadbolt over hard and fast and loudly. She did slide the deadbolt into place. She just didn't want him to hear it and know she did it. Becca walked slowly out of the kitchen, feeling as if Conrad could see her through the lacy curtain over the door.

The text was from Melanie, asking if she could swing by, and offered a bribe of breakfast sandwiches from Sugarbush. She had found some videos of square dance competitions from so long ago they were only on videotape. Did Becca have a VCR at her place?

Becca texted her to come over, welcome, yes, she had the old tech. Even though she really needed to wash and dress for the day, since Melanie would be there in probably fifteen minutes, she went down into the basement. A few seconds later, she hurried up the second flight of steps into Devona and Rufus's side of the duplex. She peered through the blinds on their living room windows, then the driveway side windows, to see if Conrad was still walking around outside. No sign of him, but she saw a black pickup parked across the street, just at the bend in the road, partially hidden by Mrs. Oglethorpe's overgrown rhododendron.

"Conrad, you are such a creep," she whispered.

No way now was she going to admit that she had Devona's spare key, just like Devona had her spare key. Plus, there was the agreement to keep their basement doors open, so they could get into each other's side of the duplex in an emergency. She might have told the Conrad she knew before her trip, but not the man he had become under Simone's influence.

If Conrad was going to sit and wait for her to leave, so he could creep around again, he had a long wait ahead of him. She had no plans to leave her house all day. Or at least, until it was time for the dress rehearsal for the Labor Day Parade.

She sighed, as the black pickup pulled out in a wide arch and turned around in Mr. Cranston's driveway, before heading down the street and away. "Okay, so maybe I was wrong, but the guy is just acting weird. I should have Rufus check if there's a pod in his basement."

~~~~~

When Saundra stepped into Book & Mug late Saturday afternoon, she wanted nothing more than to order a triple Mo'Klah and collapse in that back corner booth and vegetate. She certainly didn't want anyone to ask her about the break-in at the library that morning, speculations on what had or hadn't been stolen, and who might have knocked out Officer Carruthers. So that begged the question why she was here at all. Kai and Eden would ask how she was feeling, if she had heard anything, if she was worried, and who was this Nick who came out of nowhere twice in as many days to be her knight in shadowy armor.

To her relief, the coffee shop side had only a handful of people, all of them gathered around several tables that had been pushed together, laughing and talking over each other. From what she picked up as she walked to the counter, they were trash-talking each other about ... dancing? The difference between tap dancing and square dancing?

The contrast of the insults to the smiles and laughter certainly raised her spirits. Maybe she would visit the bookstore side of the shop before ordering a decadent drink. Devona's licorice-dark head of hair was visible above the shelves, in between stacks of books sitting on top of the
~~~~~

bookcases. Saundra watched her for a few moments and decided the young woman was shelving the books. Probably a new haul from an estate sale. All the more reason to spend more time getting to know Devona. Bibliophiles needed to stick together.

"Hey, how's it going?" Olivia stepped up behind the counter. "Kai was hoping you'd stop in."

Saundra offered up a weary smile. "How bad has the gossip been?"

"Well, the stories are so wide apart, a lot of people are dismissing most of them as crazy rumors and wishful thinking." She wrinkled up her nose, eyes sparkling with mischief.

"Wishful thinking?"

"That *you* clobbered Carruthers, instead of that mystery guy. A few of the bigmouths want to know who he is and if he's staying long enough to run for trustee."

Saundra muffled a snort. Yeah, right, as if Nick West would ever settle anywhere, forget long enough to run for public office.

"Anyway, Kai left something for you. I was threatened with losing access to the coffee-flavored whipped cream if I let you order anything." Olivia snickered and held up a finger, signaling Saundra to wait. She stepped back into the kitchen and came out just moments later with a frosty, tall glass. "Don't tell him I told you, but when he's ticked or wound up or worried about something, he experiments. He wants your opinion on this." She slid the glass across the counter to Saundra, then leaned sideways to snag a straw and a long-handled spoon.

"What is it?" The pale amber creamy mass was swirled with reddish-brown and green streaks. Saundra picked up the glass and took a deep sniff. "Cinnamon and ... apples?" She hoped that was the green. The other choice was spearmint.

"He's calling it frozen hot apple cider for now." She shrugged. "Yeah, he's leaving it up to the Guzzlers to give it a better name."

"How can it be frozen and hot?"

"Don't ask me. Ask the guys who sell frozen hot chocolate and get away with it."

"Thanks." Saundra was saved from having to say anything more when two couples came in, calling greetings to Olivia. She wandered to a table along the glass block wall of the bookstore and settled down to sip and unwind and wait for Kai to show up.

This was nice, having a place where she was expected to show up after a stressful day and people looked out for her. She wasn't sure if she should be glad or flattered or feel odd about Kai experimenting on her. Maybe she liked knowing he wanted her feedback on his creative effort, working off his stress over this morning's library attack.

She sipped and closed her eyes and let herself slump a little in her chair. Consciously relaxing wasn't as easy as it should have been, because *making* her muscles untense was a little bit of a contradiction. The cold drink melting on her tongue and sliding down her throat helped. Apple and cinnamon, maybe some nutmeg. It wasn't overly sweet. That was a mistake in most instant cider mixes. Too much sugar.

A bite of heat made her open her eyes. She guessed Kai had put pepper of some kind in the drink, swirled through the cinnamon and other spices. That gave a whole new interpretation to "hot" in the "hot frozen apple cider." Saundra wasn't sure she liked it. Cayenne in extra-spicy Chinese, yes. Cayenne in the dragon's breath tea Kai served, yes. On apples, and in apple cider?

Movement on the sidewalk across the street caught her attention and pulled it off the slight sting on her tongue. A man was pulling open the door into the building across the street. Her finely tuned survival instincts, thanks to the Mulcahy family and irate, entitlement-attitude library patrons, told her she knew him. Dark, curly hair, wide shoulders, dark pants and button-down shirt. Not the jeans and Ts that seemed to be the uniform on weekends. Just before he vanished into the shadows inside, she recognized him as a man who had been arguing with Lisa Pascal in the municipal parking lot two days ago. Saundra had caught something about "attorney-client privilege" and "confidentiality," before the man stomped away. Lisa had pulled out her phone and ran back up the street, holding the phone to her ear.

Saundra wondered what he was doing in that lobby, this late in the afternoon, when half the shops on Center were already closing up for the day. After everything that had been happening since arriving in Cadburn Township, Saundra was ready to suspect him of being up to no good. He just looked like someone skulking and waiting to cause trouble.

Another man appeared from the left of Book & Mug. Saundra guessed he had come up the sidewalk from Apple. Pale hair, jeans, somewhat familiar just from that sideways glimpse she had of his features. Especially that scowl. He glanced both ways and hurried across the street, aiming for the door the first man had gone through. It swung open, and the first man stepped out to block the second man from entering. Saundra held her breath as they both glared at each other. Then the first man stepped back, vanishing into the shadows of the lobby, and the second man followed him.

Saundra shook her head and turned her attention back to her drink. There were enough odd things going on, she didn't need to get distracted by some disagreement that was none of her concern. The smart thing to do would be to go home and get a good night's sleep, put this strange day behind her, and enjoy the holiday weekend.

"Hey, how are you doing now?" Kai brushed his hand across her shoulder as he came from behind her, and then settled into the chair facing her. "Everything calmed down over at the library?"

Saundra rolled her eyes, startling a laugh out of him. She liked it that she didn't need to say anything. He understood. The library and its staff were a world unto themselves, in some ways. He certainly had more experience with Twila and Carruthers than she did. Twila had grown cold and nearly silent as the day wore on, and she got one phone call after another, presumably from Carruthers or someone else in the Trustee Cadburn camp. Saundra had been surprised that Twila didn't explode at one point and accuse her of attacking Carruthers. Thanks to Nick's self-defense training, Saundra could have knocked the man out, if she had to. She just hoped she would never be in a position where she would need to.

"Have you decided if you're coming on Monday?"

For a moment, she blanked, then remembered that Eden had invited her to join the cousins for a day of relaxing on the roof of their building.

"Yes, definitely." The new brightness in his eyes made her fluttery inside. She focused on the drink, which was half-empty now. When had she drunk all that? "This is incredible."

"Yeah? I always try to come up with something for the fall street festival that doesn't add to the overdose of pumpkin spice whatever."

"My hero."

That made him laugh. She asked about the flavors he included. She must have winced when he got to the cayenne pepper because he chuckled and shrugged.

"Yeah, Eden thought that was a step too far, too."

"Maybe you can offer an extra-spicy option? For people -- That's weird." She pointed at the pale-haired man coming down Center from the right. The bag he carried in one clenched fist swung sharply with the force of his stride. "He just went inside maybe ten minutes ago, and I know I didn't see him coming out."

"Who?" Kai turned around to watch the man open the door to the lobby and go inside, wearing an even darker, deeper scowl than the first time. "Huh."

"Do you know him?"

"Conrad Price. He's kind of ..." He turned back around to face her. "He owns the building. Or rather, his family owns it, and a lot of other buildings in the township. They're kind of competing with the Cadburns to be top landlords or whatever, but only the Cadburns think so."

"Is he a magician or something? Because I know I saw him go in, but not come out, and now he's going in again."

"Oh, that's easy. There's a balcony on the other side of the building, looking out on the creek, and outside stairs at both ends of the building. Conrad probably left by the outside stairs and came back through the front door. Was he carrying that bag the first time you saw him?"

"No ..." Saundra laughed quietly at herself. She wanted to say Conrad wore a different color shirt, but she couldn't remember what color he was wearing the first time she saw him. Maybe the change in light, just in ten or fifteen minutes, made the difference.

"There you have it."

"Hey, Vo?" Rufus wheeled around the corner from the elevator nook. "Red alert!" He winked at Saundra and zoomed past her through the opening in the wall between the coffee shop and bookstore.

"What's up?" his sister called, her words punctuated by a thud of books hitting the wooden floor of the bookstore.

"Jerk alert."

"Guess Conrad getting in his face didn't do any good, huh?" Kai stood up to look down the street at a man striding toward the door. He looked like a much younger version of the first man Saundra had seen waiting for Conrad.

The door swung open and he walked in.

"How many times do we have to tell you to get lost?" Rufus shoved his wheelchair forward to block the man.

"Get out of my way, freak," he said. He sounded more tired than angry, to Saundra's ears.

"The term is 'gimp,' and I'm not going anywhere while you're in here."

"Fine." His mouth pursed like he was going to spit.

"If you're not here for coffee or a book," Kai began.

"Why can't you people just butt out? This is between me and Devona, okay?"

"No, it's not okay," Devona said. She stepped out of the bookstore side, arms crossed over her chest. "I don't have anything else to say to you, Raymond."

"Why? Will you just explain to me why?"

"Miss Sarah said so. That's all the explanation you need."

"Look, I'm not trying to get the inside scoop on the estate, okay? Yes, my dad's being a total jerkwad and poking his nose where he's got no business after the way he treated my grandparents. I don't care. I don't want anything."

"Except what you can't have," Rufus snapped.

"We gotta talk. That's all I want. You and me, Devona, straightening things out." He took a step back. "When everything is settled with the lawyers, okay?"

"We'll see," Devona said, so quietly Saundra thought perhaps Raymond didn't hear her.

Then he nodded, once, and turned and stomped out of the coffee shop. Saundra's face warmed as she realized that almost everyone else in the shop had stopped their conversations to listen. The soft thud of the door closing seemed like a switch, allowing the other conversations to resume.

Sunday, September 4

Lisa tapped Becca's shoulder as she was heading down the hall from the Singles' classroom to the sanctuary for the morning service. She beckoned with a tip of her head when Becca turned to see her, and they stepped out of the flow of traffic.

"I spotted some of the Fontaines here, looking for Conrad."

"Why?" Becca almost laughed, even though it wasn't really funny. "He hasn't come to church in months."

"I know, but they know this was Miss Sarah's church, and he should be here and ..." Lisa shrugged. "Anyway, you need to be warned. Once they give up on him, they'll probably be looking for you."

"What do they want?"

Another shrug. "I heard them asking people if they had seen Frank, but ..."

"Frank?" A chill ran up her spine. "The oldest brother?"

"They were supposed to meet him, or he was supposed to call them yesterday, but no one has seen him."

"Weird."

"Tell me about it." Lisa gave her a little shove. "Go hide. You do not want to be caught between the Fontaine brothers and Conrad."

"Thanks."

Lisa checked the crowd one more time, then headed down the hall, away from the sanctuary. Sighing, Becca waited for the stream of people to thin out a little before stepping back into the flow. She didn't wonder, until she was in her usual pew on the piano side of the sanctuary, why Lisa wasn't going into the service. Unless she was being careful to keep the Fontaine brothers from seeing them together? It had to be rough, working for the law firm handling the complicated terms for the family estate. Especially if a family feud made things tricky and unpleasant.

Lisa's warning was still at the front of Becca's thoughts when Jenny, Amber, and Pippin, members of the Singles group, slid into the pew in front of hers. They had decided just since class to visit Put-in-Bay today. Did she want to go with them? She only had to think for maybe ten seconds before accepting. The excursion would certainly get her out of the house and away from anyone searching for her.

Definitely, she needed this day away from everything and everyone.

She would deal with Conrad, and his uncles, and the family feud, and whatever it was Sarah wanted her to do, along with finding rehearsal space for Four Corners on Tuesday, when the holiday weekend was over. And not a moment before that.

~~~~~

Becca couldn't hear her phone in her purse. She checked her phone when she got off the ferry at the Catawba docks at the end of a long, sunburned, fun day and wasn't surprised to find nine missed calls and four voicemail messages. She didn't feel a moment of regret. She had a right to relax and enjoy a day of freedom from the tyranny of the phone, didn't she? Five days a week, she was on call for all her clients, and handled her tasks six days a week, often ten hours a day. That was what being a virtual assistant meant. Sunday was hers. They were free to send her emails, with the understanding that she wouldn't even read them until the work week started. Anyone who got upset that she didn't make an exception for them weren't clients for very long.

That didn't mean she didn't check the numbers, to see who had called and might need a reminder conversation about the rules.

Two messages were from Conrad. The other two were numbers she didn't recognize, with area codes she didn't know off the top of her head. The first Conrad message was just a sigh before hanging up. The second was a gruff, "I need to talk to you. Yeah, the Tuesday night slot is open at Windows. It's yours. When we open for business again. Not sure when. I'll see you tomorrow after the parade."

He didn't say where. She had to assume he would be waiting in front of the Windows building, or maybe in Windows.

Becca didn't check the other two messages until Amber pulled her car off the ferry and everyone got back in for the two-hour ride home to Cadburn. Both were silent, though she thought she heard some background noises, like muted voices or maybe a car engine. Why would someone leave the phone connection open and not say anything? Becca saved those to listen to later, when she didn't have voices around her, and the sound of Amber's car engine, and she wasn't wiped out. If they were wrong numbers, shouldn't they have hung up as soon as she stated her name and gave her office hours? She considered just deleting the non-messages. On the other hand, they might be people looking for a virtual assistant, who had gotten her number from a current or even a previous client. She saved the numbers as new contacts and gave them the code she had made up to help her remember the details. In this case, NOO: non-message, outside office hours.
~~~~~

Chapter Eight

Monday, September 5

The Labor Day parade went off without a hitch. Four Corners performed their abbreviated routine perfectly to much applause. If TippyToes tried to give a sample routine without stopping the forward momentum of the parade, Becca didn't even try to look. She saw signs for Fontaine Realty hanging from two barricades, but there were enough people packed together along the parade route, she couldn't see if there were any more. Becca speculated on Conrad grumbling, as he had in other years, that some of Trustee Cadburn's sycophants had taken down some of his signs. She braced herself to be supportive and sympathetic when she met up with him after the parade. After all, Conrad had said Four Corners could return to Windows. Best to stay on his good side.

She nearly let that sourpuss, Heinrich, distract her as Four Corners marched past the Windows building. He glowered at everyone from the curb, fists jammed into his bony hips, looking like he might leap into the parade at any moment and start punching.

Too late, she tried to avoid eye contact with him.

"Tell that idiot boyfriend of yours, now they're smashing the security cameras!" Heinrich shouted.

She nodded. It wouldn't do any good to shout back that she wasn't Conrad's girlfriend. That wouldn't make Heinrich leave her alone. He was just a grump who felt the world owed him. That nod seemed to placate him because half his scowl wrinkles smoothed out. Then she was past him, and the marker was coming up on the parade route for Four Corners to do one more routine before they reached the township park and the end of the parade. Becca hoped Heinrich shouted the same message to Simone.

Conrad wasn't waiting in front of the Windows building when she walked back down Center more than half an hour later. Becca waited twenty-five minutes total. For the first ten minutes, she stood outside in front of the door. Then she went inside, and since the stairwell door was open, she climbed the stairs. The shades were down in the big room, the sliding door was locked, and no progress had been made on the new small room. Three more boards were sitting loose across the opening in the floor, in a different spot from the last time she had seen boards pulled up. What was Conrad doing? Would those boards be replaced in time for Four Corners to start using the room again? Maybe this was an excuse to keep refusing to book the room?

Finally, she came back downstairs and sat on a bench on the sidewalk where she could watch the traffic, coming and going, and hopefully not be obvious that she was waiting for someone. It helped to have a book on her phone, so she could look like she was busy. On the bright side, sitting there in her turquoise gingham shirt and ruffled skirt, she attracted attention, easily identified as a square dancer. Five people asked about joining Four Corners, because they looked like they were having so much fun. And the dance steps looked easy enough to learn.

At twenty-five minutes with no Conrad in sight, Becca sighed and got up to go home and change and get her bowl of pasta salad and six-pack of peach seltzer. She had a relaxing afternoon in the Kenwards' backyard waiting for her.

Last year, she had spent the day with Sarah, Albert, Conrad, Devona, and Rufus. Today, the siblings said they were going to their mother's cottage to get some repair work done. Becca assumed Conrad and Simone had plans. Chances were, Simone had found out Conrad wanted to talk to her and had delayed him or made him change plans.

Nope. She wouldn't let either of them ruin her holiday.

She would deal with Conrad on Tuesday.

Tuesday, September 6

Much against her better judgment, Becca tried to call Conrad before she went to bed Monday night. The realty office voicemail had finally changed. She nearly hung up when she heard Simone's voice cooing the message, encouraging callers to leave a message and Conrad would get right back to them, their business was so very important. Praying Simone wasn't monitoring the calls, she left a message telling Conrad she would stop by around 10am to sign the lease for Four Corners.

Of course, Conrad didn't call back. That didn't mean anything.

Her first errand of the day took her to Lumber Village, to get sizes of lumber, finishes, and estimates of costs for a few renovation projects for Tracy Adams. She owned the strip of shops on the south side of Cadburn Creek, appropriately called Creekside Shops. Heinrich slouched on a stack of heavy-duty buckets next to the front counter, jawing with Mo, the owner, father and grandfather of everybody who worked there. The curmudgeon sniffed loudly when he saw Becca approach the counter with a notebook full of questions.

"He don't listen to you any better than he listens to his renters, does he?" the old man snapped.

"Excuse me?" She knew exactly who Heinrich was talking about, but she was just irritated enough to pretend she didn't.

"Conrad Price." He spat the name like it should be a curse word soon.

"Considering I can't even get him on the phone?" Becca wasn't in any mood to be charitable and not add to the gossip. Conrad was on her dirt list. Again. Still. Yet. "Anyway, you're out of the loop. I freed myself of Conrad months ago."

"Good for you," Mo said, and for emphasis wiggled his enormous jug-handle ears. He winked when she muffled a giggle. That old trick had worked since she was in grade school. "What can I do for you, honey?"

"Tracy needs more price estimates and what quantities you have on hand and if Kyle's team is available to do the renovations." She handed over the notebook.

"Love that girl. She's gonna keep me in business. Not like those other two." Mo's lip curled up and he rolled his eyes expressively before stepping away from the counter. "Back in a couple." He stepped through the door into the lumberyard office, where Becca could see several of the next two generations working on computers and dealing with paperwork.

"Yeah, smart, getting rid of that slacker," Heinrich mused. "The pieces got picked up, but nothing's been done about replacing the cameras. How's a man supposed to keep his business going safe without some security?"

Becca shrugged. She knew better than to point out that Heinrich had yelled about the broken cameras just yesterday, a holiday. For all she knew, Conrad was out buying the replacements right now. She thought about commenting that they needed security cameras to protect the security cameras. That probably wasn't a smart thing to say, just smart-alec, and she didn't want to encourage Heinrich to keep harping on the subject.

The man did have a right to be concerned, since his business dealt with coins and gems, and buying gold and silver. Still, he didn't have to be so loud, telling the entire street his business. How secure was that?

"Now there are all those barrels sitting on the stairs," Heinrich continued. "Did he at least do right by you and buy them here?" he shouted, leaning back to aim his comments through the office door.

"Eh? What's that?" Mo leaned out of the doorway, frowning.

"Those barrels of whaddayacallit? The stuff for drying and fighting off stink. Did Conrad get those from you? Or did he shaft you and get them from somewhere else, like last time?"

"Last time?" Becca flinched, knowing she had made a mistake, encouraging Heinrich to talk. Still, she was curious.

"June, when Windows had that pipe break and Conrad said there was all that mold. Barrels of the same stuff, sitting on the stairs. And other stuff. Sand. Who fights ceiling leaks with sand? I tell you, there better not be that same weird stink this time around as there was that time." He nodded sharply for emphasis. Hard enough, Becca heard his neck crack. "No leaks got through to my place. Or anybody else's place. But there was Conrad, ripping up boards, putting down new boards, giving old Mo there the shaft. Albert always used Lumber Village for all his construction. Complaining about black mold. Acting high and mighty, a regular snot-faced kid with people who've been renters for decades. And that weird smell. That was not a mold smell, I tell you."

"Yeah, but you gotta admit, the new-fangled stuff they're coming out with, supposed to be good for the environment, it don't smell any better," Mo said. He came out waving the printout sheets with the answers to all the questions Becca had given him. "A lot of times, this natural stuff smells a whole heck of a lot worse. Just be grateful Conrad is stopping the leaks from getting to you and your shop. He hasn't raised the rent to make up for losing income from Windows, has he?"

"No," Heinrich grudgingly admitted. He pursed his lips, deep in thought, and glared at a spot on the floor.

Mo tipped his head toward the door and waggled his bushy eyebrows. Becca took the hint: this was a good time to make her escape. She thanked him and hurried out of the building.

Despite Heinrich's words, which made her expect to hear hammering and the scream of wood being pried apart, silence greeted Becca when she stepped into the lobby of Windows more than an hour later. The stair door hung ajar a few inches. That had to be a good sign. She headed up the stairs, walking quietly, listening for sounds of activity. She most definitely did not need to come upon Conrad and Simone preparing for another picnic, or worse, snuggling and kissing.

She took a few testing sniffs as she climbed the stairs. No odd smells. Maybe Conrad had caught the mold or other damage before it got bad enough to smell? She tried to feel sorry for him.

Was that a footstep? Did she hear a muffled voice? She couldn't tell if that was supposed to be a man or woman's voice.

"Conrad? It's Becca. I hope you have that paperwork ready to get down to business."

Something thudded to the wooden floor. Heavy feet shuffled. Becca took the remainder of the stairs two at a time, determined that this time she would not get up there and find the entire place empty again. What was with Conrad, playing games like this? She reached the room and stumbled slightly as she left the stairwell, trying to turn to see everything, and catch whoever had been up here.

All the boards that had been pulled up the last time she was here had been put back in place. That was a good sign. She didn't see any signs of damage. No barrels of drying agent. No buckets of stain and sealer, to fix what had been damaged by the repairs. No weird smells. Just some bankers boxes piled up against the wall, and other boxes sitting haphazardly across the floor, open, with papers strewn out from them.

"Oh, hey, you must be Becca, right?" a woman called from the other end of the room.

Becca wondered if this was what whiplash felt like as she turned her head fast enough for her neck to ache. At first, the speaker was just a silhouette against the bright morning sunlight, streaming through at the top of the window. Then she stepped closer and resolved into a young woman in jeans and a green plaid flannel shirt, the sleeves rolled up, hanging open over a black tank top. Her glossy, blue-black hair was coiled up at the back of her head with strands sticking out, plastered to her face with sweat, and she had a streak of something dark across one wide cheekbone. It seemed to make her gray-blue eyes stand out even more.

"Hi, I'm Conrad's cousin, Agatha." She chuckled and wiped her hand on her thigh before holding it out to shake. "Sorry. Along with coming on as office manager, I'm also overseeing the renovations."

"There's a lot of that going on," another voice said, coming from the door out onto the balcony. This speaker was a young man, also in jeans and flannel, the same thick, curly, blue-black hair. He had Albert Fontaine's hooked nose, so Becca didn't experience a moment of doubt. "Hi, I'm Chris. I get to do the renovations while my big sister nags me."

Agatha snorted. She gestured at the accordion files and other paperwork strewn across the floor. "Sorry about the mess. Connie's out and about, but he did leave instructions … although not very clear. Could you bring me up to speed?" She stepped over to the paperwork.

Becca followed her, with Chris right behind them.

"I want to lease this space for my square dance club, every Tuesday night, from 7 to 10, and the first Saturday of every month from 9 to noon."

"Wow, that's a lot of rehearsal time. You guys pros?"

Becca barely managed to muffle a snort. "No, we just have a lot of fun, and the first hour or so is meeting for dinner and socializing. We probably won't need all that time, but it pays to look ahead and plan for emergencies."

It also paid to make sure Simone and the nasties in her tap dance group couldn't play tricks like scheduling a rehearsal late in the evening, showing up "accidentally" an hour early, and then sitting there, talking loudly enough to interfere with the caller. They had done it before. Having meetings scheduled to run later than Four Corners actually needed ensured no one could come in and use the space after them.

And to be honest, Becca and some of her friends had pulled the same trick on Simone in revenge. But also, to be honest, they had been much younger when they did it.

"Sounds like fun. Mind if we hang around some time to see what it's all about?" Agatha went to her knees to sort through a stack of papers.

"Sure. We're always open to new recruits. What kind of dancing do you usually like?"

"Who has time for dancing?" She gestured at the paperwork and hooked a thumb back toward Chris. "Figuring out what our grandmother wanted us to do with the family business is turning into a full-time job."

"It's really nice to finally meet Conrad's cousins," she ventured. "I mean, nobody ever talked about the rest of the family, what with the family feud and all that. I guess Raymond's plan to heal things is finally working, huh?"

"Yeah …" Agatha paused and looked away.

"Too bad you never got a chance to meet Miss Sarah. She was incredible." Becca forced a smile when she suddenly felt like crying, which made no sense. "I really miss her."

"She thought a lot of you. I mean – well, she left letters for some of us. And she mentioned you."

"Oh, yeah, I've heard about those letters." Becca shuddered.

"You have?" Agatha frowned, finally turning back to her.

"Never mind. I'm just glad you're getting along with Conrad."

"We've got an awful lot to make up for," she murmured. "Hah!" She snatched up papers off a pile that threatened to slide sideways and spread across the floor. "Here we are. I knew I put them somewhere."

More than an hour passed from the time Becca climbed the stairs until she was out the door again, with a signed leasing agreement. Four Corners could officially begin meeting at Windows on the River next Tuesday night.

Chris kept her busy, asking about Four Corners, about Conrad, about what it was like growing up in Cadburn Township, while Agatha ran downstairs to borrow a copy machine. She laughed, despite being out of breath when she came back, and gestured around, as if she had to point out that most of the office hadn't been moved over here yet.

"We're just lucky we had the right paperwork here, and we didn't have to go to the office to get it," she said. Chris immediately hurried to the sliding door and outside. He didn't say goodbye.

Still, considering how Conrad had been treating her lately, his cousins were much more pleasant. They probably had a lot of things to take care of. Maybe they were just nervous about working for Conrad. Maybe they were feeling pressure from some of their uncles? Maybe they were here without the rest of the family knowing, and they were worried about getting caught? Maybe she should just write off the whole family as slightly odd?

Still, she wasn't going to look too closely at the circumstances of this miracle. She had successfully booked Windows for Four Corners' use. Short of convincing a judge to cancel the contract, there wasn't anything Simone Radcliffe could do to take that time slot away from them. Well, anything legal. There were lots of nasty tricks she could do, and had done, to frustrate Four Corners in general, Becca in particular.

In triumph, Becca decided she could indulge in a frozen whip version of Kai's new drink and headed through the open doors of Book & Mug. She had some time to kill before meeting with Charli Hall. Becca pulled out her phone once she had her drink, and created an email to everyone in Four Corners, to make the big announcement. A knot of tension loosened in the base of her skull, and the relief still spilling through her made her feel almost giddy. Or maybe it was the combination of chocolate and coffee and all that sugar, rushing through her blood.

Thursday, September 8

Thursday was the Guzzlers meeting. Becca was glad to sit back and just listen to everyone else talking, sharing about their end-of-the-summer activities, plans for the fall, looking ahead to the next street festival, in October. She especially enjoyed watching the interaction between Saundra Bailey and Kai. There was something growing between them. At least, Becca hoped so. More than just that connection that happened when people went through stressful situations.

The gossip around town wasn't too bad, considering that the man who had fallen from the fire escape and died while apparently trying to break into Book & Mug in the middle of the night had been harassing Saundra, too. The speculation on what he had been looking for had taken some strange and interesting turns. Mostly because Roger Cadburn had blown a few fuses publicly, and then per his usual habit, tried to blame Kai and his cousins. Elections were coming up, and Trustee Cadburn had used up all the good grace and respect earned by his ancestors. He was going to be very surprised when he wasn't re-elected.

Becca wondered what it would take to get Kai or Eden or Troy to run for office. All three were popular and respected. Still, she couldn't imagine Kai handing over the reins of Book & Mug to someone else so he could focus on running the township. Eden was too busy as a private investigator, as evidenced by her hiring Becca to help her. As for Troy, the man wasn't as visible as his cousins, but he seemed to be far busier than could be accounted for by the health food store he ran, and the greenhouse on the roof of the Mug building. What was he involved in that seemed to require trips on a regular basis, staying away two and three days at a time? Becca liked the cousins too much to pry into their private lives and possibly hurt feelings or alienate them.

Kai announced that he had solved the annual problem of coming up with a fall-themed drink to serve during the fall street festival. He pretended to be weak with relief that he had managed to avoid the over-used pumpkin spice flavor. Everyone agreed that the frozen hot cider was nearly perfect. No one could think of any additional ingredients, or variations to offer. There was some teasing argument over whether Kai should put the cayenne pepper back in, or how many sales he would generate if he made it an optional variation on the drink.

Around then, Becca noticed how quiet Curtis was, how little he interacted with anyone at all. He spent a lot of the meeting time watching Saundra, with a sad, thoughtful expression. Becca believed Curtis was far more aware and intelligent than most people gave him credit for, but something had damaged him long ago and he had retreated into a somewhat childlike state in self-defense. The way Kai and his cousins had taken Curtis under their wings and looked after him, almost from the day they came to town, said a lot for their character. And just highlighted what an egotistical, use-'em-and-lose-'em jerk Roger Cadburn was, in Becca's estimation. She couldn't figure out why Curtis was so loyal to the Cadburns, other than some long-standing rumors that his family was an offshoot of the Cadburns.

Bottom line: Curtis was an underappreciated treasure in the township. Becca had learned long ago that anything she wanted to know about the inner workings of the township, the buildings and history, and the truth behind the rumors and tall tales, she could get from Curtis. The man observed everything, remembered everything. He simply never told anyone what he knew unless someone asked. When Curtis died, many secrets and wonders would vanish and die with him.

She made a mental note to talk to Curtis about the stories of Underground Railroad tunnels under the town, and the rumored secret passageways that opened onto Cadburn Creek. There were also stories she wanted to follow up on, of a Cadburn daughter who had never returned from serving in the Civil War, disguised as a boy. Someone should take the time to sit Curtis down, give him all the peppermint and chocolate drinks he wanted, let him talk as long as he wanted, and preserve those stories before it was too late.

Maybe Saundra was the one to do it. She certainly seemed to fascinate Curtis. Could the elderly man have a crush on her? Becca hoped not, because of that something sweet she sensed growing between Kai and Saundra.

Such ruminations kept Becca almost as quiet as Curtis. She muffled a chuckle when Kai officially adjourned the meeting and sent the Guzzlers home. How had the time passed so quickly? Several people asked her about Four Corners as they were gathering up cups and napkins and pushing the tables and chairs back into their normal configuration in the back of the coffee shop. Becca was delighted to announce that she had re-acquired Windows for Tuesday meetings, starting next week.

"That might be fun to try," Saundra said. "I think I've gotten over being traumatized by square dancing in gym class," she added with a chuckle.

Becca urged her to consider joining them. Kai looked interested in joining Four Corners, too. If Becca read his expression correctly. Maybe he was more interested in spending time with Saundra than square dancing.

She had a lot to think about as she made her farewells and headed out the door.

Chapter Nine

Friday, September 9

Book & Mug was buzzing with speculation and what few facts were known about the events the night before, when Becca stopped in for her morning cup of cinnamon latte and to check in with a hard-to-reach client. She stayed half an hour longer than she intended, listening to people and taking notes, to narrow down who to talk to.

Who would have thought it? Curtis was the accomplice to Jacob Styles, the man who had fallen from the fire escape at Book & Mug. Becca knew there was more to the story than what people shared. Demanding facts never calmed down excited gossips. She would learn more by sitting quietly and listening.

The story that really caught everyone's attention was how Roger Cadburn had threatened Saundra with a gun. He wanted some books he insisted she had stolen from the library, or from his family. The details weren't clear on that part of the story. He was now under arrest. Someone said Saundra was part of a trap set up by the FBI, and Cadburn was suspected of a lot of crimes. Someone else said Curtis had attacked him to defend Saundra. Others insisted Curtis was innocent, and Cadburn had framed him for the death of Styles. No one could agree if that fall from the fire escape could be considered accident, murder, or self-defense.

Becca's head was close to swimming, when she finally put her mug in the bus pan on the end of the counter and left Book & Mug. She wasn't sure where she wanted to go, but just walked, until the aromas escaping Sugarbush Bakery caught her attention and gave her an idea. Something constructive to do. She went in, bought a dozen chocolate chip cookies, then took them to the police station and asked if she could visit Curtis.

The woman at the front desk smothered a grin when she saw the clear plastic bag of cookies. She said she would have to get Captain Sunderson's approval, but she didn't think there would be any problem with giving the cookies to Curtis.

Becca understood more when she was escorted to Curtis's cell. Other people had already been by to visit him. He had a stack of snacks sitting on the shelf that ran down one side of the cell, several books, comic books, and a pillow and blankets that were clearly not standard jail issue. This was why she loved living in Cadburn Township. Despite all the political bickering and other, sometimes childish rivalries and squabbles, the people of Cadburn looked out for each other. She was pleased to see that other people appreciated what a treasure Curtis was.

The big man burst into tears when she walked up to his cell door and offered him the bag of cookies. What she could make out through his sobs and sniffling, he knew he had made his father sad, and he had done a bad thing. He was only trying to help. He didn't know Styles was dead, he just thought Styles had gone away because he was mad at him.

"Curtis, he was trying to shoot Kai. You stopped him. That's a good thing. You didn't mean to land on him, did you?"

He went so silent for several seconds, Becca thought maybe he had even stopped breathing. Then Curtis shook his head and wiped his face on his sleeve, sniffed hard, and shook his head again.

"But I still did bad. I have to go to jail forever."

Becca didn't know what to say. She knew better than to give the big man false hope. With his luck, he would be given a public defender who wouldn't make any effort to defend him, just walk through the steps and pick up his paycheck. Or the prosecutor would be one of those activist extremists who vindicated the obviously guilty and made villains out of victims. He would try to make his career on sending Curtis to the electric chair for something that anyone could see was entirely an accident.

For one thing, Curtis was too clumsy to perform the kind of gymnastics required to throw a man off the fire escape and ensure he landed on top of him. Common sense said Styles' death was entirely an accident. Then again, with all the research Becca did for Charli Hall, she had abundant proof that common sense was often lacking in the justice system, along with mercy and charity.

She did what she could to stop Curtis's tears, even if she couldn't fully cheer him up, and headed back to Book & Mug. Curtis was a Guzzler. Maybe the Guzzlers could do something. At the very least, they could investigate the public defender and prosecutor, when Curtis finally went to trial, and make sure he got a fair trial.

Becca nearly laughed aloud when she wondered if anyone was this concerned about Roger Cadburn. Somehow, she doubted he had the money required to buy his way out of trouble. Not like in his grandfather's day. Of course, Jerome Cadburn hadn't needed to buy his way out of trouble. He lived up to the reputation of his ancestors who had founded the township.

She crossed Center at Apple and caught sight of Eden coming out the side door of the Mug building, carrying a canvas shopping bag. Listening to intuition, Becca detoured to walk up to meet her.

"For Curtis?"

"He likes puzzle books." Eden shrugged and held out the bag for Becca to look inside. A half-dozen books, an assortment of pens, and a bag of peppermints. Becca knew how Curtis loved peppermint.

"Do you know if there's anyone putting together something to help Curtis? Like make sure he gets a good lawyer? Post bail? Something?"

Eden smiled. "Talk to Troy. He's our money man."

This was why Becca loved Cadburn Township.

~~~~~

Mid-afternoon, Becca went to Windows. Despite the leasing agreement in her possession, she listened to gut instinct, which said she needed to talk directly to Conrad. The stairs door was locked. She heard thudding, so someone was up there.

A man swore. That didn't sound like Conrad, more tenor than a medium baritone. Footsteps moved across the ceiling. Becca tipped her head back to follow the sound. What was going on up there?

She had almost an hour until she had to drive to Medina and meet a possible new client. Her irritation with Conrad guided her. The sounds from upstairs were muffled, so that meant windows were closed, and probably the doors onto the balcony. If she was careful, no one would see her, and she could get an idea of what was going on. If this was one of Simone's nasty tricks, Becca didn't want to be caught flat-footed. She wanted enough warning to cancel Tuesday's meeting. And maybe talk to one of the junior lawyers at Worter, Worter & McIntosh, to see if she could sue for damages or wasted time or something.

Becca went through the lobby to the back of the building and the deck over Cadburn Creek. She took the outside stairs and walked slowly along the balcony to the sliding doors overlooking the water. The sheer curtains were in place. Looking from sunshine into shadow, she could still make out two men in the shadows. She nearly touched the glass of the sliding door with her nose, to get a better look at the men. One stood, while the other knelt, reaching into the gap in the floor where at least three boards had been removed. A chill squeezed the back of her neck. She associated that chill with a warning from her guardian angel to get out of there.

This is so stupid. I need to move.

Curiosity held her there a few more seconds. Just as she was about to take a step backward, the man who was standing turned, putting what he held in his hands into the light from the skylight. Becca muffled a gasp and checked – no, she wasn't casting a shadow into the room. That would be stupid, wouldn't it?

She couldn't see what the man held. The man kneeling on the floor pulled something out and handed it to the standing man. Then he stood up and leaned in to look closer. They talked, pitching their voices soft for a few moments before bending down and putting the boards back in place, covering up the holes in the floor.

Then they headed for the sliding door. Becca froze. Now she could
~~~~~

see the gap, less than an inch, between the sliding door and the track. There were scratches on the track. They had probably broken in.

What was she doing standing there?

She turned and darted down the balcony, running on her toes, praying the boards wouldn't bang or creak. The sound of the door sliding open reached her just as she darted around the corner.

Please, please, please, go down the stairs. Don't come this way.

"I'm taking this to my connections downtown," a man with a baritone voice said. "You need to go find your brother and sister and get out of here. It's getting too dangerous, you got me?" The footsteps moved away from her, and Becca prayed she was right, they were going down the stairs.

"What about my father?" the tenor voice asked. A squeak-creak punctuated his words.

Becca knew that sound, it was the fifth step down from the balcony.

"I think he's with Conrad."

"And that's supposed to make me feel better?" The footsteps stopped. Then they moved again. The fifth step squeak-creaked. He was heading up again.

"Hold it."

"Let go of me!"

The footsteps stopped.

"Shut up," the baritone said. "You don't want to let the whole building know what's going on, what we've found. Because we don't know what exactly we've found yet. You need to get out of here, get out of this, because we're on really shaky ground. I don't mind telling you, the local police won't be happy to see me any time soon."

"So you've been lying to me?"

"Kid, you have no idea the lies being told around here."

"Maybe I should go tell Conrad what you're looking for. How about that? And the cops."

"Fine. Who do you think they'll believe? The kid whose father has been making scenes, threatening people? The same kid who's been pestering that pretty little girl in the bookstore? What are you going to do? Throw accusations at Conrad?"

"But what we found—"

"What did we find? I'm convinced right now Conrad didn't put it there. We're all a lot safer if we keep this quiet, and you go hide out and lay low with the other kids. Okay?"

"Okay?"

"Okay," came the grudging tenor response.

Footsteps started moving again.

Becca peered around the corner, praying with all her might they were going down the stairs, not heading around the balcony and about to discover her there.

She caught a glimpse of them before their heads vanished from sight, under the edge of the balcony. One was Raymond Fontaine. The other could have been another Fontaine, but he didn't have Albert's hook nose.

That was all she could see and note before they were gone.

She waited, listening until the footsteps faded away completely. Then she crept down the stairs, half bent over to look down ahead of her. In case that intense man with the baritone voice was waiting for her to appear. She envisioned him coming out of the shadows of the lobby, hitting her like a fullback with a tackling dummy, and sending the dummy, her, over the railing and down the rocky, steep walls into Cadburn Creek. There wasn't enough water to drown anyone, but she could break bones and get cut up pretty badly on the way down.

Becca prayed hard, though she wasn't quite sure what she called out to heaven in the panicky recesses of her mind. She held her breath and stepped into the lobby, crossing with the softest footsteps she could manage. A long pause in the doorway out to Center, to look in all directions before stepping out onto the sidewalk.

All that made sense from what she overheard was that Conrad was in trouble. Whatever those men had found in the floor, he hadn't put it there.

How could Conrad defend himself if he didn't know what was going on? Should she tell him? Would he listen?

For a few seconds as she waited to cross the street, with the goal of retreating into the safety of Book & Mug, she considered not doing anything. After all, she couldn't be sure of what she had heard. This was a mess, but she might make the mess worse. She was ashamed to admit she wanted him to pay for his thoughtlessness and stupidity. And choosing Simone. At the same time, if this was something serious, Conrad didn't deserve whatever kind of trouble might fall on him if he didn't get some kind of warning. He deserved a chance to defend himself.

Becca prayed and planned what she would say as she walked to her car. She prayed more once she was in her car, then called Conrad.

She had to leave a message. Again. This time she didn't mind. She prayed Conrad would be all right, and this would turn out to be something stupid, something entirely opposite of what she feared and refused to put into words. Hopefully Conrad would laugh at her, rather than be angry with her.

Her phone rang just as she turned onto the on-ramp of I-71 heading south. She glanced at the screen once she was safely in the center lane and saw Conrad's office number displayed on the screen. For the first time, she felt a flicker of regret that she hadn't set up the Bluetooth in her car, to take calls while driving. Even with the hands-free option, she simply preferred to have her driving time free to listen to the radio or just have blessed, rare silence and freedom to think.

Her phone blipped at her, meaning Conrad had left a message. Of course, he would want to talk the one time all day she wasn't free to talk. Maybe Conrad was irritated by the number of messages she had left, he thought she was a nosey, interfering twit, and was chewing her out.

She got to her meeting place, in the park on the Square in Medina, ten minutes ahead of time. No sign of the hopeful client. She braced herself and listened to Conrad's message.

"Hey, thanks for the heads up," he said, his voice low, free of the rasp that irritated her so much lately. "I appreciate you looking out for me. I owe you, Becca. Big time." Conrad exhaled loudly, so his breath whistled into his phone. "I'm heading over there to deal with it. But thanks. We make a good team, don't we? How come we didn't work out? Granny would have been happy to see us together, you know?"

"We didn't work out, you testosterone-damaged dweeb, because you never follow through, you don't answer your phone, you call me Becks when you know I hate it, and you picked that skanky cat Simone." Becca's face warmed. Had she just said those things aloud? Carefully, she glanced to the right and left, trying not to move her head.

Whew. No one was staring at her. It looked like nobody was close enough, crossing the Square and the lovely little park, to have heard her. She hoped. Of course, she hadn't looked directly behind herself. With her luck, there was someone standing there, staring, wondering if they should call the police to take care of this crazy woman.

Conrad didn't call back to say what had happened when he went to Windows. Becca knew she didn't really have any right to know, but she had been helping him out, right? It would have just been courteous to let her know what kind of trouble she had helped prevent.

~~~~~

"I have the strangest urge to apologize," Eden said, as she and Troy followed Kai into the lobby of Saundra's apartment building that evening.

"Huh?" Troy looked up from his smartphone and half-stumbled, as if he was surprised to find they were inside already. He had been tapping away at his phone, dealing with texts and emails, since they got in Kai's car and headed up Longview. "For what?"

"I feel like we're chaperones for their first real date." She snorted when Kai reached for the button of the elevator, turned sharply to look at her, and missed.

"This is not—" Kai sighed and tried to laugh at the sudden racing of his heart. "Now that things are calming down, Saundra just wants to ..."
~~~~~

He shrugged. "You know, we've had her over a few times, now it's her turn. We're celebrating the whole Cigar Man mess getting cleaned up. It's not a date," he muttered half under his breath, as the brass cage elevator rattled to a stop and creaked and squeaked open.

"That's good, because we might end up asking a lot of awkward questions," Troy said. "Can't wait to see that greenhouse."

"I'm willing to bet that it's entirely a coincidence," Eden said as they stepped into the elevator. "Saundra is into plants, and Patty told her about this apartment with the greenhouse on the balcony. It just worked out that it was vacant when she needed to move." The elevator started up with a shake and a clatter.

"I hope so," Kai muttered.

"I don't," Troy said. "I would love to have a few connections, so we can ask questions and get real answers after all this time."

"If there are connections, then Saundra isn't exactly the person we think she is, and that could ruin a lot of things," Eden said. The elevator banged to a squeaky stop for punctuation. She patted Kai's shoulder as they waited for the door to slide open, so they could step out.

The apartment door hung open, allowing sweet-spicy-fruity aromas to waft out into the hallway. Kai's stomach rumbled in response. He remembered some cartoons, where streamers of enticing aromas wrapped around people and picked them up and yanked them into a room.

"Knock knock," Eden said, pausing in the doorway.

"Come on in!" Saundra appeared in the doorway of the balcony off her living room. "I think I made a mistake setting up on the balcony. The wind picked up and is trying to blow away my napkins and placemats." Laughing she spread her arms. "Welcome. My first official dinner party."

"Ouch, and we're way under-dressed." Troy gestured down at his jeans and boat shoes.

"Nope, you're all perfect. Hope you're hungry." She stepped into the kitchen while gesturing at the sofa and chairs. "Make yourselves comfortable. We'll be ready in like ten minutes."

"Hungry and heading for starving," Kai said, and followed her into the kitchen. He hoped there was something he could offer to do to help. "Whatever you made smells incredible."

"On that note," Eden said, right behind him, "can we help with anything?"

"Confession time." Troy gave Kai a nudge. "We're all curious about that greenhouse, after you asked for advice and leads on supplies. Mind if I take a look before we eat?" He ignored the glare Eden shot him.

Kai held his breath, silently chanting a command for Saundra not to get suspicious. Part of him wished he had never told his cousins that she had taken the apartment that once belonged to Sybil Orwell. He had never had a chance to search the place, the few times he had been here since she moved in. If Troy messed things up and tonight was a disaster, he might never have a chance to look for anything the mysterious woman might have left behind. Such as information on the three cousins' true identities and why they had been deliberately lost in the system.

"Go ahead. If you spot anything I've done wrong, or that needs fixing, I would be so grateful." Saundra tugged on the latch for the sliding door off the kitchen, pulled it open, then stepped aside, clearing the way for Troy to go out into the small greenhouse.

The aromas of wet soil and some acidic plant food and the warm perfume of green growing things filtered into the kitchen, thin threads woven through the smells of their dinner. She performed a simple, swirling dance around the island unit in the center of the kitchen, picking up serving plates and bowls and filling them from the stove and oven. Eden slipped in easily, taking the empty cooking vessels and putting them in the sink or stacking them on the counter. She handed the full platters and bowls to Kai. He didn't need to be told to put them on the table.

The three of them were sitting down, while Saundra filled tall glasses with lemonade poured over ice cubes with raspberries in them, when Troy came in from the greenhouse.

"Please tell me you're not growing some exotic new drugs in there," he said, once he had settled in the last empty seat, facing Saundra.

"I wouldn't know." She laughed when Eden and Troy both frowned at her. "Most of those plants, what they're for, what they'll do when they've been analyzed and processed or whatever, I have no idea. Later," she said, waving her hand to effectively stop the questions ready to spill off Kai's tongue. "Troy, would you mind giving the blessing?"

"Ah …" He leaned back a little, glancing at Eden, then at Kai, then back to Saundra. "Sorry, that's not really … one of my strong suits."

"Oh. Sorry if I made you—I just assumed …" She flushed a little. "Would you mind if I prayed?"

"Please do," Eden said. "At one of our foster homes, our parents had us hold hands when they prayed. I kind of miss that. Yes, I do," she added, wrinkling up her nose at Troy. "Don't give me that look. Just because I don't make you heathens join me over prayers at every meal doesn't mean I've gone heretic." She held out her hand to Saundra, sitting to her left, and to Troy, on her right.

Kai wiped his hand on his jeans before taking Saundra's outstretched hand. He fought a grin when he felt hers tremble slightly. He liked the feeling of her hand, warm and strong and smaller than he would have guessed. He didn't pay much attention to what she said, as he searched back through his memories to which set of foster parents Eden was referring to. She had said "our," so there were only two foster homes where all three of them had been together. Yes, he could remember holding hands, but not understanding who those people were talking to.

Then Saundra finished, and he held onto her hand a few seconds longer, so she had to gently tug it free. She blushed a little, and he knew he was grinning like an idiot. If Troy gave him a hard time over that when they went home, he wouldn't much care.

Eden asked about the recipes, and Kai had a surge of completely irrational pride when Saundra said she hadn't used a recipe, per se. She experimented and played with herbs when she cooked, and only remembered to write down what worked about half the time. Troy used the mention of herbs as an opening to bring up the greenhouse. Did Saundra grow her own herbs for her cooking? She admitted that yes, one section of shelves of pots were her personal plants. Those, she knew the names and uses, and dried herbs for cooking all through the year.

"Most of the greenhouse is Aunt Cleo's domain. I'm just her remote-control gardener. She sends me the seeds and cuttings, and I take pictures and measurements and carefully record all the different levels of watering and fertilizer and the effects and ... whatever." Saundra shrugged.

"Why?" Kai asked. "I mean, you said you don't even know the names? How does that happen?"

"My aunt travels all around the world, doing all sorts of research. She sends me the seeds and cuttings, and she confers with other people who know more about the plants, what they're supposed to provide or the seeds or leaves or stems or roots or whatever are supposed to do."

"Don't you want to know?" Troy said. "Aren't you curious?"

"After all this time?" Saundra shuddered and her hand tightened on the handle of her fork. She shook her head. "It's crazy, but I feel a little safer, maybe some barriers around me if I don't know. If I treat the plants as just a hobby, I guess. I rented greenhouse space, back where I used to live. It wasn't safe having these plants in my apartment because my cousins were just these selfish, prying creeps. They felt it was their right to come into my home and dig around and take whatever they wanted."

"Yeah, I know what that's like." Troy jerked sideways, away from Eden's slap, and laughed. "I'm thinking of foster brothers and sisters. No privacy. No way to protect what's yours without raising a big, ugly fuss."

"So what happens when they come visit here?" Kai said.

"Oh, I hope they don't. They should be angry enough with me, first for changing my name and then leaving town without their permission ..." Saundra chuckled. "Hopefully they've finally gotten the message that I don't want to be part of their family anymore, so leave me alone."

"Changed your name?" Eden's expression didn't change, she didn't move, but Kai felt the tension shoot through her. "Bailey isn't your real name?"

"Oh, it is. Legally now. It was my mother's maiden name. No, my father was a Mulcahy." She huffed a little chuckle. "Mulcahy-Dresden Pharma? Which, if you know anything about the pharmacy industry, explains why Aunt Cleo doesn't want my father's family to have any access to those plants."

"Wow. Ever get the feeling we got off lucky, not knowing where we came from?" Troy muttered.

Eden kicked him under the table. He muffled a yelp. She stuck her tongue out at him. Then, to Kai's relief, all four of them laughed.

The only further reference to those plants in the balcony greenhouse was when Troy offered to give it an inspection to winterize it. He recommended some additives in the watering system that he had been experimenting with. The goal was to help the plants resist drops in temperature that couldn't be completely prevented by the heaters currently sitting quietly on the floor under the grow tables. Kai was proud of him for not asking for samples of the plants, and even more proud that Troy didn't try to sneak into the greenhouse to take some leaves and buds, when Eden and Saundra were standing on the living room balcony, discussing the view.

"Notice anything familiar in there?" Eden asked later that evening, on the drive home.

"Didn't get a chance to look that close," Troy said.

"I trust her," Kai said.

"We haven't said we don't," Eden said.

"But you're going to investigate anyway."

"I have to. Especially since my first check of her – don't get hyper on me, Kai, you know it's second nature for anyone new to town, anyone who becomes part of our lives or businesses. I trust your gut instinct, and mine says she's genuine, but … well, she changed her name."

"To separate herself from, and probably deliberately to hack off her slimebag relatives," Troy said.

"I hope so."

"What if she's a plant?" Kai said, knowing that was what his cousins were thinking.

"We need to get a good look at her friend Charli's heart locket," Eden said.

"Huh? How did we get from Saundra being a Mulcahy to—"

"If Saundra is a long-term plan to earn our trust and get at the seeds in our lockets, then her friend Charli is either another target, or she's part of the plan. Earn our trust by making us think that we've found someone else with a heart locket."

"We need to get our hands on it and look inside, see if she still has the seeds," Troy said.

"Who says any of the other lockets have seeds? Maybe other things are hidden in them. Maybe messages, explanations." She shrugged and slumped lower in the front passenger seat. "Maybe the truth of what's going on."

"Suppose those plants she's growing come from seeds hidden in a heart locket. Did she take them from her friend's locket? Or did Saundra or her aunt have her own locket? What if every heart has different seeds? If so, we can't prove anything, if her plants aren't the same ones that came from our seeds."

"You guys are giving me a headache," Kai said.

"I need to do research into Charli Hall. More research," Eden corrected. "It's a pretty sad story. She's one tough lady." She inhaled deeply and sat up, as Kai pulled the car into the alley behind their building.

"Well, yeah, working for an investigator," Troy said.

"Carson Fletcher. I've worked with him. Not face-to-face, but on the phone, sharing information, insight. He's sent a few clients to me. No, I'm talking about her personal life." She tugged on the latch to open the car door. "Upstairs."

She didn't wait for either of them to respond but headed for the door. Kai had to check in with the staff who were on duty tonight before he could head upstairs. The lights were off in the office, but Eden's apartment door hung open and light spilled out, inviting them in. Troy wasn't there when he tapped on the open door and stepped in. Eden came out of her kitchen with a tray of glasses and a pile of cookies. She gestured with a tip of her head back into the kitchen. He stepped in and retrieved the pitcher. The milk had a beige tint, and he sniffed and caught a whiff of mint and cinnamon. The aroma came from a powder Troy had come up with after years of growing the seeds taken from their three lockets, experimenting and pollinating and crossbreeding. Without being sure what those plants were supposed to be. The mixture helped them relax while keeping their thoughts clear. He wasn't sure if she chose the powder from habit, unthinking, or she was reminding them of what they had been fighting to defend and understand most of their lives.

"Have you done any research on Charli Hall's grandmother?" Kai settled down on the couch facing the one where Eden could usually be found stretched out, either reading or surfing the web or half-asleep, exhausted. "Seeing as how the heart is hers, according to Saundra."

"And just when did you find that out?" Troy asked, having just joined them. He tossed a bag of chocolate and peanut butter drizzled popcorn to Eden. The bag barely cleared the glasses. She scowled at him, then stretched out on her couch and untwisted the closure to open it.

"Lots of talking. Listening." Kai shrugged. "So that means you haven't checked her out?"

"I'm still trying to figure out Charli," Eden said.

She took a handful of the popcorn, twisted the bag closed, and tossed it back to Troy. Then she told them what she had learned about Charli Hall. She had married in college. Comments from classmates and teachers and friends about her very short marriage and the senseless death of her husband in a convenience store shooting. Kai felt some concern when Eden related the reports of what Charli had done to track down the shooter and bring him to justice. He wondered what drove her. A sense of justice, a hunger for revenge?

"No clue yet to what name she writes under," Eden finished, after going through other details of Charli's life since then; the writing conferences she attended, her closest friends, also writers, and the work she had done with Carson Fletcher. Kai reported some of the things Saundra had told him about Charli's career problems. There was precious little he could tell them, because Saundra was very careful to protect Charli's alter ego. He had to admire her for that.

"I need to be careful researching her. She obviously has professional help in protecting her pen name, keeping a thick wall between it and her real identity," Eden said. "And quite frankly, hearing how she went after the guy who killed her husband, something tells me I don't want to rile her. I don't think she'd be violent, but she could find out things about us and make us vulnerable to whoever out there doesn't like us."

"Wish it was as simple as finding someone with a huge glass heart collection," Troy said. He tipped his head back and tossed some popcorn up high. He jerked to the right as it came down, but the chocolate-covered glob bounced off his nose.

"Actually …" Kai grinned when his cousins turned to him.

"Spill," Eden said.

"He's got a couple suspects," Troy guessed.

"Just one. And the character she's known for has an origin story that's something like Charli's," Kai admitted. "Carlotta Vandevere has a glass heart collection that she features on her website. Fans send her glass hearts. I've never seen a picture of anything like our lockets, but that makes sense if it's an heirloom, and she has an idea how valuable it is."

"The question is if she knows about the seeds. Or if she has seeds in hers," Eden quickly added, nodding to Troy when he opened his mouth. "And more important, if Saundra got the seeds she's growing from her." She sighed and reclined again. "Tonight did not give us the answers I was hoping for."

"Just what we need, more mystery and questions surrounding Saundra."

"Yeah, but I think we really need to be careful of that spook, Nick,"

Troy said. "He just shows up a little too conveniently, whenever she needs him." His weary expression turned to a nasty grin. "Knight in shining armor is kind of your gig, isn't it?"

Kai just shook his head. He had no right to get irritated with Troy. Especially since there was some truth in what he said. He was grateful Nick was there to help Saundra whenever things got tense, but he couldn't help feeling a little ... well, not jealous, but worried. He hadn't known her long enough to have anything solid between them. He had never really wanted to get serious about someone, until Saundra, so he wasn't sure what to do, how fast to move, and how soon he needed to take out a contract on Nick West to get him out of the way.

All right, that last part he could blame on the really long day and all the craziness they had gone through the last week or two.

"I don't think you have anything to worry about with Nick," Eden said.

"He is more your type," Troy countered.

"Is not!" She sat up again and reached for the last cookie. "Okay, we're all getting punchy. I'm going to call it a night and get to work on digging into the Mulcahy clan in the morning. I need to verify Saundra's story, especially when she changed her name, and the subtext that she doesn't get along with her cousins."

"I believe her." Kai hoped he hadn't said that too quickly. Or too often.

"I really hope what you find out ties into the last excavation job you did on them," Troy said. "I don't remember his name, but there was one Mulcahy son who was considered the black sheep of the family."

"Meaning he was the only decent one in the entire brood. Yeah." Eden nodded. "We need to move slowly and carefully."

"Like ... duh?" Kai muttered.

He remembered that first, and hopefully only encounter with Bridget Mulcahy, soon after that botanist Troy had consulted sold them out. At first glance, she was dazzling and magnetic, but that didn't last long. Like artificial whipped cream, leaving a bitter aftertaste. She showed up about a year before they discovered Cadburn, when they were all living separately. Eden was still learning how to erase their trails, and Troy was using his rapidly growing investments to pull strings and pay for records to be sealed as quietly as possible. They had turned the tables on the people who had been blocking most of the avenues they found to track down their pasts. Then they had traced those faceless, usually nameless people's footprints backward.

Bridget had found Troy because of the botanist, and she followed him to the coffee shop Kai managed as he worked his way through college. She targeted Kai, probably because he was younger and more visible. As far as the three of them could tell, Bridget and hopefully the rest of the Mulcahy clan didn't know about Eden.

Kai still wasn't sure what had tripped the alarms for him, other than how quickly Bridget became a regular and wanted to know all about him. He was only flattered for maybe ten minutes. A sleek, wealthy, cultured young woman showing interest in him set off alarms for Kai. Careful watching proved she wasn't interested in him. She always seemed to be there, busy with her phone, checking social media, when Troy came in for lunch and to talk every other day. They were lucky that Eden never came to that coffee shop for lunch. Usually, they met at her apartment. Kai gave Bridget's credit card information to Eden to check out.

All their alarms went off. She was identified as an executive-in-training at Mulcahy-Dresden Pharma, almost at the same time Troy's investigation of the suddenly silent botanist revealed his regular communications with the pharmacy corporation. Troy went with two friends who were newly graduated lawyers to confront the botanist and take back whatever remained of the seeds that had been entrusted to him for analysis. He admitted he had germinated most of them. The lawyers threatened to file legal claims and complaints and destroy the botanist's reputation in the industry. More important, they got custody of the plants grown from the seeds.

Troy stopped coming to the coffee shop. Bridget lost interest in Kai soon after. When she started haunting the lobby of the building where Troy rented space for his office and makeshift greenhouse, Eden called in some favors and filed a restraining order against Bridget. She had a public meltdown in the lobby when Troy presented her with the order, and a threat to take her family corporation to court for theft of intellectual property. The botanist hadn't identified the plants, to determine if they were unique, or simply a new variant. Mulcahy-Dresden was unable to file for patent on the seeds and resulting plants. Eden and Troy worked with several friends with more experience in such things, and filed provisional patents on the seeds, to at least put in a "place marker," and a time stamp, if the day ever came that Mulcahy-Dresden tried to claim they had genetically engineered the seeds.

Interestingly, the botanist vanished altogether. Rumors said he had fled the country. Eden didn't take the time to find out if they were true.

Learning Saundra was related to those Mulcahys had felt like a hard punch in the gut with spiked gloves. Knowing she had changed her name to escape them was some help, but not as much as Kai needed.

~~~~~

Becca groaned when someone thumped, hard, on her back door just seconds after she turned off the kitchen light to go upstairs and finally go to bed. She had that early morning breakfast meeting with Valerie Carter
~~~~~

and had stayed up late organizing all the research she had done for her.

"Hey, babe," Conrad said, when she pulled the door open. "Sorry for stopping over this late. Do you know where Devona and Rufus are?"

Becca almost pushed the screen door open to look to the other side of the duplex. She hadn't heard either of her neighbors moving around. A glance past Conrad showed Devona's car but not Rufus's van.

"No. They mentioned meeting someone for dinner ... sorry. Have you tried calling them?"

"This isn't something to handle on the phone. I'm looking for Raymond. I figure, you know, Devona might know where he's staying. He's not answering his phone. Do you know where they went?"

He shrugged, offering a crooked grin that sent a totally inexplicable chill down Becca's back, and braced himself with one arm against the door frame. She was glad she had the screen door between him and her. The movement put the underside of his arm into the light, revealing several long, fresh scratches, some of them deep enough to be scabbed. This time last year, she would have ordered him to come inside so she could put ointment and bandage strips on the cuts. But that was last year. The Conrad standing on the other side of her door wasn't someone to invite into her house at nearly 11pm.

"Uh ... no, I don't. Sorry."

"This is really—" A spark of something hot in his eyes sent a deeper shiver down her back. "Hacking me off," he said after a few seconds, when she was sure he was going to blurt words Sarah Fontaine would have slapped her grandson for using. "I just want to talk to him about what you saw this afternoon, and the guy is suddenly nowhere to be seen. I was hoping since he can't take no for an answer, he'd be tailing Devona, but ..." With a growling kind of sigh, he pushed off the doorframe and stepped back. "Thanks."

"Sure. Sorry I couldn't help."

"Well ..." He winked. "We could talk about you making it up to me." A muffled chiming sound had him growl something that sounded foreign, and he snatched his phone from his back pocket. Whatever he saw on the screen deepened the scowl lines around mouth and eyes. "Later, babe. Gotta take care of ..." With an angry sigh, he turned and stomped off the porch, down the steps, and out into the darkness.

Becca stood in the doorway for several minutes, waiting to hear the sound of an engine starting, then the car driving away. She had the awful feeling she wasn't going to get to sleep any time soon. More than anything, she needed to talk to Sarah. Conrad had changed so drastically.

She knew what Sarah would say, though. She would counsel Becca to pray hard for Conrad. Maybe pray for God to use His two-by-four on him, if that was what it took to straighten him out.

~~~~~

When the three cousins split up for the night, Kai suspected Eden wasn't going to sleep very long. She tended to keep working and hunting until she got answers. He tried to relax enough to sleep, but he was only able to doze, lightly enough that he heard the bells in the clock tower, maybe five miles north on Sackley Road, when they chimed midnight, then 12:30, then 1am. He wasn't surprised when he padded down the stairs in his bare feet, in sleeping shorts and still pulling on a T-shirt, and found the light on over Eden's workstation. She barely glanced up when he stepped into the office, as if she expected him to show up.

"Cleo Bailey certainly earns her Frequent Flyer miles," she muttered.

Kai settled into his swivel chair and leaned back, to just the right angle where he could read over her shoulder.

"World traveler?"

"And then some. Got some pictures of her and Nick West, when they were involved in helping to expose some shady dealings overseas." She glanced over at him with a crooked little smile. "That sort of verifies what Saundra told us about him. Investigative work, protégé of her aunt. Like Troy said, spook."

"Anything about the rest of the family?"

"Little enough to be suspicious. Like someone took steps to erase their history, too."

"Yeah?" Kai sat up with a thud and scooted his chair over closer to hers. "Did they do it, or was it done to them?"

"No way of knowing this early in the investigation."

"So you are investigating?"

Eden shrugged. "But it's interesting the society page hits when I researched her sister and brother-in-law."

"Society page?"

"Gossip. Supports the impressions I got before. Saundra's father is the black sheep of the family. Nice guy, but either he hated the business and wanted nothing to do with it, or the rest of the clan locked him out. Saundra was basically in the shadows her whole life. I found some school records, commenting on how her cousins and their yes-men bullied her."

"Good for us, or bad?" Kai finally said, when Eden continued studying the documents called up on her screen and didn't make any more comments.

"What does your gut say?" She didn't turn to look at him.

"I want to believe her."

"But?"

"But ..." He sighed and leaned back in his chair again, to study the painted images on the ceiling tiles. "But this could be her chance to finally get accepted by the family. Despite erasing our steps, they followed me
~~~~~

and Troy here to Cadburn, without us detecting them. Which means they probably know about you now. And ... they've learned enough about us to send Saundra to ... No, I don't want to believe she's a Mata Hari. My gut says she's exactly what she says she is, but ..."

"But there's the odd coincidence of her friend Charli having a heart locket. And looking something like us. Enough to be a relative," she added, her voice dropping nearly to a whisper.

"So what do we do? Confront Charli? Plant some bugs in Saundra's place, hack her phone, so we can overhear her reporting on us?"

"Let me do more digging, find out about Charli and her aunt Cleo. And just spend more time getting to know Saundra." Eden sighed and turned halfway to face him. "My gut says she's the real thing, too, but we can't afford to take risks without more information."

"So ... if we find out Charli having the locket is just coincidence, and Saundra is safe, what then? Ask what they know? Ask to talk to her aunt? Find out where she got the plants we saw in her greenhouse tonight?"

"We'll know what questions to ask when the time comes." Eden glanced sideways at him and snorted, amused and weary.

Chapter Ten

Saturday, September 10

"Well," Saundra drawled, leaning into the gap between door and frame to look out of her apartment. "Think of the devil and he appears. And here I thought you had taken off for more interesting places."

"I would, if there wasn't work and more keeping me here. And it's not you. For a change," Nick West returned with a slight smirk. Not as large a smirk as she expected, after he had swooped in and rescued her, like he had done when her cousins had rallied the school bullies against her. He raised the cardboard tray with two large, sealed take-out cups and a paper bag that bulged with promise. Grease smears darkened the logo for Deli-licious. "Are you going let me in while the food is still hot?"

"A man who brings breakfast when I don't feel like cooking. How did I luck out?" She gave up fighting her smile and stepped back, pulling the door open. "But what makes you think there's trouble? Carruthers has orders to stay away from me, and Roger Cadburn has to wear an ankle monitor. And don't you dare say Curtis is a threat."

"None of them." He handed her the bag that smelled of cheese and sausage and bread, and reached with his free hand to tug open the sliding door to the balcony. "Hate to break it to you but checking up on you wasn't my first reason for coming to this sleepy little town."

"Really? Why do I feel relieved rather than insulted?"

"For starters, you're intelligent and humble. I have no idea why you resent my brotherly concern." He gave her a wide-eyed look of mocking innocence.

Saundra doubted Nick had ever been innocent, even when he was a wriggling baby in diapers. She followed him out onto the balcony. "I've been wondering. Which intelligence agency do you work for?"

"Don't know what you're talking about. I work for your aunt."

She chose not to comment on that. "So, what or who brought you to town, and why do you have time to handle my new bullies without ignoring your prime mission?"

"What do you know about a guy named Conrad Price, who runs Fontaine Realty?"

"Besides threatening to run against Roger Cadburn, which would normally make him the town golden boy?" She shook her head, distracted when Nick unwrapped the sloppy, incredible-smelling breakfast bagel sandwiches that oozed cheese and onions and an interesting greenish sauce, nearly hiding the hash brown patty and sausage and bacon. "Why are you investigating him?" She hoped he would talk and not ask her questions for a while. This definitely needed to be eaten hot.

"An old friend tracking some money followed a trail here, and there's been some hijinks with some highly skilled manipulation of electronic records. What do you know about your friend Eden and the computer geek who works with her?"

"Just about that. I haven't been in town that long." She took a bite and seriously considered kissing him. But that would mean smearing some of that mouthful on him, and she didn't want to waste anything.

"Long enough to get someone to try to kill you."

"Threaten. With a squirt gun. Big difference."

"Not where I'm standing. Not when I have to answer to Cleo if you get scratched." He took a bite and let out a groan. "Oh, yeah," he said around the mouthful. At least Nick knew how to talk with his mouth full without spraying. "Definitely a repeat customer. That man knows his stuff." He chewed a few more times, then swallowed. "Conrad Price. Have you run into him?"

"Not really. I've heard some of the gossip. His grandmother died recently. His grandfather died last winter, and some estranged sons showed up and tried to muscle Conrad out of running the family business. Why? What does he have to do with this money trail?"

"Don't know yet. I find it interesting he had a lot of communication with your friend Eden, and her pet geek has been doing a lot of security work for him."

"This is about Eden, not about Conrad Price, isn't it? You're just looking for an excuse to go digging around."

"Why would you say that?"

"Eden is an investigator, and Rufus does computer programming. That doesn't make them guilty of anything if Conrad is doing something illegal. Until we figure out what's up with Eden's heart locket, I think we should keep a low profile. We don't know what side of the conflict she and the guys are on."

"What conflict?" Nick's tone turned cool. He put down his sandwich to study her, all mischief gone from his gaze.

"Well, duh, I may be Cleo's research geek, but I do pull my head out of the computer and the books often enough to figure some things out. You two wouldn't be so secretive about the lockets and where the seeds came from and what they are if there wasn't danger and people fighting over the seeds and ..." She shrugged. "Whatever."

"So you don't trust your new friends?"

"I trust them. I just don't know if they should trust us."

"If they don't trust you, there's something seriously wrong with those people." He let go of his sandwich long enough to squeeze her wrist. Considerately keeping from interfering with her grip on her sandwich that kept trying to explode out from the bagel and spill onto the wrapper spread on the table.

He lost all those points he had earned when he waited until she was taking another bite, then said, "Especially Kai."

Saundra choked. She couldn't twist enough to jab him with her elbow, so she settled for stomping on his foot. Nick snorted in the middle of his own mouthful. She hoped he got some onions and cheese up his nose, at the very least.

"So, tell me what you know about Conrad, ignoring what connection Eden might or might not have with him."

By the time they finished their sandwiches and she refilled their cups twice with coffee, she had related to him everything she knew. Mostly gossip. Conrad didn't come into the library, and he didn't attend Cadburn Bible Chapel, even though his grandmother had been an active member of the congregation. She knew how Nick worked, and told him everything she had heard, which wasn't very much. About Becca and Simone's rivalry, both the dance clubs and over Conrad. The breakup between Raymond Fontaine and Devona, before most people realized there was a romance starting. How Sarah had gone on a vacation with Devona and Rufus and never came home. People were still talking about how odd it was that she had donated her body to science at a local university, and there was no body to view at the church service. The rumors that the estranged Fontaine sons had threatened to take everything away from Conrad. Frank Fontaine had been seen skulking around town just a few days ago, then his brothers showed up, claiming he had disappeared.

Saundra couldn't make out any clear picture from all the bits and pieces. She hoped it helped and triggered some insights for Nick. Whatever he was working on.

~~~~~

Kai really hoped he was just suffering from a sleepless night, meaning bad waking dreams, when Nick West walked up to the counter just after 9am. He finished an order of white chocolate frozen whip for a party of six while Libby stepped up to wait on Nick.

This was just stupid. He shouldn't feel resentment, maybe even a sense of threat, when Nick walked in. Without his intervention, Saundra would have been hurt several times. Roger Cadburn might have done something even more moronic than threaten her with a squirt gun, to get hold of books Saundra had never taken from the library in the first place.

"Hi. Kai, right?"

Kai barely kept from jumping when that smooth baritone voice
~~~~~

seemed to come out of nowhere. He turned to see Nick holding a tall, plain coffee and leaning on the counter a few steps away.

"That's right. What brings you back to town?" He really hoped Nick wouldn't say Saundra, because he might have to throw someone out of Book & Mug for the first time since he opened the coffee shop.

"I've got some questions for your cousin, Eden. Is she available?"

Kai didn't have to think long. Nick probably had some last threads to tie up, whatever part he was playing in the investigation. He nodded and pulled out his phone to text. Just in case Eden was on a phone call or video chat or something that shouldn't be interrupted.

Saundra's spook is here. Wants to talk to you. Free?

Just a few seconds later: *No. Very $$$. B right down.*

Kai laughed. "She's on her way." He suggested Nick make himself comfortable, either the stools at the far end of the counter or in the big booth in the back, then spent the next couple of minutes wondering what plain coffee said about him. Nick didn't make use of the insulated pitchers of creamer or any of the multiple sweeteners on the service counter.

A group of high schoolers came in to cash in their points from the summer reading program. When Kai looked around again, Eden was sitting across the corner of the counter from Nick, with her own tall cup of iced coffee. He said something Kai couldn't hear, but Eden sat up and started to shake her head. Nick reached in his pocket and brought out a folded paper. He handed it to her and waited while she unfolded it and read through it. Several times. Then, to Kai's surprise, she slid off her stool and gestured for Nick to follow her.

~~~~~

Saturday morning, Becca had a breakfast meeting at Morning Folks café with Valerie Carter, a former sales rep at the Strongsville weekly paper. She had launched her own boutique advertising and promotions agency and had hired Becca to do preliminary searches for her: office space, equipment, software, online resources, office supplies, and printers for letterhead and business cards. Since she planned to hit the library and do a couple hours of searching archival books for Charli before spending the afternoon working with Eden, Becca parked in the municipal lot on Apple, rather than starting out in the parking lot across the street from Morning Folks. She resisted the urge to give Windows a possessive little good morning wave as she crossed the bridge over Cadburn Creek, to turn left on Creekview to walk to Morning Folks.

The morning radio DJ had been talking about a forecast of several days of rain, prompting Becca to glance down into the creek as she crossed the bridge. Several people had been talking about how high the water would get in the creek with the fall rains. It was the same slight flurry of worries every fall, but no one's basements ever flooded because the water
~~~~~

never rose more than three feet in the creek. Some people were saying this was the driest summer in the last fifteen years, maybe more. Some of the people who still tried to find the Underground Railroad tunnels joked about praying for high water levels in the spring and fall, just to reveal those tunnels. The people who lived downstream, where the bank was much lower, didn't think it was funny. Especially when insurance rates got yanked higher, in anticipation of possible flooding and flood damage claims. Here in the center of town, it was a good thirty-foot drop from the bridge to the creek bed, but heading east down the creek, once it passed the township park, the channel dug out by flowing water widened and the landscape lowered. Meaning greater chances for flooding.

All those worries seemed far away right now. Becca noted the dry ridges of rock, and spots where debris had collected in piles, stranded when the water level went down. She couldn't remember the last time she had looked down into the creek. There certainly seemed to be more rock than water, right there under the bridge supports.

A woman called her name. Becca turned to look ahead, then behind herself. A woman waved her arms and broke into an elegant little half-trot to catch up with her. Silver-streaked sable hair and a sleek figure, gray-blue sun dress, trailing her trademark three, long, filmy, rainbow-streaked scarves. That was Valerie.

Something snagged at the back of her mind. Becca waved, but she was already turning to look down into the creek. Was that … no, that couldn't be.

"Hey, I thought that was you. Walking off whatever the breakfast special will be today?" Valerie said as she caught up with her. "You okay?" She rested a light hand on Becca's shoulder.

"Please tell me I need to get my eyes checked." She pointed down to a dark shape that lay in a leaf-clogged puddle, partially in the shadows of the bridge.

"I hope somebody is playing a really sick joke." Her grip tightened.

"Do you see a man, lying face-down in the water? Gray sleeveless shirt, jeans, work boots, curly black hair?" She raised her gaze from what she still hoped was just an optical illusion, or maybe a mannikin some stupid college prankster had thrown in the water, two months ahead of Halloween.

Valerie nodded. Becca swallowed hard and reached in her pocket for her phone.

There was some comfort in the police station being just a few blocks down the street, and the fire station just around the corner from the township park. Captain Sunderson and Allen Kenward were the first to jog down to the bridge, just moments after the siren sounded. Allen exchanged glances with his captain, then continued to the other end of the bridge. The building sitting right there on the corner had a deck extending out over the creek, and switchback stairs of railroad ties and bricks built into the slope of the bank. It was the fastest way down to the creek, without taking a dive off the bridge itself. Probably like that man down there had done.

Sunderson pulled out her phone, turned on the recorder, and got Becca and Valerie's statements while Allen was climbing down. The rescue truck pulled up on the bridge and three firefighters in T-shirts, boots, and their turnout gear pants, held up with suspenders, climbed out and leaned over the railing. They conferred for a few moments before pulling a metal stretcher from the back of the truck and heading for the same stairs to follow Allen down.

"No pulse," Allen called up to them. "He's cold, and there's a pretty big dent in the side of his head. Lots of blood pooled in the water here."

"Recognize him?" Sunderson called after a few moments of watching the rescue workers climbing down.

"Maybe."

"Meaning?" She cocked an eyebrow and glanced at Becca.

"I think I see his wallet. Let me check." Allen pulled a wad from his shirt pocket, shook out plastic gloves, and put them on. Then he leaned forward, bracing himself so he didn't touch the body, and tugged at the man's back pocket. In a few minutes, he had opened whatever he found and looked through the contents. "Raymond Fontaine."

"Well that just sucks," Sunderson muttered. She walked back to the Center Avenue end of the bridge as she pulled out her phone.

Becca watched the rescue workers climb down to the creek bed and pick their way among the shallow puddles and piles of waterborne debris. Something felt odd about the scene. Bob Endicott, with the stretcher tucked under one musclebound arm, stepped into the water by the body's feet, and went in to his ankles. That sparked something.

"What are the chances he just happened to fall into the only water deep enough to partially hide his body?" she said, more thinking aloud than talking to Valerie.

"Coincidences aren't," the other woman murmured. "You know ... I'm just not up to breakfast right now. It's too early in the morning for something really strong. If I were about to start drinking. Which I hope I'm not. Just saying ..."

"The Mug might have just what we need. Heavy on sugar and cream," Becca suggested.

"Sold." She offered a thin smile and interwove their arms. "Why aren't they doing anything?" She gestured with a jerk of her chin at the officers just standing around the body.

"Probably waiting for the coroner or whoever is qualified to examine it and record everything before they can move him."

"Obviously, I don't watch the right kind of TV."

"Did I hear right?" Sunderson said, rejoining them. "You're heading over to the Mug? Good," she continued, when Becca and Valerie both nodded. "I'm pretty sure I've got everything, but if I can get hold of you for any follow-up, once we get the body moved, I'd appreciate it."

"But don't talk to anybody?" Becca looked past the police chief. Several people were standing at either end of the bridge, looking their direction. The fire truck was enough to generate questions. When the coroner's vehicle showed up, that would really get the talk going, and bring more gawkers. The sooner she could get out of sight, the better she would feel.

"The fewer details you share, the better. Appreciate it." She nodded to them and gave that cool, polite smile that was probably taught at the police academy, for those who would be dealing with the public and the press. At least, that was what Becca decided, as she and Valerie walked down to Center and retreated into the shadowy shelter of Book & Mug.

Devona and Rufus were barreling out the door as they came in, and the four nearly collided. Rufus muttered an apology and tipped back on his main wheels, pivoting to get around them. Devona stopped.

"Were you – did you see?" she said, reaching out like she might clutch at Becca's arm. "Captain Sunderson said one of the cousins." She swallowed hard. "We need to identify him and help contact the others. Mama Sarah would – we have to tell the family. Do you know who?"

"Allen looked in his wallet. He said it's Raymond."

Devona went so pale, Becca expected her to fall over. The younger woman shook her head, took a deep breath, and hurried after her brother. His wheelchair was already across the street and heading up the sidewalk.

Becca guided Valerie to a table tucked far at the back of the coffee shop, behind the bookstore half-wall, where they would be hard to spot. Then she got to the counter and ordered their drinks; the richest, biggest frozen whips she could think of. It helped being a Guzzler and knowing all the recipes. She and Valerie needed espresso and chocolate and cream and syrup and caramel. Lots of it.

When she turned to take their tall drinks to the back table, she risked glancing out the front window, and saw the coroner's truck sitting on the bridge. Knowing the body would be moved soon, out of the sight of gawkers, made breathing a little easier for her.

She and Valerie focused on discussing the business that was the reason for meeting today. She was relieved to have something else to think about. A few times they caught each other turning to look over the half-wall, to the picture windows at the front of the coffee shop and up the street to the bridge. The police SUV was still there even though the coroner's truck and the rescue team had left.

They finished all the work they had hoped to get done over breakfast, and stayed seated, waiting, making phone calls to get some errands done that Becca would have normally handled in person. Such as talking to the landlords of several possible locations for Valerie's business. The phone calls used up time and also saved time. Two storefronts she planned to visit with Valerie were no longer available, just since she made the list on Friday.

"I'm disappointed in this one," she said, after the third phone call, and tapped the address on the list with the end of her pen. "This is right next door to Morning Folks. It's adorable. Or at least, it will be once it's cleaned up. The previous tenant was a nightmare for Tracy and the other shop owners on the strip. Tracy was constantly sending him notices that he had violated the terms of the lease, pulling down built-in shelving, and painting without permission. One time he had new electrical sockets installed without permission and blew out the wiring in the units on either side of him, and then sent her the bill. He's still fighting with her, insisting that she owes him several months refunded because business was so bad for him."

"No landlord can ensure good business," Valerie said, punctuated with a snort. A sparkle of her usual wry humor had returned to her eyes.

"Especially when his nastiness to customers drove them away, and the shop owners on either side of him are claiming that the smells and noises coming from his store drove their customers away."

"So the place is a mess? That's why you don't want me taking it?" She looked slightly confused.

"No, it's mostly cleaned up. But the Tweeds just signed a lease agreement. They're planning on opening up a candle shop."

"That sounds like fun. Do they have a name chosen yet?"

"Brighten Your Corner."

"Sounds adorable. I don't suppose the place across the street is still available to look at?" Valerie leaned forward to tap at the address next on the list. "I'd love to be close to a shop like that."

"That one is still available, and Tracy is the landlord for that strip too. She'll wait for you to come check it over, but she says to hurry. A couple other hopeful businesses have been asking to look at it."

"I could go over right away ..." She glanced at the front window, then shrugged.

Becca turned to look out the window, but her gaze caught on Captain Sunderson walking along the glass block half-wall toward them. The woman looked grim enough to make her mind race, wondering what sort of bad news she had brought.

"Thanks for waiting." Sunderson paused to rub at her eyes with the heels of her hands. "The coroner was able to make a preliminary confirmation of what we suspected when the body was moved. The victim was unconscious before he hit the water. The blow didn't kill him, but the damage from the fall would have if he hadn't drowned."

Becca shuddered. There were so many questions she could ask based on all the crime investigation and forensic shows she had seen over the years. Charli Hall referred to the assumed medical and scientific knowledge as the "CSI effect," which made real-life investigations and especially court cases difficult. TV viewers just assumed that every police lab could run DNA and fingerprint analysis in a matter of moments. Such misleading, unreal knowledge made court cases doubly hard for the defense and the prosecutor.

"Did Devona and Rufus positively identify him?" she asked instead.

"Yeah. Pretty rough on them. Wish I didn't have to call them, but they've been seen talking with the victim on multiple occasions." The captain rubbed at her neck. "Thanks for your help. There's no telling how long he would have laid there before someone else noticed, and it's supposed to rain pretty heavy tonight. That would have changed the scene and destroyed evidence."

She didn't say anything about the rising water level in the creek washing away the body, and Becca was grateful.

~~~~~

The morning sped by for Kai, with all the activity on the street, and talk about a body found in the creek. Even without that excitement, it would have been a normal warm September Saturday, people busy with errands in town, buying drinks to take with them as they walked the sidewalks or went to the park to enjoy the weather. Nick reappeared during a busy time, and Kai hoped one of the other baristas would deal with him.

No such luck. Once the counter area cleared, and Mike and Libby stepped away to take care of bus pans and replenish supplies, Nick stepped up to the far end and nodded to him.

"Refill?" Kai asked.

"My back teeth are sloshing. I don't know what it is with you and Saundra and coffee." He smirked. Kai decided his professional, polite mask of welcome wasn't fooling him. Nick knew his presence bothered him. And he enjoyed it.

"Something else you need to clear up?"

"That's a good way of putting it." Nick looked over his shoulder, studying the main seating area and the door beyond. No one was approaching, and from the murmur of voices, everyone was busy with their own conversations and not listening to anyone else's. "Me and Saundra. I look at her like my kid sister. Okay?"
~~~~~

Kai nodded, fighting not to react, despite the light, rising sensation in his chest and head.

"So don't hurt her, okay?"

"I—"

"Yeah, I know you don't mean to, but ... the world is full of people who mean well, but they turn out to be jerks. The ones who should be watching out for you, they're the ones who hurt you the most. Family pretty much sucks, for Saundra. All she's got is her aunt and me, and I'm not even blood, but our family history ..." One corner of his mouth twitched upward, just for a second. "She's finally free of some really bad luck. Anyway, you look after her, I'll look after you. Deal?"

Kai wouldn't have been surprised if Nick held out his hand to shake and seal the agreement. He thought for a long moment before nodding. He considered asking Nick about the Mulcahys, then decided just asking would be giving away too much of his family's problems with them. Would taking the risk open up the door to sharing about the heart lockets?

It would be nice if someday, they could all just sit down and tell the truth and expect the truth in return from Saundra and Nick and her aunt and get everything out in the open.

Nick nodded, that smirk grew a little higher, and he got up off his stool at the counter and walked out without looking back.

That gave Kai a lot to chew on, until the after-lunch lull, when he could leave the counter in the hands of Libby and Keith. He headed upstairs, only partially thinking about what to make for lunch. He willed Troy and Eden to both be in the office when he got there.

They were. And even better, they had ordered from Celestial Dragon and got his usual. He bowed to them both before he slid into his usual chair at the conference table and opened the first carton. His stomach rumbled loudly as he caught the first whiff of the kung pao chicken.

"Interesting morning, huh?" Troy said, once Kai had chewed and swallowed his first mouthful.

"And then some. I got the big brother talk from West." Kai filled his mouth while his cousins thought over that bit of information. He swallowed and washed it down with a slug of lukewarm tea, then repeated the conversation as much word-for-word as he could remember.

"Uh huh." Troy settled his own mug on the table and leaned back. "Think it's safe to ask Saundra about the Mulcahys? Is this a sign that she's not a spy? Or is Nick just backing up her cover story?"

"You're killing my appetite."

"Poor baby." Eden smirked over the rim of her mug. "Let me do my dig into Charli, figure out where the locket came from, maybe by then we'll be that much more secure with Saundra, so we can start asking the really sticky questions."

~~~~~

By mid-afternoon, Becca had a new appreciation for the discretion of Captain Sunderson and the loyalty of the officers under her command. Well, most of them, anyway. Carruthers was on administrative leave indefinitely, thanks to his part in the whole Trustee Cadburn mess. He would have been a hard leak to plug, because the man had a reputation for shooting off his mouth.

What mattered to her now was that her name and Valerie's weren't mentioned when news of the body found in the creek got around to the local media outlets. The few people who had been on the street at the time either didn't recognize her and Valerie standing on the bridge, or they were kind enough not to mention them right away, as the gossip started spreading. People who had seen them later talking with the police chief figured out that they had been involved. After the third call fishing for details, Becca set her phone to vibrate and let everything go to voicemail.

~~~~~

"Hey, where've you been?" Rufus called, drawing Saundra's attention away from the trivia game she was playing with him and Kai and Eden that evening in the back corner booth of Book & Mug.

Outside, the predicted rainstorm was a deluge, pounding against the side windows. She felt especially cozy, indoors with friends, indulging in another of Kai's decadent experiments in coffee drinks. She was going to have to walk everywhere, just to avoid gaining weight from acting as his test subject.

She was sitting on the end, so it was easy to turn and follow Rufus with her gaze as he wheeled away to the coffee shop door. A few moments later, Devona came into view, dripping wet, followed by Patty Hill, lowering her dripping cardigan that apparently had given its life to partially protect her from the driving rain. Rufus followed so closely behind them the footrests of his wheelchair came close to hitting the backs of their calves.

"I thought a little walk in the park would be helpful, get away from people," Patty said. "We should have brought umbrellas."

"You should have brought a life raft," Eden said.

Devona tried to smile, then caught her breath and her face crumpled like she fought not to burst into tears. Eden nudged Kai and barely gave him time to slide off the bench, to allow her out.

"You're coming with me and getting into some dry clothes." She wrapped an arm around Devona. "How about you?" she added, looking back over her shoulder at Patty.

"Fine. Wash and wear hair." She let out a gasping little laugh as she gave her cardigan a gentle little shake. "Sorry about that." Raindrops spattered for several feet around her. Fortunately, there were no customers sitting in this part of the coffee shop at that moment. She hung up her cardigan on one of the hooks conveniently waiting at the end of each booth divider wall. Saundra slid over, silently inviting her to sit. Patty let out a sigh and closed her eyes as she settled down.

"You need something hot. What'll it be?" Kai said.

"Surprise me?" She opened her eyes long enough to give him a little smile and grateful nod.

"How's she feeling?" Rufus asked.

For punctuation, and almost as if in answer, the rain pounded harder against the front windows.

"She really hasn't said much, but my impression is she feels ... guilty," Patty finally finished with a shrug.

"For what?" Saundra kept her voice down and glanced around. This would be the perfect time for the wrong person to come upon them and overhear what they shouldn't. "From what I've heard, she broke up with him before things really got started, and he won't take no for an answer. Wouldn't," she corrected herself.

"Sarah asked her to dump him," Patty said. "I can't see how Devona feels any guilt. If only Sarah were here, we could get some answers." She sighed. "And she could help Devona get over this. It's so sad, because they did look so happy, the few times I saw them together."

"Yeah, well, it's not doing that much good ..." Rufus groaned and rubbed his face with his palms. "This doesn't go past this booth, okay?" He leaned in closer, just as Kai came back with a tray with four steaming, frothy drinks, smelling strongly of cinnamon. He grinned and leaned back and pivoted out of the way so Kai could slide into the booth facing Patty and Saundra.

"Thank you." Patty held the tall mug under her nose and inhaled the fragrant steam. "It wasn't so bad when the rain was warm, then it got frigid and felt like bullets. Fall is definitely here, far too soon."

"This is perfect." Saundra sipped and smiled. "Hot version of frozen apple cider?"

"Ouch. Needs a better name than that." Kai winked at her and slouched back in the booth, cradling his mug. "So, what big secret were you about to reveal? Is this one of those, 'I'll tell you but then I'll have to kill you' situations?"

"Close." Rufus took a big gulp from his mug and set it on the end of the table. "Mama Sarah just about had a heart attack, when she saw Raymond and realized who he was, and then realized he and Devona were really hitting it off."

"Why? I can't imagine she'd hold a grudge against her grandson for whatever his father did, all those years ago," Patty said.

"Nope, it's nothing Raymond or his father did, but ..." He looked around again. "Nobody else hears this, okay? I don't want to get into all the ugly details, but … Mom is a Fontaine. Close enough that Raymond and Devona, dating? Pretty much illegal everywhere you go."

"Oh." Saundra took a deep breath and gripped the edge of the seat cushion with one hand, fighting the sudden dropping sensation that turned into aching for Devona. "She never explained to him why she broke it off, did she? That's what's making her hurt so much. He died angry with her."

"That poor girl," Patty whispered.

Rufus focused on the drink cradled in his hands, and the other three looked at each other, questions they couldn't speak filling the air.

"We've got a little bit of a problem," Eden announced when she returned to the booth.

"How's Devona?" Saundra asked.

"I convinced her she needed a hot shower. Rufus …" Eden's eyes narrowed. "She says someone has been trying to break into your house."

"What?" Kai sat up straight. "Hey, are you two okay?"

"Yeah, we're …" Rufus scrubbed his face with his hands and slouched back a little in his wheelchair. "The first few times, we thought it was just Raymond, being a jerk, stalking Vo. I was putting together a boobytrap kind of thing. Mostly to embarrass him. Then I got a brainstorm and it's turning into a burglar alarm. It went off once while Raymond was here, trying to find her, so definitely not him."

"Burglar alarm? And you didn't ask me to help?" Eden said.

"Want in now?" He grinned. "I'm about ready to ask Becca if I can put it on her side of the house, in case the jerk tries to get into her place and come up through the basement to our side. We're gonna make a mint when we finally get it patented and on the market."

Saundra managed a chuckle when Eden just shook her head and rolled her eyes.

"What could this guy be after?" Kai said.

"Honestly?" Rufus leaned closer and lowered his voice. "Mama Sarah had her lawyers distribute a bunch of letters to different people, to protect or whatever, and bring to the official reading to explain the trust and all the changes she made before she died. We figure, the creep thinks we got one."

"Who knows about the letters?" Saundra asked, prompted by a shiver and a half-formed idea she couldn't quite put into words yet.

"No idea. See, the lawyers had to fire somebody they caught taking pictures of documents. The idiot claims she didn't get a chance to send to anyone, but who knows? I've caught some gossip that's pretty close to the truth. Mama Sarah made a whole bunch of changes before we went on that trip and she …" Rufus grimaced. "Then there was all that fuss last weekend, some of the sons looking for the oldest one, Frank. He was up here, investigating, but he's vanished. Frank is Raymond's father."

"It's getting kind of dangerous to be a Fontaine," Kai murmured.

"Maybe we should try to identify whoever has been trying to break in," Eden said.

"You'd do that?"

"Really?" Devona said, startling all of them.

Saundra flinched and looked over at the younger woman, with her hair slicked down, making her eyes look huge in her pale face. She nudged Patty and moved over, so Devona could slide into the booth with them.

"You'd do that for us?" Devona said.

"Once I get over being mad at you that you didn't ask for help sooner," Eden said, and wrinkled up her nose at her.

That wrung a choking little gasp of laughter from Devona.

"You know, there are so many Fontaines suddenly visiting Cadburn. Maybe they're after more than your letter?" Patty chuckled when the others gave her confused, questioning looks. She told them about a chance remark from Becca Sheridan, about her good luck running into two Fontaine cousins who were helping Conrad, and the girl, Agatha, who said she was going to be his leasing agent. "The poor girl was so relieved to finally have Windows nailed down as the Four Corners' meeting spot again, I just didn't have the heart to tell her I found it a little suspicious. Especially with the way Conrad has been dodging her, every time she tries to get a straight answer from him."

"I agree. Suspicious. I'm inclined to think they were lying," Saundra said. "Find them, and you might not just get answers, but maybe they're involved in what happened to Raymond."

"No," Devona and Rufus said almost in unison. They locked gazes, then he sighed and slumped back in his wheelchair and gestured for her to go on.

"We know who they are," she said, after several moments of studying her clasped hands resting on the table. "They have no reason to break into our place."

"Who?" Kai prompted.

"Emily and Benjamin. Raymond's brother and sister." Devona hurried on while the other three digested that revelation. "They used their middle names, that's all. At dinner yesterday, we were laughing at the trick. They were trying to find paperwork to prove Conrad isn't ... There's this guy who says he's investigating ..."

Her gaze flicked to Eden, who cocked one eyebrow at her. Saundra had an impression of silent communication. Unfortunately, she couldn't read minds.

Devona sighed. "It doesn't really matter, does it? They were there and found a contract in the files. Emily scrambled around and covered over the information to make a new contract, for Becca. Just to cause trouble for Conrad and bring things out in the open."

"Would they have been tearing up the floor?" Patty asked. "Becca mentioned something about the floor being ripped up, not just construction to wall in an office space."

"Yeah, they thought something was hidden under the floor," Rufus said. He shuddered. "And then Raymond went back last night because he had this awful idea he wanted to check out. Whatever he found out, it must have been bad, because now he's dead."

"Where are Emily and Benjamin now?" Patty asked. "Do they need help? First their father goes missing, now their brother is dead. It must be awful for them."

"They're staying with —" Devona caught her breath. "Yeah, they're making arrangements and talking to the police, to find out when they can take Raymond home for the funeral."

Chapter Eleven

Sunday, September 11

Greg McMaan, an usher, tapped Becca on the shoulder when everyone stood for the opening prayer at church that morning, and handed her a note. She didn't recognize the steeply right-slanted scrawl. Her name was almost illegible on the front of the triple-folded piece of paper. She had a hard time focusing on Pastor Roy's prayer and waited until the announcements were being made before reading it. What was she going to do if one of the Fontaines had finally caught up with her and was waiting in the back of the sanctuary?

Why was she worried? They couldn't do anything to her in public, with so many witnesses. Unless Conrad was stupid enough to let slip to Raymond, when he confronted him over tearing up the floorboards at Windows, that she had seen and tattled on him?

She definitely needed to stop reading mysteries before turning off the light to go to sleep. Her imagination was starting to run away with her.

The note inside was just as illegible as her name written on the front. She nearly said "No way," out loud, when she read Conrad's name at the bottom. This wasn't his handwriting.

Maybe Conrad had had a stroke? Could that explain his change in personality?

Then she read the note and she was willing to believe he had suffered some kind of brain damage.

> *We need to talk. I've got things to do today and Monday. Meet me at 8 at Windows on Tuesday. But don't come upstairs. Wait in the lobby.*

Why would he ask her to meet him at 8 on Tuesday, when Four Corners started their meetings at 7? Didn't he remember that the club would be there on Tuesday? Or didn't he talk to his cousin, who gave her the contract? What made him think she was going to come downstairs when she would be busy with the meeting?

"You okay?" Saundra asked, when they met up outside after the service.

"Hmm?" Becca blinked and looked around, and her face warmed as she realized she had been moving on automatic pilot. "A lot on my mind."

"Tell me about it. Eden said you visited Curtis. Thanks."

"I wasn't the only one."

"Yeah, but Troy said you had an idea for the Guzzlers to kind of team up to help get him through this mess, and that's ..." She shrugged. "I'll be glad to help. Oh, and Charli suggested we get together. She hopes we can work together on a new series she's brainstorming."

"You don't mind? I mean, you're the children's librarian, not the reference librarian." Becca looked around, just in case anyone was close enough to overhear, and softened her voice. "Do you know about her being ..." She waggled her eyebrows suggestively.

"Her pen name?" Saundra laughed. "Oh, yeah. And the trouble she's having with her publisher wanting to change her character, and the new agent waiting in the wings. I just hope she isn't starting over from scratch, new pen name, new look, all that."

"It's nice someone else is in the know. Do you have plans for lunch? Frenchy's has a great all-day breakfast buffet on Sunday."

"Oh, thanks, but I've got plans with Patty and Pastor Roy."

"Join us," Patty said, stepping up just in time to catch the last part of the conversation.

Becca didn't have to think long to accept. The foursome had a relaxing afternoon enjoying the late summer weather on the back porch of Pastor Roy and Patty's house, just down the street from the Chapel.

~~~~~

Kai came back to Book & Mug from running to Sugarbush to restock the bakery offering. The apple and cinnamon scones were a big hit and had sold out before the afternoon got started. Allen Kenward, looking grimly official and on duty, practically followed him through the door. A prickle of some sense of warning made him slow as he headed for the kitchen area to give the boxes of fresh scones and cinnamon whoopie pies to Amy to put on display. He looked back to see the police officer following him.

"Help you with something?" Kai said.

"You don't happen to know where Rufus is, do you?" Allen kept his voice down and glanced around as if to make sure no one was listening.

"Ah, yeah, I do. Why?"

"Please tell me you can vouch for his whereabouts Friday night."

Kai stiffened as a chill hand seemed to grip the back of his neck. "You're not trying to pin Raymond Fontaine's death on him, are you?"

Allen raised his hands to chest height, palms outward, and took a step back. "Trying not to. We got an anonymous call, saying the two had a shouting match last week, about staying away from Devona."

"Yeah, several." He gestured for Allen to wait, stepped into the kitchen with the bakery, then led him to the elevator. "He and Devona spent Friday with Raymond's brother and sister."
~~~~~

"Is that a fact?" Allen followed him into the brass cage and they were both silent until the door opened on the office upstairs.

"How's that look?" Eden said.

"They'll never know what hit them," Rufus said, and nodded at the computer screen in front of him.

Allen looked around. Eden was nowhere in sight. Kai gestured for the officer to follow. They came around the big circle of the cousins' workstations, to show Eden on one of the monitors, her features distorted as she reached up to the camera. The picture tilted for a moment and she nodded.

"That's better. Tighter. Check the manual pivot?"

Rufus tapped on the keyboard and the image shifted slowly to the right as she stepped out of the way. It showed a quiet street of small front yards and wrought iron and white picket fences and a few places where homeowners had put out fall decorations already. Some of them looked battered from last night's torrential downpour.

"All green," Rufus said.

"Okay, let's do a check of the motion sensors, and I think we're done."

"Thanks. We owe you big-time." He stuck the tip of his tongue out of the corner of his mouth, caught between his teeth in concentration as he tapped furiously on the keyboard. With one final stroke, he nodded. "Good to go."

"Okay, I'm making a counter-clockwise circuit of the house." Eden stepped out of the camera view.

"What's going on?" Allen asked, gesturing with his chin at the monitor.

"Someone's been trying to break into their house, so Eden insisted on installing a prototype security system one of her clients asked her to help them test drive," Kai said.

"This is sweet. Ten times better than what I was cobbling together." Rufus gestured at the screen, where the image changed to show a view of the side yard of the duplex he and Devona shared with Becca, and Eden walking through. He snatched up a tablet and tapped on the keypad that appeared on the screen, then worked his way through several screens that followed. With a grin for Kai and Allen, he tapped one final key and the images vanished from the computer monitor and appeared on the tablet. "I can see you," he half-crooned.

Eden turned around and stuck her tongue out at the camera. She gave him a thumbs-up and walked out of the image. A moment later the scene changed. She appeared, walking through it.

"Wow, that's impressive. Probably got an impressive price tag, too." Allen tipped his head slightly to the right. "How come you haven't reported the attempted break-ins?"

"Family honor?" Rufus shrugged. "We promised Miss Sarah about … well, keeping silent until things got really ugly lately, just seemed the easier way to handle things. And we want answers, so …" He gestured at the monitor. "Trap and getting it all on video for evidence."

"Okay, I'm loading up the car and heading back," Eden said.

"Hey, pick up some of those pulled chicken sandwiches they've got on special at Frenchy's, will you?" Kai shouted.

"It's your turn to cook, and that doesn't mean carry-out," Eden called back. She crossed her eyes at the camera, waved, and stepped out of view.

Rufus tapped a few more controls on the tablet, then on the computer, then gave out a loud sigh and slouched in his wheelchair. "And done. A lot faster than I thought it'd get done. Really, Kai, me and Devona, we owe all of you." His weary smile faded as he looked back and forth between Kai and Allen, who looked uncharacteristically somber. "Uh, something up?"

"Sorry, Rufus," Allen said. He settled into one of the old-fashioned wooden rolling chairs. "This problem with the Fontaines is getting a lot more serious than some hurt feelings and fighting over the estate."

Kai ached a little for Rufus when his confused expression turned wary. He settled down at his own workstation, with his back to his computer, and listened as Allen explained about the anonymous call and asked the expected questions. He admired Allen for being official, but still kind. To make things easier, he told Rufus what he had told the officer about being with Emily and Benjamin.

"Yeah, we let them stay out at the cottage Pop Albert gave our Mom. It seemed like a good place for them to stay, out of the way, avoid being spotted by their uncles, who can be even bigger jerks than their father. And no, Raymond wasn't staying there. It was kind of awkward, with him still trying to get Devona to take him back, and Mama – it was just more comfortable if he stayed in a hotel, okay? We gave the hotel number to Captain Sunderson."

"Yeah, and the hotel people confirmed his coming and going. Raymond was seen on security cameras leaving the hotel late in the afternoon, and never came back. So what were you and his brother and sister doing?"

"Sharing news, what we had found out, all the digging they had been doing. Some odd things they discovered when they were poking around at Windows, looking through files, discrepancies in bills for supplies for all that work they did in June, replacing the floors."

"Funny thing about Windows." Allen flipped through a few pages scribbled in blue ink and glanced at them. "It's supposed to be locked up all the time, according to Conrad, but some of the other tenants have been complaining about people walking around upstairs and hearing wood being pulled up, but no sign of repair people at work. Now you say these cousins of his have been digging through office files? What were they doing there, instead of at the realty office? How did they get in?"

"Oh, they had a key. Mama Sarah gave me and Devona keys to everything before … look, we're trying to help, and they're the good Fontaines, and Conrad is being a jerk, so we decided to mix things up, help with the digging." Rufus shrugged.

Kai noticed he didn't look either of them in the eyes, but fussed with his equipment, shutting down various electronics that had been part of setting up the security system at the duplex.

"How late were you four together?" Allen asked after a few moments of silence, as if he was waiting for Rufus to offer more information.

"We stayed overnight at the cottage."

"Can I talk to them, have them vouch for you?"

"No. I mean, yeah, you can, but I don't know where they are. They're really busy with phone calls, and letting the family know, and trying to track down their uncles, and whatever. They left this morning."

"Okay." Allen sighed and rubbed his hands over his face. He clearly hadn't liked going through this questioning any more than Rufus had, and Kai admired him for doing his job and trying to keep friendship out of the mix. It was a hard balance to maintain.

Monday, September 12

"There you are, Becks. Glad I caught up with you." Conrad braced himself on one arm against the glass block half-wall next to the table at Book & Mug, where she had settled not ten minutes ago.

"Why?"

She bit back a handful of responses, starting with asking why he called her *Becca* and *babe* one day and *Becks* the next. And ending with asking what part of, "No, I can't talk right now," he didn't understand. He had texted her five times in the last hour, wanting to know where she was, and if they could talk. She had texted back each time, saying she was busy. Testing him, she hadn't mentioned his note about meeting Tuesday night at Windows. What was so important that he needed to talk to her before then? After the last text, she responded that he could catch up with her at the picnic when the Fall Street Festival Committee met. If he hadn't forgotten that he was part of the committee. There were so many things he had forgotten over the last six months.

She supposed he had been across the street and saw her going into Book & Mug. Then her gaze caught on his bared arm. It didn't have those deep scratches she had seen Friday night. Had she been looking at the other arm?

"We need to clear the air, y'know? Can I get you something?" He pulled out the chair facing her at the table and started to sit down.

In silent answer, she moved her three-quarters full snickerdoodle frappe to the center point of the table.

"Oh. Sorry." He chuckled and finished sitting.

"What did you want to talk about?" She caught her breath when the answer shot into her head: he was going to say he had changed his mind, or rather Simone had whined and badgered him until he changed his mind and cancelled the contract Agatha had given her.

"Just ..." He shrugged. "I want to apologize."

"For what, exactly?" She kept her voice even, when part of her wanted to grab him by the collar of his T-shirt and shake him until his eyeballs rattled.

No, she would prefer to do that to Simone. What had she ever done to Simone to make her such a persistent, nasty adversary all these years? It wasn't like Simone and Alicia Monroe had been such good friends, but every few years, Simone spat her name out and came close to shooting lightning from her eyes, as if Alicia's emotional breakdown over that unwashed idiot, JD Ryan, was somehow Becca's fault. And she still had to pay for it all these years later. Becca had never dated him. Not once. She wouldn't even share a table with him in science class. So how could Simone justify blaming her for what the creep did to Alicia?

She shook her head, realizing she wasn't listening to Conrad. A few seconds of him stammering and saying "umm" and "y'know" assured her she hadn't missed anything. At least, nothing coherent.

"Conrad, we're ancient history. Let it go."

"That's the thing. I'm not allowed – I mean, hey, I feel bad. You're a great gal."

Gal? Who says gal nowadays? Becca took a long pull on her frappe to keep from laughing.

"I just want you to stop being angry at me. Y'know?" He shrugged.

"No, I really don't. Look," she hurried on, when a flicker of something she swore was fear dug wrinkles around his mouth and eyes, just for a moment. "If you feel bad, I forgive you, okay?"

"I wish you'd do more than just forgive me." He reached to put a hand on hers on the table. "Maybe we can be friends again?"

She looked at his hand, just waiting, until he withdrew it. Why did Conrad's hand feel so cold? And damp? She remembered times he had held her hand. His had always been dry and warm and calloused from all that work he did, managing most of the upkeep of all the Fontaine properties. Had Conrad changed so much it affected his body, too?

"If you want to be friends, how about giving me back the other half of the Mizpah coin?"

"The what?"

He blinked, his face twisting in a helpless, silly kind of grin. The kind guys wore when they didn't want to admit they had no idea what was going on.

The Conrad she had said goodbye to in January had never worn that ridiculous, weak expression. He should have immediately corrected her, reminding her that Sarah had given him the coin to give her half, so they would both remember to pray for each other while she was in Bosnia.

Becca had no idea why she had implied she had given him the coin. This was one of those times when she was working entirely on instinct. She shuddered a little, as instinct told her she wouldn't like what she discovered if she dug for the answer.

"Devona?" Eden called, coming around the coffee shop counter, heading for the bookstore area. "Is Rufus there with you?" She stepped around the tables in the open floor area between the booths and the glass block wall, studying a tablet clutched in both hands. She skidded sideways when she nearly ran into a chair that hadn't been pushed into the table and looked up. She grinned at Becca and opened her mouth to speak. Then her gaze shifted to Conrad. She looked down at the tablet in her hands, back up to him, then hurried into the bookstore.

Conrad's phone chimed. He yanked it from his pocket and looked at the screen. Frowning, he stood up.

"Look, something came up. But think about it? Being friends again? It's kind of important."

"To who?"

Again, just for a moment, she saw that fear. Then it morphed into that stupid, clueless smile that was so very not the Conrad she had known.

"Yeah, I really miss us joking around, playing mind games, Becks. I'll catch up with you later. We still gotta talk. I'll call you." He turned, waving blindly at her, and hurried out of the coffee shop.

"Mind games? In what parallel universe?" Becca muttered. She closed her eyes and knuckled her temples to fight off the threatening headache. So, did this mean Conrad's arrangements to talk to her on Tuesday were off, or did he still expect her to be there, downstairs at Windows, when she needed to be upstairs, leading the meeting?

Who was playing mind games now?

"You okay?" Eden asked.

"Yeah, fine. Just feeling like a real idiot." Becca opened her eyes to see Eden and Rufus watching her. Looking concerned. "Oh. Ouch. How loud did that get? Sorry."

"Not that loud." Rufus shrugged. "Kind of made a little problem, though."

"Ya think?" Eden snorted and stepped around his wheelchair, to slide into the chair facing Becca. "There's something weird going on, and you're in the middle of it, so ..."

"Ever have one of those days when you really hope you'll wake up any minute and find out the last few weeks were a bad dream?" She clamped her teeth shut, instead of spilling the odd bits of puzzle she couldn't put together yet in her mind: Conrad calling her Becca, then Becks again. Forgetting about his grandmother's Mizpah coin. The scratches on his arm healing much too quickly. And now, it struck her that he had been referring to Sarah as Granny, when she had always been Grandma.

Maybe he really had fallen down, broken his skull on something, and reprogrammed his brain? His entire personality?

"All the time, lately." Rufus gave Eden a wide-eyed mock innocent look when she just shook her head. "Show her." He gestured at the tablet she held upright, facing herself.

"What's going on?" Becca asked.

"We finally got some answers – well, more proof than answers, and validating some suspicions ..." Eden turned the tablet to put it screen down on the table. She rubbed her eyes with the heels of her hands, then sat back and proceeded to tell about the attempted break-ins and the prototype security system she had installed on Rufus and Devona's side of the house. "So, just now, the alarms went off and ..." She shrugged and turned the tablet over, woke it up, and set it so Becca could see three still images on the screen.

She assumed it was three different angles of the same man trying to pick a lock on Rufus and Devona's back door. She looked at each image a second time. Then a third time.

"You said this was just now? While I was sitting here, talking with Conrad?"

"Yeah. Unless this prototype is so advanced, it's getting reception from a parallel universe," Rufus muttered.

Becca sat back, with both hands bracketing the tablet. She couldn't yank her gaze off the three images of Conrad. With those scratch marks visible on his arm again.

"Did he get in?" she asked, to pull out of her spinning thoughts.

"The alarm went off, and one of the programmed responses kicked in, a recording of Rufus calling out, asking who was there. He ran, getting out of the range of the motion sensors, just seconds before the system would have notified the police. That's something that needs to be adjusted," Eden added. "There should be an option to cancel the call or delay it until the owner can check the cameras, to be sure it isn't one of their kids who lost their key, or a squirrel or something else activated the motion sensors."

"Okay, makes … sense. But …" Becca swallowed and fumbled for her drink. Her mouth was dry, and her throat felt even drier.

"How can he be two places at the same time?" Rufus said.

"Proof," Eden said. She turned the tablet over again, and that somehow helped Becca yank her thoughts out of the spiral of questions.

"Proof of what?" Becca asked.

"Did Conrad tell you he was twins? Well, actually triplets, but we haven't been able to track down the third brother past a couple of consecutive terms in juvie."

"Triplets?" She tried out the word. It didn't make sense in her mouth. "He mentioned getting contacted by his brother, Steve, but he didn't mention … before we just entirely lost contact."

"Steven Harris and Nathan Stemple. The triplets were separated at two months old when their mother got sent up on a really long list of criminal charges and no relatives would take the boys. Nathan followed in their mother's footsteps, or at least he tried. He's a pretty pathetic would-be criminal genius. He needs a keeper. A very slippery grasp on reality and common sense. Steven, on the other hand, went military and then graduated into intelligence work. Lots of sealed records, but I've got a few friends who pushed the envelope, telling me what they could without getting both of us in trouble." Eden shrugged. "Maybe three years ago he seems to have gone into private practice. Every time someone tries to nab him for something nasty, he has a rock-solid alibi. Then he just seemed to vanish about five months ago. We have to guess that his intelligence connections helped him get into sealed records, he found Conrad and made contact."

"And chances are good it's been him, hacking into the company computers and emails and playing with bank accounts," Rufus said. "All this time, we were spinning our wheels, thinking the uncles were playing nasty."

"But what does that have to do with …" Becca gestured at the tablet and the hidden camera images. "And Conrad acting so different. And …" She ran out of words. She didn't know what she was thinking. She had the awful feeling if she took her gaze off Eden's face, she would discover the coffee shop was spinning around her.

"Well … looks like Conrad was providing an alibi, if anybody spotted Steven trying to break into our place," Rufus said.

"To get what?"

"Evidence," Eden said.

"And that letter people think Mama Sarah left with us. And … well, that's proof too, if you think about it," Rufus said. "If the scumbag suspects anything, he's looking for her. I mean, that's the whole reason we put the plan together, because she figured out some things, and he was getting nasty, and she was afraid he'd try something."

"Who?" Becca nearly shouted the word.

Rufus and Eden locked gazes for a few moments, then Eden nodded. "Yeah, it's time."

"I'll drive," Rufus said.

They were heading down I-71 when something occurred to Becca. "You're not going to show those videos to the police, are you?"

"Not yet." Eden glanced back from the front seat of Rufus's van. "We're working with someone who's coming at it from a different angle. We need him to see it, decide if it'll ruin things to give this to Sunderson. Although we can trust her to keep things quiet if we need to. It's just ..." She sighed. "There's money laundering involved, and possibly a whole lot of other nasty things. We started out just trying to figure out what happened to Conrad, if someone was putting pressure on him. We thought maybe Miss Sarah was being threatened, and if we got her out of the way, that would shut everything down, but ..." She shrugged.

"Get her out of the way?" Becca lost her breath for a few seconds. "Where are we going?"

"It's a cottage Pop Albert gave our Mom. It's in her name, and chances are good the creep doesn't know about it, so it's about the safest place we could think of to hide in," Rufus said.

Becca swallowed the question that neither of them seemed willing to answer just yet: *Hide who?*

Eden spent most of the drive asking Becca about the progression of events, the breakdown and breakup between her and Conrad, starting when Becca went to help the missionary schools. She was especially interested in the appearing and disappearing scratches on Conrad's arm. Whichever one of those men was Conrad. She was also pleased when Becca mentioned the several times she had encountered Conrad supposedly visiting Rufus and Devona, always when they weren't home, and the times he had made comments that seemed to indicate he was still interested in a relationship with her. Plus, the flip-flopping between calling her Becks and Becca, and the new detail she had caught: Conrad had changed from calling Sarah Grandma to Granny. They agreed they needed to set up a calendar to mark all those dates and times, to try to establish a pattern, and perhaps identify which man had been Conrad and which had been his brother, Steven.

Becca's head hurt from constantly turning the questions over in her head. What sort of awful blackmail did Steven have on Conrad, to force him to play along and share his life? Maybe Conrad had started acting so strange to get people to notice and question if something was wrong? But nobody had? Simone had taken advantage of his changed behavior, but everyone else, including Becca, had written him off as a jerk.

If only Miss Sarah hadn't died. She would have noticed before everyone else, and she would have done and said something.

Was that why Sarah had died? She noticed something, and Steven ... did something about it?

They got off the highway at Chippewa Lake. Becca remembered the lake community from when she was very young, and a classmate's family had a cottage there. She had memories of long, lazy weeks at the cottage, playing in the lake, and the tiny amusement park near the water. It had been slowly getting run down since before she was in elementary school.

Rufus followed the perimeter road through the cottage community, to the far side where trees had grown up, hiding the homes there from view, and hiding the lake from the view of the residents. The cottages were farther apart and kept up better. The driveways were concrete instead of gravel, and the lawns were neatly mowed. Rufus pulled into a concrete driveway and up into a turnaround behind the cottage.

"I called before we left and warned her we were coming, and why," Eden said. "Please don't freak out. She feels bad enough as it is that she had to do it to you, but we hope you understand. And honestly ... she could use more company than we've been giving her."

"Please," Becca whispered, as the van door slid open. The mechanism lowered the folding ramp so Rufus could wheel out. She stared at the back door and windows of the cottage, screened with sheers, so all she could catch was movement, a shape waiting in the shadows. *Lord, please, is this a day for miracles? Is everything going to change, starting now? I'm sorry, I know I haven't prayed as much as I should, but ...*

She couldn't continue, because Rufus was out of the way and she got up to follow him, and the back door was opening.

Then her first miracle in a long time stepped into view.

The next few minutes were a mess of tears and clinging to Sarah Fontaine and both of them holding each other up. Eden and Rufus hurried them all inside the safety of the cottage where no one could see or overhear them.

"Oh, my dear," Sarah said, when she and Becca ended up in a big, overstuffed chair together, holding hands. "You were the part of the plan I regretted the most. I'm so glad Eden decided to bring you in on the conspiracy. I'm sure this has been awful for you. Will you eventually be able to forgive me?"

Becca choked on a multitude of responses and ended up laughing and wiping tears off her face.

"I'm just so glad to know you're alive, how can I be angry?" she finally managed to say. "Whose idea was this?" She laughed, not surprised at all, when Sarah hunched her shoulders and slowly raised her hand. "How? Why?" She flinched as an idea hit her hard, so it felt like something had slammed against her ribs. "Are you hiding, you faked your death, because you're afraid of Conrad?"

"Not of Conrad, no." Sarah shook her head. "Afraid *for* him. Afraid of the awful man who followed him back to Cadburn. Right after that trip to Virginia, to meet his brother face-to-face, and determine what exactly this man wanted, contacting him after so long. We both should have suspected something when his brother knew far too much about the problems we were having with the business.

"Something happened. There in Virginia, and then when he came home. He was tense, secretive, short with people. I think now he realized he was in trouble, and he was trying to push people away, so they wouldn't be hurt if something happened to him. Suddenly he stopped coming to see me, stopped checking in, and he was very rude when I stopped in at the office. People were coming to me, asking what was wrong with Conrad. Then I knew he was in awful trouble when he called me Granny."

"I knew it." Becca's face warmed. "Sorry, but it just struck me a little while ago that he always called you Grandma, but ever since I came back, he referred to you as Granny. Why would he change?"

"That was our warning signal." Sarah blinked rapidly and released one of Becca's hands to yank a tissue out of the box on the coffee table in front of them and dab at her eyes. "When he first started working for Albert, there was all sorts of nastiness coming from the economic downturn. People assumed a high school boy having so much responsibility could be bullied and used to their advantage. They'd tell him Albert or I said one thing, and they'd tell us Conrad said something else, and try to lock us into things we didn't agree to. We each had a trigger word we'd use in front of people we suspected of playing crooked little games. I don't know how many con men we caught out who would come to me. 'Oh, yes, Conrad told us, "My Granny will just love this opportunity".' And I'd tell them what I thought of their opportunity, or Albert would, because Conrad let us know they were cheats." She shook her head. "So when he started calling me Granny, I was sure it was a signal that something was wrong, he was protecting me, so I backed away. I gave him space to figure things out. Until suddenly my Conrad wasn't anywhere to be found."

"Rufus got all sorts of warning flares from the firewalls and the boobytraps we had set up in the company network," Eden said, taking up the story. "We tracked it to someone using the office computers, and Conrad's home computer. We had put up a lot of shields when we had signs of people trying to hack their way in and change things, back when we thought it was the uncles trying to take the company or wreck it."

"Then one day I looked in the eyes of that man who was the mirror image of Conrad, but wasn't my Conrad, and I was suddenly afraid for my life. It wasn't anything he said, but just this threat in the subtext," Sarah said. "I asked Eden and Devona and Rufus to help me set up a trap, so to speak."

"Do Worter & McIntosh know anything about this?" Becca had to ask.

"Bill does. And Lisa. We needed to make all sorts of changes and addendums and legal loopholes and figure out how Miss Sarah could die on vacation, and nobody would ask questions if there wasn't a body to bury." Eden shook her head, giving the elderly woman an admiring smile. "You should have worked in intelligence, or private investigation. You're one sneaky, clever old chick."

Becca sputtered, suspecting Eden had substituted *chick* for something a little less flattering or amusing.

They settled down to compare memories of odd actions and words from Conrad, trying to determine when they had seen the real Conrad, acting under pressure, and when they had seen his brother. Becca played with the idea that Conrad had taken up with Simone to alert everyone who really knew him that something was wrong. Or else that was his brother Steve. She recalled the times various people had made remarks about how much Conrad had changed. Comments like "total personality transplant" didn't seem so bitterly amusing now.

A shadow appeared against the sheers, and a moment later someone knocked on the back door. The four fell silent with an almost audible click like a switch had been flipped. They looked at each other. Eden studied the shape, sighed, then got up and went to the door.

"Why am I not surprised it's you?" She stepped back to let a man come into the cottage.

Becca's first impression was that he looked enough like Kai and Troy, he had to be a relative. Eden watched him as he paused and studied the three, and a crooked smile spread across his face.

"The late and beloved Sarah Fontaine, I presume?" he said. A slight accent Becca couldn't quite place lay under the amusement in his baritone voice.

"This is Nick West." Eden stepped around him to take her seat. She gestured at the two chairs sitting to one side. Nick dragged one over to join their group. "He's something of a private investigator."

"Something of?" Nick cocked one eyebrow at her.

"I don't know what exactly you are."

That earned a chuckle from him.

"He was involved in that whole mess with Curtis and Trustee

Cadburn, and he's a friend of Saundra's, so …" She shrugged. "I'm willing to give him a chance."

"Don't forget that Rance Harcourt vouches for me," Nick said.

"Who's that?" Rufus leaned back in his chair, with a narrow-eyed look that clearly said he wasn't ready to accept Nick's presence just yet.

"Former FBI, the guy who helped me get my start," Eden said. "He helped me get past a few firewalls and legal walls, to find out about Steven and Nathan."

"Ma'am, I'm glad to know you're not dead. I was afraid I'd have to add proving Steven Harris killed you to my to-do list before I was finished here," Nick said. Sarah and Becca both flinched. His smile died. "Sorry, I didn't mean to scare you."

"No, no, it's all right." Sarah kept her hand pressed over her heart. "It's just startling, I suppose, to realize that my fears were justified."

"He's done a lot worse things to get what he wants."

"What else can you tell us about the brothers?" Eden asked. "Have you found Nathan yet?"

"No, and considering the power behind the agencies involved in this operation, that says something. But that was Steven's specialty when he was inside. The theory now is that he's been regularly erasing Nathan's activities and records, using his brother as a shield and alibi if he gets spotted during his operations."

"Just like they're using Conrad, you think?" Sarah said.

"Ma'am, either they're blackmailing your grandson into cooperating, or they've got him prisoner somewhere and they've both stepped into his identity and life. As I told Eden, we're sure Steven is using Fontaine Realty to cover up money laundering, at the very least. That's what brought me to town." He turned to Rufus. "I need to work with you directly now. Those firewalls and that labyrinth you put up around the computer network are pure genius. If you're not careful, you're going to get recruited and probably have a handful of agencies fighting over you."

"Uh huh." Rufus glanced back and forth between Nick and Eden. "Should I be worried?"

"If he gives you a hard time, just sic Saundra on him," Eden said.

"I'm losing my touch," Nick murmured. "Seriously, though, Steven most likely fingered you for Raymond's death. If we don't find Frank soon, I'm afraid his body is going to show up next, and there will be real proof that you're responsible this time. He's going to step up the offensive soon if he can't figure out how to get you out of the way and shut down the firewalls and the fail-safes you built for Conrad. The fact he can't get through them means he hasn't gotten that information from Conrad. Bottom line is, you and your sister need to get out of town, out of his reach, so he can't use you against Conrad like he was using Miss Sarah at the start."

"That's a good idea," Sarah said. "In fact, I need to go to Columbus and face down my boys. I've enjoyed getting to know Emily and Benjamin and Raymond, and I'd like to get to know my other grandchildren before this whole ugly mess takes more of them. It's time we end this ridiculous feud, and I'm sorry, my dear, but you and Devona are in the middle of it."

"How?" Rufus shook his head, very visibly lost.

"I'll explain on the way down. How soon do you think we should leave?" she asked Nick.

"The sooner the better. Now for you." His smug smile as he turned to focus on Becca made her want to slap him. She refrained and sat up, waiting for him to continue. "I need your help putting the pressure on the brothers, figure out which one is Conrad and which one is Steven, and if Nathan has entered the mix."

"Makes sense." She could guess what *putting the pressure on* might entail. "I might have something useful already."

She described the scratches that disappeared and reappeared on Conrad's arm. The times she ran into him and he flipflopped between indicating he wanted to resume their relationship, the times his interest made her feel uneasy, and the times he was completely under Simone's thumb. Even when she wasn't around.

"Is that a fact?" Nick mused. One eyebrow cocked up and that smirk returned. "Useful. One of them wants you, the other wants or at least is trapped by Simone. If we could use you to put a wedge between the brothers, or at least make them mess up ..." He snorted. "At the very least, we'll hack off that sparkly little Simone. Think you can do it?"

"Oh, yeah. I've needed some justification to give some of hers back. But what if they're not Conrad and Steven? What if they're Steven and Nathan? How do we separate them enough that we can find Conrad?"

"Where could Conrad be?" Sarah said.

"Well ... using the security system boy genius here created," he nodded to Rufus, "we've been checking out each of the properties Fontaine Realty owns. There are a couple with no cameras, and no traffic, no renters. Those are the best locations for holding prisoners. Chances are good that Frank got too close to whatever Steven is doing, and he's being held in the same place as Conrad."

"That boy has always been the biggest mouth ..." Sarah sighed. "And the biggest heart. Of course he'd take risks and go solo, to protect his brothers. Are chances good that both of them are still alive? If that ... that creature would threaten me, so you thought he would kill me, wouldn't he kill Conrad, and Frank?"

"Ma'am, Steven has a set pattern. He's done this enough times that it'd take an awful lot for him to break the pattern. Killing Raymond is a big break from that. It was likely an accident. He probably figured the boy was dead already when he tossed him, or he was too badly injured to keep alive in the same prison he's holding Conrad and Frank. His proven pattern is to take over other people's lives and businesses, then blackmail them into cooperating. He's laundered money and used trucking companies to smuggle. His victims step back into their lives with no evidence, no backup to defend themselves. They take the fall, he gets clean away."

"Not entirely," Eden said. "Otherwise, you wouldn't be onto him like this."

"No, not entirely. But not enough evidence, not strong enough proof. Until now, we hope."

"So they need Conrad alive." Sarah smiled and her hands trembled, so Becca reached over to catch hold of them again.

Becca saw something in Nick's gaze that made her doubt. Or maybe it was that he doubted his own words. Something was wrong, something was different this time around.

Then she knew, while Sarah and Rufus and Nick got to work talking about how to sneak the three out of town.

The victims of Steven's schemes hadn't been his identical brother before. That could change a lot of things. She decided to wait until she could speak privately with Nick, to verify that he had already thought of that troublesome detail. Then he gave her something else to think about.

"We need to get more access to Windows," Nick said, while Rufus was on the phone, contacting Devona to get ready to leave, and Sarah was in her bedroom, packing. "Money has been taken out of the business, physically, to make it hard to track. We've got security camera images of Steven taking bundles from banks. All outgoing packages have been searched, so that money is still physically around, somewhere. Plus, Steven is suspected to be in possession of several million in small bills. He needs a place to stash it until it's safe to move. With all that flooring pulled up and replaced around the time he took over Conrad's life, it has to be at Windows."

"That was you I saw on Friday with Raymond, wasn't it? You were pulling up the boards, looking for it," Becca said. "You found some, too. Who were you taking the money to when you left? I heard you arguing with Raymond, telling him to wait."

"Yes, we found a little. Harcourt has it. He's the one who got me involved in the first place, gave me Eden as a contact. And there are several hundred square feet yet to look under. Before time runs out and Steven is spooked and makes a run for it." Nick's expression darkened as he met her eyes, then Eden's. "We don't want to know what stupid things Steven will do when he's spooked enough to run."

Chapter Twelve

Tuesday, September 13

Conrad never called Becca, either in answer to the messages Nick had her send him as tests, to all his phone numbers, or to pull the rug out from under Four Squares' meeting that evening. She wished she could rely on silence to mean there was no problem with the room. He wouldn't wait until the last minute to tell her the boards hadn't been put back, would he? Or, she realized around 5:30, maybe Conrad had been so busy with the whole mess of Raymond Fontaine's body being found in the creek, he hadn't had the time or attention to devote to fixing the damage to the floor. She had a recurring vision of reaching the top of the stairs, coming from behind the half-wall, and seeing most of the floor torn up instead of just those few boards that Raymond and Nick had pulled up.

Or, considering how clearly Eden didn't quite trust Nick, Becca supposed the chances were good he and some federal agents went into Windows while Conrad's, or more likely Steven's back was turned, and pulled up all the flooring. And Four Corners would have to deal with the damage and inconvenience.

Becca felt a squeezing sensation in her chest, every time she remembered telling Captain Sunderson about seeing Raymond and calling Conrad to let him know what his cousin had been doing. Before she knew about the lookalike. Had she called Conrad, or had she called Steven and alerted him that his game was starting to unravel?

Had she given Steven an alibi, telling the police captain about his visit to the duplex so late at night, trying to find a way to contact Raymond? Had she been talking to the killer, using her as an alibi?

She had told Nick what she had done, when he drove her and Eden back to Cadburn, so Sarah, Rufus, and Devona could head to Columbus immediately. He didn't try to persuade her she wasn't to blame, but he pointed out that Raymond had been reacting without thinking the last few days. He could have gone to confront Conrad and run into Steven. Or Steven caught him going back to Windows to look for clues to what had happened to his father. He could have investigated one of the buildings where there weren't security cameras, despite Nick ordering him to wait until authorities could do it properly, and again, been caught there by Steven. The bottom line was that Raymond hadn't done what he was told by those with experience. He wasn't to blame for his own death, but he wasn't innocent, either.

"In situations like this," Nick had said, sounding weary, his voice taking on grit, "nobody is innocent, nobody is smart, everybody makes stupid mistakes. It just seems like the innocent always have to pay."

Becca didn't know what to think, what to feel, when Allen called her back about the information she had given them. Conrad had an alibi for the time period when the coroner said Raymond had been knocked unconscious and then dumped over the bridge. More than half an hour before Steven, if they were right about which brother was doing what, had showed up at her back door. This version of Conrad had been caught on camera having a screaming fight with Simone in front of the Rampant Lion, a bar with a reputation for regularly disturbing the peace on the Cleveland side of Brookpark Road. A dozen people had captured the fight and posted it on social media. Most of the comments were mockery. At the height of the name calling, with Simone swinging at him, missing, and falling off her stilettos, Conrad went to his knees and begged her to forgive him and marry him.

The thought of Conrad having a screaming, name-calling fight in public like that made Becca sick far more than the idea of him marrying Simone.

This was so much not Conrad, yet it had to have been him, because who had been killing Raymond if Steven had been fighting with Simone? What had his brother done to him?

With Simone apparently calling the shots now in Conrad's life, Becca fully expected to get a last-minute call full of lame excuses. She turned her ringer off after she parked three slots down from the lobby door that evening, arriving early to set up for the Four Corners meeting. Too late to pull the rug out from under her now. If Conrad/Steven wanted to block them from using the room, as per the contract she had signed, he would have to do it in person. From the back seat of her Jeep, she pulled out a bag of paperwork and printouts of the footing diagrams of an old dance step her research had uncovered maybe two months ago. She had been saving it for a special occasion, and tonight certainly qualified.

Daryl called to her just as she reached the door, and she turned to see him coming up Apple, hauling the old, trusty boom box loaded with CDs. It was amazing how much square dance music was out there. If she knew Daryl, he had found a new song for them to dance to, in celebration. She waited for him to catch up with her and silently admitted that she wanted someone with her if she got to the stairs and found the door locked. With a note on the door saying that, in light of the family tragedy, Windows on the River was closed until further notice. Again.

No sign on the door, which was closed to within an inch of the frame. Becca wondered why she got a shiver up her neck. The door out to the street creaked open, and she looked back to see Ginny and Peggy and several others coming inside. They waved, faces bright with excitement. Becca swallowed a chuckle.

"What—" The T was so sharp it echoed all by itself. "—are you doing in here?"

Simone stomped through the door, pushing aside Bridgette and Clyde, two prospective members from the University of Akron. They had come up to Cadburn last week, doing research on local ghost legends, and stayed to watch the Four Corners learning a new dance in the park.

"Uh, we're having our weekly meeting," Jack said, coming up behind her and making her jump.

Becca considered turnabout fair play. She fought a smile.

"In the lobby?" Simone's voice went nasal with disdain.

"No, we're heading up to Windows."

"You can't. It's still closed." She gestured at the door.

She clearly didn't see it was ajar.

"Not according to the contract Becca signed last week," Ginny said.

"Connie put me in charge of all contracts, so you didn't sign one." Simone's tone of voice threatened she would stick out her tongue any second, and probably blow raspberries at them.

"When was that?" Becca fought for a calm expression. This was the roof falling in on them she had been anticipating the last few days.

"Yesterday!"

"Well, the contract I have was signed last week, by Conrad's cousins, Agatha and Chris." She reached into her tote and pulled out a photocopy of the contract. She had learned by bitter experience to never put the original documents of anything in danger of being snatched and ripped up or ruined with an "accidentally" tipped over cup of coffee.

"That's—that's—" Simone let out a shriek like a steam whistle. "I don't care what his cousins told you. Or what they signed," she hurried to say, when Becca waved the contract with the signatures clearly to be seen, in turquoise and purple ink. "Windows is closed. Locked up tight. Nobody is allowed in or out."

Becca swallowed hard to keep from grinning or maybe laughing. She felt warm air gushing through the gap between door and frame, meaning the sliding door was open upstairs. She thought about doing an end run around Simone by going through the lobby and up the outside stairs and getting in through the sliding door.

"It's fake!" Simone finished with a triumphant toss of her head. As if that sealed everything.

"Prove it," Jack drawled, like a gunfighter daring the town bum to meet him in the street at high noon.

"How about we call Conrad and let him decide?" Becca said.

"Fine. Just make a fool of yourself." Simone dug in her glittery purse and stomped across the lobby, making a show of needing privacy.

Becca pulled out her phone and tapped the number Conrad had given her for their almost-date.

"Hey, Becca," he almost purred, answering the phone after only two rings. "What can I do for you?"

"Hi, Conrad, I'm sorry to bother you. You're probably eating—"

"Nope. Can I talk you into joining me?"

"Thanks, but I have my Four Corners meeting tonight. In fact, that's why I'm calling you."

So, he had totally forgotten about that note asking her to meet him tonight. Which one had sent her the note?

"Babe, I'd do a lot of things for you, but square dancing is not my thing. I'm scared I'd fall flat on my ugly mug."

She shuddered, wondering why that choice of words scared her, just for a second. Conrad *had* come dancing maybe half a dozen times before she went to Europe. He had said he loved it, even if it did bring back traumatic events from elementary school gym class.

A chuckle that had to be half-hysterical escaped her. Why did everyone she talk to about square dancing always refer to the horrors of elementary or middle school gym class, and having to square dance with the creepiest kid?

"No, you don't have to dance with us. But we have a little problem. I was at Windows last week, and your cousins signed a contract to let Four Corners have our meetings here, starting tonight."

"Who did?" His voice went hard.

"Your cousins, Agatha and Chris. And I'm here right now with my club, and we're about to go upstairs. But Simone is here, and she says she's in charge of contracts now at Fontaine, and she says we can't go up. I say the contract I signed last week means we can. Who's right?"

"I'll be right there. I'm five minutes away. We'll get this fixed in no time."

"Thanks, Conrad. Now I owe you."

"Fake!" Simone shrieked and reached for Becca's phone. "You faked that phone call. You nasty little lying slut! Who do you think you are, pretending to talk to Conrad? He's on his way here and he'll settle you. Just you wait!"

"Funny," Becca said, raising her phone high over her head, out of Simone's reach. "That's exactly what Conrad just said."

"Becca!" Conrad's voice came through, loudly enough to make the phone buzz in her hand. "Give the phone to Simone. Now."

Simone's eyes got wide, and she backed up two steps. Her hand shook as she took the phone Becca held out to her.

"Connie? Sugarbaby, what's going on?" She turned her back on everyone, hunching her shoulders as she listened. Three times she started to say, "But Connie—" And each time he cut her off.

Sniffling, she turned around and handed the phone to Becca. The pathetic confusion making her eyes look like a kicked puppy transformed in just a few breaths to the usual vindictive, gloating Simone.

"Just you wait," she snapped, backing up a few steps. She didn't seem to notice when she ran into people. "Conrad's going to fix you. I don't know what sneaky tricks you're playing, but it's over as of now. You hear me?"

"What is over?" Melanie said, with just a touch of Southern syrup in her voice. "Simone, honey, a whole lot of us are just wondering, what's your problem with Becca, anyway?"

"My problem?" She pointed one glittery finger at Becca. "Ask her."

"I have no idea," Becca said. She thought about retreating up the stairs. She suspected opening the door when Simone had insisted everything was locked up might just be the straw that would break her hold on reality. "Simone, I'm telling you in front of all these witnesses, Conrad is all yours. I'm not fighting you for him."

"Yeah, that's what you say," Simone grumbled. "How you gonna prove it?"

"She doesn't have to," Ginny said. "Common sense says—"

Conrad stomped through the door. People stepped aside, creating an aisle to the center of the lobby where Becca and Simone faced each other.

"Connie!" Simone wailed. "You promised me you'd never ever again let these clodhoppers use Windows."

"When?" Conrad barked. He reached up, raking a hand through his hair, and pausing so Becca thought he might tear out handfuls. The move revealed the scratches on his arm. "When did I make a stupid promise like that?"

"Yesterday." She wriggled and simpered and scampered up to him and reached to rest a hand on his chest. Conrad stopped her with an icy glare. "When we got engaged," she finished on a whisper.

"We got—" His throat visibly convulsed. A low growl rose from him. Conrad turned to Becca. "You know what? I'm just hacked off enough right now ... Windows is yours. Rent free. Whenever you want it."

"But Connie!" Simone wailed.

"Just shut it. Get in my truck. Now." He pointed out the door.

Simone whimpered and scurried out of the lobby. Several people clapped.

"Look, Becca ..." Again, he raked one hand through his hair. "We need to talk. Clear things up. Get away somewhere, just the two of us. Y'know?"

"You know where to find me," Becca said. She shivered and hoped she didn't show it.

"Yeah, but we're running out of time ..." Conrad cleared his throat and looked around. "So ... you're all set, right? Starting next week, no problems. I'll take care of Simone." He snorted. "If I have to ship her off to outer Mongolia, she won't get in your way again."

A few people chuckled. Conrad shrugged and shot Becca a glance that made her feel scorched, and icy at the same time. He finally turned and walked out.

"Wow," Greg whispered. "Please tell me somebody got that on their phone?"

Chuckles helped brighten the atmosphere that felt clogged with whining and sharp voices and a threat of getting clawed by Simone's glittery fingernails.

~~~~~

Kai turned the shop over to Amy and was nearly to the front door when Saundra appeared in the picture window, walking up Apple from the municipal parking lot. He hurried to swing the door open and step out before she got there.

"Ready for a fun night of dancing?"

"I don't know." She visibly fought a smile. "I've been having flashbacks to seventh grade gym class. I always got stuck with the sweaty boy with dirty hands."

"Promise. I wash regularly." He held up his hands, palms facing her. "I even put on deodorant today."

"Ewww." Laughing, she let him hook his arm through hers, and they went to the corner to cross the street.

"Looks like a lot of people are here already." He gestured across the street to Windows, where people were walking down the sidewalk to the lobby door, just as Simone Radcliffe came stumbling out looking like she was being chased. "Huh, I wonder if she tried something at the last minute."

"That's the girl with the tap dancers?"

They watched Simone stagger down the sidewalk away from them, arms wrapped around herself, to stumble to a stop next to a black pickup.

"Yeah. She's got it in for Becca."

Just as they crossed the street, Conrad came stomping out the door. He gestured at Simone. She pulled open the door of the pickup and struggled to get up into the passenger seat while Conrad walked around and got in the driver's side. The passenger door was still hanging open as he pulled away from the curb with a squeal of wheels.

"Wow," Kai said.

"Ain't that the truth?" Greg Wells said with a chuckle from the
~~~~~

doorway. "I honestly don't know who won that one."

"Easy," Ginny said, and stepped out from behind him. She tipped off a salute toward the departing truck. "Becca got us Windows again, so we win. Becca finally got that twinkletoes to shut up, and Conrad got her, so he got what he deserved. And from the way he's snarling at her ... she got what she deserved. We all win!" Chuckling, she stuck out her elbow. Greg hooked her arm with his, and they stepped back into the building.

"Huh, that sounds like an interesting story," Kai said. "Shall we?" He and Saundra followed them through the door.

Nearly a dozen people had stopped in front of the closed door at the base of the stairs.

"Hey," Becca called to them as she pulled the stairwell door open. "Good to see you. Ready for a night of adventure and thrills?"

That earned chuckles from several people. Some stepped aside to let Kai and Saundra start up the stairs after Becca.

"My suspicious mind says you're not really interested in square dancing," she said, pausing on the third step. "After all the weirdness going on, I'm fine with that. I figure you're here as Eden's eyes and ears if something else happens."

"Hmm, pretty much." Saundra crossed her eyes at Kai, making him choke as he fought not to laugh.

A stream of warm air spilled down the stairs to him, and he thought he heard footsteps upstairs. Running. He was about to call out, warn Becca to be careful, to stop and let him get ahead of her, when she paused and frowned, studying the top of the stairwell.

"Does it look ... I don't know, dusty?" She gestured at the early evening sunlight spilling across the opening of the half-wall at the top of the stairs.

Kai tipped his head back and squinted. "Yeah, it does. I thought I heard someone moving around up there."

"Oh, just great." Becca dropped her bag on the step in front of her and vaulted up the stairs, two at a time.

"Wait!" He nearly ran into Saundra, trying to move faster and stop her. Saundra raced after Becca. Kai wished for about the space of four steps that Nick West was there. The man was handy to have around. That gun would be welcome, if only to protect Saundra.

"Oh, heck, now what?" Becca called.

Kai emerged from the stairs a moment later and stepped around the half-wall.

The air was heavy with dust, and some bitter smell he couldn't identify. Boards were tossed down in a haphazard pile near the wall, and a gaping hole in the floor maybe six feet wide seemed to be the source of the dust. It looked like a pile of dirt filling the hole, streaks of black and tan and white.

"What is going on?" She went down on her knees at the closest end of the hole and reached in.

"Maybe you shouldn't touch anything," Kai said. "I can see some tools on the other side. If I heard someone leaving, then they dropped them on their way out. Maybe the police can get fingerprints. This could be dangerous."

"Why would they fill the floor ..." She shook her head and struggled to her feet. "No, this was already here. He didn't rip up the floor to drop sand and whatever else that is. What did he find?"

"I'm calling the station." He dug in his pocket for his phone.

Becca nodded and stared at the pile in the hole. Saundra stepped up next to her. They stood there with their backs to him as he dialed and asked the dispatcher to send Allen, then notify Chief Sunderson. While he was talking, more members of Four Corners reached the top of the stairs. Greg, Hank, Ginny, and Marianne. They gathered around the hole. Will walked over to a box by a pile of bankers boxes and dug in it. He came back with a ruler and half-knelt on the edge of the hole. Before Kai realized what he was doing, he started digging in the sand or dirt or whatever it was with the ruler.

"Don't! Sorry," he hurried to say to the dispatcher. He had yelled pretty loudly. "Send somebody over quick, will you? We've got people wanting to dig around. You bet," he said, when she asked him to keep people away from the scene. Then she hung up. "Hey, don't change anything."

"Will you look at that," Greg blurted, and pointed at something yellow and blue and white that had emerged through the displaced dirt or sand.

"What is it?" Ginny said.

"Hey, guys, the police are coming. Don't mess with it, okay?" Kai said.

"Is that—I don't believe it." She took a step back, shaking her head. "I knew something strange happened, but I couldn't prove ..." She glanced at Becca, her gaze troubled.

"What?" Becca said. "Ginny, are you all right?"

"That's the logo I designed, and Charlene printed up, one of the first things she made with her fancy gizmo that makes iron-ons for clothes. But why would someone put it under the floor?"

"Logo for what?" Greg said.

Will glanced at Kai, his mouth twisted in a smile that was part defiance, part guilt. He swiped at the dirt with the long side of the ruler, moving more of the grainy black and tan and gray mixture off the colored patch.

"Fontaine Realty." She nodded once for punctuation. "Sarah asked me to redesign their logo, to put on T-shirts and bags and such. They sponsor a couple youth teams each year, and they wanted a nice big, bright new one. Charlene printed up a sample shirt for Conrad."

"I remember," Becca said. "He sent me the new logo. He couldn't wait to see it on the shirts."

"Could have fooled me. I took it over to his office, and then didn't hear boo from him. He got irked with me for asking, and claimed he never saw it." Ginny shook her head.

Marianne stumbled backwards so quickly she tripped over her feet. Will and Hank hurried to try to catch her, and the three of them nearly all went down together. Marianne's face was white, her eyes wide.

"Is she all right?" Allen Kenward's voice startled all of them. He must have arrived during the scuffle.

Marianne pointed at the hole. Her voice came out a strained whisper. "There's a skull."

Will raised his arm like he would throw away the ruler he still clutched. Then he sighed, walked over to Allen, who had come to a stop at the side of the hole, and handed the ruler to him.

"We kind of moved a little bit of it around." He hunched his shoulders when Allen gave him a long, assessing look.

Kai stepped up next to Allen. Marianne had better eyes than he did, because those gray and tan streaks through the black and brown warped the shape and made details hard to see. It wasn't exactly a skull, because there was dried flesh still attached to much of it. Like a lot of the mummies that had been unwrapped to examine on Smithsonian specials. She was right, though. The forehead and left eye socket and cheekbone were a little easier to make out once someone said he was looking at a skull. Knowing that stylized fountain, blue streams of water on a yellow background, was on a T-shirt made it a little easier to make out other details. The arm bone and some of the hand bones, with dark, dried flesh attached to them, emerged from the remains of the sleeve.

"Okay, I'm going to have to ask for your help," Allen said. "None of you can leave until I get your statements. If you could make sure nobody else comes up here, without telling them what happened? Appreciate it."

"I was going to call Conrad next," Becca said. Her voice sounded even, just a little softer than usual.

"Yeah, good idea." He glanced over at Kai. "Have you done any work helping Eden with her investigations, gathering evidence?"

"Take pictures?" Kai gestured at the hole with his phone.

"And crowd control." Allen gestured at the door out onto the balcony. "We need someone there to make sure people don't come up the back way."

Greg and Will volunteered for that duty, both of them stationed at the bottom of the stairs outside. Hank took the bottom of the stairs inside the building. Another half-dozen members of Four Corners showed up before the crime scene team made it up the street from the police station. Kai listened to Hank's drawl thickening as he assured everyone that nobody was hurt. There was just some damage to the room. They would all meet next week, just like always. Everything would be cleaned up and fixed, no problem at all. He wondered if Hank realized that his accent went deeper South the more stressed he became. Who wouldn't be stressed, finding a body in a hole under the floorboards?

Allen put on gloves and took advantage of the ruler being there and got measurements included as Kai took dozens of pictures. Becca and Saundra helped, turning on the overhead lights to brighten the scene and uncover more details. When the team arrived, Kai stepped back with everyone else. Ginny and Marianne had retreated to the farthest corner, where someone had unfolded some chairs, to sit and hold hands. They were both unnaturally silent.

The investigators took more pictures. They took samples of the different colors of materials surrounding the body. They took more measurements, and Allen asked Kai to come back and help by recording the steps as they slowly brushed away the material from the body, uncovering it bit by bit. T-shirt, jeans, leather boots. Nothing in the pockets, no jewelry other than a corroded chain around the neck, with a flat bit of gold metal hanging on it, round on one side, jagged on the other, like a disk had been cut in half on a zigzag.

The woman on the team noted that the ring finger on the left hand was broken and speculated that the deceased had been wearing a ring, and whoever buried him under the floor had taken it.

Once the body was completely uncovered, Allen asked Ginny to identify the T-shirt she had made for Fontaine Reality.

"Any response from Conrad yet?" Allen asked Becca, while Saundra and Greg supported a pale Ginny back to the corner to sit down. She breathed loudly through her nose and swallowed repeatedly.

"Nothing. I've called the realty office and his cell."

The sky was dark and the breeze blowing through the open door had grown chilly by the time the team figured out how to remove the body and a large portion of the sand and dirt with as little disturbance as possible. Digging down around the edges of the hole in the floorboards, they discovered that several thick sheets of construction grade insulating plastic lined the hole. Allen theorized that some of the sheeting they found tucked up between the pile of floorboards and the wall had been over the body. It had kept any stray liquid from decomposition from escaping to penetrate the ceiling to the rooms underneath.

"There wasn't a lot of liquid," Ed Wilcox, one of the team members observed, when they discussed that discovery. "I'd hazard a guess all these different colors of materials are a mixture of some kind of silica gel for preservative, sand, industrial strength desiccating compound, and salt. Like what you'd use for sidewalks to cut down on ice. The body is more mummified than decayed. Something to control the smell, probably activated charcoal. It dried up instead of rotting."

That got a gulping sort of whimper from Marianne.

"Sorry. And see here," he hurried on, pointing to different areas around the body, where the T-shirt and jeans had rotted away, and other areas where they were stiff with salt, discolored in spots. "Dried and preserved. Someone knew what they were doing. Gotta wonder where they got that large an amount of silica gel and activated charcoal."

"Did you say desiccating compound?" Becca stepped up and looked down at the body, her eyes shadowed and wounded. "Heinrich was complaining just a few days ago about all the barrels on the stairs. And Conrad bought barrels of it a few months ago. The last time he claimed there was a pipe break ..." She shuddered once and wrapped her arms around herself.

Kai ached for her, so tightly controlled.

"You think they opened up the floor to add more to the body?" another member of the crime scene team asked. Someone Kai didn't know.

"The body's not going to stink. It's too dried and preserved," Wilcox said. "Maybe they're getting ready to ... Uh, no."

"What are you thinking, Wilcox?" Allen said. He looked around the room. "You're thinking another dead body? A new one?"

Marianne moaned and ran for the balcony door. Muffled coughing and gagging sounds came through the sounds of several other women hurrying to follow and put their arms around her.

"Knowing what they needed to deal with ... could be an indicator this was done deliberately," Allen mused, staring down at the body. "Not an accident. I've read about more cover-ups that made people look guilty when the original damage was an accident. They reacted in fear, thinking no one would believe them, and just made themselves guilty, when they could have walked. This, though ... and that kid thrown off the bridge ... and the same story about broken pipes, but no one sees any water ... I don't care if I get written up for slander and false accusations, my gut says this was planned out ahead of time. Maybe the murder took place right here."

"I've heard grumbling about how the flooring was replaced back in June," Becca offered. Her voice strained, hinting how she fought for control. "The people who normally would have been hired to do the work were left out of it."

"Yeah," Will said. "And the way the shut-down of this place was handled. People being kept in the dark, contracts canceled without warning. Lots of grumbling from the folks downstairs, too. The noises and odds smells. And face it, Conrad's been a bear ever since June."

"Covering up things," Wilcox offered, voice soft. He went down on one knee and brushed away some of the dirt or whatever that dark, grainy mixture was, from around the skull.

"Can't believe Conrad would hurt anyone, even with how much a jerk he's been," Greg said.

"Maybe he was being blackmailed or forced to help someone," Dave Alderman said.

Several people flinched and looked around. Dave hadn't been among the original people who found the body. Kai thought the number of people in the room had grown. He didn't blame members of Four Corners skirting Allen's orders and letting some of their numbers up here anyway. This was big news for Cadburn Township. Even after the excitement with Curtis and Roger Cadburn and Jacob Styles.

"How do you figure that?" Allen asked. His scowl deepened for only a moment as he looked around the room. People were standing as close to the area around the hole and the body as the crime scene team and the barrier of their equipment would allow.

"He's been getting all that pressure from Albert's boys, and that kid who was harassing Devona, and he made those trips out of town without telling anyone what was up. And Miss Sarah was sure acting jumpy for a week or two before she died. Heck, for all we know, she was killed by whoever was making him act weird."

"His brother," Becca said.

The entire room went still and everyone seemed to turn to stare at her.

"Come again?" Allen said.

"Conrad … he wrote me a few times, when I was in Europe." She wrapped her arms around herself, staring down at the body. "When the Fontaines showed up and made all that trouble, after Albert died, he found out he was adopted. So he started investigating. And then his brother, Steven, made contact. And Conrad was having all sorts of trouble with the business. People hacking into the computers, blocking emails, missing phone messages. He thought they were trying to wreck the business. And his brother said he knew some people who could help." She jerked her gaze off the body. "You can ask Rufus and Eden. They were both helping Conrad dig into things. You can understand why he wanted the whole mess kept quiet."

"I sure like the idea of Conrad being a victim. Sure explains why he's been such a creep," Wilcox said, punctuated with a little shrug.

"Yeah." Allen sighed. "Sure does." He made more notes in his notebook. Kai estimated he had used up more than half the pages tonight.

After much maneuvering, they lifted the body and the mixture surrounding it on the multiple layers of plastic, carefully wrapped the plastic around the whole, and slid it into a body bag resting on a gurney. Everyone in the room seemed to relax a noticeable amount once the body was hidden from view. The team got to work wrapping up the preliminary investigation, cataloging the tools that had been left behind, taking more pictures of the hole now that the body was out of it, snapping pictures of the entire room. Wilcox sat down with his kit unfolded, squirting liquid on a cloth and rubbing at something. Then taking pictures of what he had been working on, tapping notes into his phone, then repeating the process with something new.

"What'd you find?" Allen asked, when Wilcox had sat for several minutes, frowning at whatever he held between gloved forefinger and thumb.

"It's the partial disk we took off the body. Looks to be gold, not very good quality, but it was partially preserved in the sand and silica. Not a tenth as bad as the chain, from being around the neck, touching the flesh." He held up the disk so it flashed dully. "I'm trying to clean it up, because it looked like there were words on it. Thought maybe it was some identification."

"It's not?" Allen bent closer, frowning.

Kai walked over to Wilcox with Allen. The technician put the disk on his palm. It gleamed dully in the overhead lights.

"It looks like … well, like something was written on it before it was broken in half," Allen said. "Kai, what do you see?"

Wilcox held out his hand further, so Kai didn't have to bend over so far.

"Ord," he read on the first line. "Tween. D thee. Il we. Again. And the numbers thirty-one with a colon, and forty-nine." Kai shook his head. "Anything on the other side?"

"Just the letters M, I, and Z," Wilcox said.

"What?" Becca slowly stood up from a group of chairs where she and several others had been waiting. Now she looked paler than Marianne and Ginny. "Can I see that?" She crossed the room to them and held out her hand, then snatched it back when Wilcox held out his gloved hand. "It's a mizpah coin."

"The Lord watch between me and thee until we meet again," Saundra said, joining them. She wrapped an arm around Becca. "Genesis 31:49."

"What does it mean?" Wilcox said.

"Let's hope it means the murder victim had his eternal life insurance policy paid up," Allen said. "Those coins were the rage for dating couples back when I was in middle school. Francine and I still have ours, kind of corroded, in one of those shadow box things she's got on the wall. I haven't seen anyone selling them for years. If you think about it, the story behind the mizpah really didn't go with the sentiment they attached to it."

"I don't understand," Kai said.

"It's a story from the Old Testament," Saundra said, "from a family argument, when Jacob ran for his life and his father-in-law Laban chased after him, probably intending to take Jacob's wives and children away from him. God came to Laban in a dream and basically told him, hands off. So, he and Jacob made a heap of stones for a witness to their vows not to harm each other, and named the heap mizpah, and called on God to watch over them and keep them both acting honorably as long as they were apart."

"Miss Sarah gave Conrad her mizpah coin, so we each had a half when I went to Bosnia," Becca said. "He joked that I took the wrong half, I should have had the miz half, and he should have the pah half. Then he said maybe he was safer taking the miz, because the implications of him being a pah were ..." She let out a long, ragged breath. "Conrad got the coin to remind him to pray for me the whole time I was gone. And remind me he was praying for me." She stared at the half of the coin, lying in Wilcox's hand. "This is crazy. I have the craziest idea in my head. What are the chances ..."

"Somebody has been buried here wearing a shirt Conrad said he never got, and his half of the coin he split with you?" Allen shook his head. "I don't know which possibility is worse. That's Con—"

"Don't say it." Becca shuddered and took a step back. "Poor Miss Sarah ..."

"I think you need to talk to Conrad and get his side of the story," Wilcox said.

"We'll offer him police protection, take him into custody, whatever we have to do to get the truth." Allen sighed. "Meanwhile, we work on identifying that body." He looked around. "I don't know if I'm wasting my breath asking all of you to keep this quiet. We don't know what the whole story is, we might not know it for weeks. Just don't tangle things any worse than they are by playing amateur detectives, all right?"

He looked around the room, making a visible effort to meet every gaze. Many of the people there nodded. Others looked away. Sheepish expressions indicated they had already started in on the wild speculations. Kai guessed some of them had already started texting or even making whispered phone calls, spreading the news. A few faces looked irritated by the warning. Those were the troublemakers who had to be dealt with, maybe have Allen's warning and stern request turned into an order. With legal force behind it, if necessary.

The team finally left with all the evidence and samples, and the body was carried down the back stairs and taken around the back of the building to avoid as many gawkers as possible. The doors were locked and sealed inside and out with crime scene tape. Kai didn't think this was the right time to say what he had thought for years: the yellow tape was just a challenge for jerks and scofflaws to intrude where they were forbidden. Allen and several other officers who had shown up in the last hour went around to everyone and took their statements a second time, adding anything they had thought of since the first interviews, reminded them not to talk about what had happened, and finally let them go home.

Saundra offered to drive Becca home. Then she blushed and apologized to Kai for assuming he would follow them and take her back to her car. He hurried to assure her it was all right, even as Becca thanked her, but insisted she could get home without any trouble.

Later, as he shared the details of what had happened with Eden, with the permission of Allen, he realized something. He liked it that Saundra took it for granted he would help, that she could depend on him for rides and other small, everyday things. Especially when it meant being kind and considerate of others.

"I don't know if I should call her or not," Eden said, after Kai told her everything that had happened, the questions the investigative team had asked, the discussions he had overheard between the witnesses and the investigators. "The simplest explanation, but the most painful one for her and Miss Sarah, is that Conrad has been dead since June."

"Come again?" Kai fought the urge to stick a finger in his ear to clean out something, because he couldn't have heard right.

"You know the law around here. I don't divulge details of jobs I'm working on until things either fall apart or it all comes out in the public wash."

"How can that be Conrad under the floor of Windows when we've seen him running around, hacking off half the town, acting like an idiot with Simone, all this time?" Kai caught his breath. "Wait a minute, how can it be painful for Miss Sarah? She's ... " His head hurt as dozens of possibilities seemed to slam into his mind.

"Things are seldom what they seem," Eden half-sang, quoting Buttercup's solo from *H.M.S. Pinafore.*

"Oh, you are in so much trouble ..." Despite himself, he grinned and sat back further, feeling some of the aching muscles in his neck and around his middle start to relax for the first time since seeing that hole in the floorboards. "Do a few people get a happy ending in all this?"

"Very few. I just wish we could guarantee one for Becca."

"Give me one clue, so I can at least try to sleep tonight?"

Eden sighed and partially bowed her head, studying him through the overgrown bangs that fell across her forehead. Another sigh. "Two words, and that's all I'm going to say. Evil. Twin."

Kai only had to think a few seconds to put the pieces together. Becca had provided the missing pieces. It made so much sense. He felt kind of sick, remembering all the grudging thoughts he had entertained toward Conrad the last few months, when an unreasonable facsimile of him had been the guilty party.

"Wow. I bet Becca is thinking of that. Hope it helps."

"Me too," Eden whispered.

"Maybe you should call and remind her?"

"Maybe. But Becca's smart. Intuitive. She's never struck me as someone who broods or works herself into knots over things. Or focuses on the dark stuff. She'll look for answers and accept them and not beat up on herself for things she can't control. She strikes me as someone who goes off by herself and has a ..." She let out a soft, brief chuckle. "Someone who has a good talk with God, and then pulls up her big girl panties and gets on with business. I wish sometimes I had learned how to pray when we were kids. It might help with things now."

~~~~~

Becca felt no guilt over lying to practically everybody who was so concerned for her. She had no intention of going home and drowning her tension in a carton of ice cream and then going to bed, with a double dose of melatonin to help her sleep. Granted, she might just do that anyway, just not right away.

She knew what she had to do, just not exactly how.

The most important step, the only one she was sure of: she got permission from Allen to call Sarah. Granted, he didn't know she was calling Sarah, he thought she was calling Devona, to let the Columbus Fontaines know what had happened. Without her, no one would think to tell Sarah until she read it in a newspaper or someone down in Columbus saw it on the Internet and showed it to her. No one needed that kind of a shock.

By the time she was three blocks away from Windows, Becca had a partial plan. She made a detour west and drove to Cadburn Bible Chapel. Pastor Roy's car was still on the side street opposite the office door. She parked behind him and went to the door. It wasn't locked, meaning there were more people than just Roy in the building. She found Patty in the office, just putting down the phone at the front desk.

"Oh, sweetheart. Come here." Patty leaped up from the desk and spread her arms.

"Who told you?" Becca's voice cracked. She stepped around the counter that separated the work area from the front part of the office where church members came for information or to drop off requests. She
~~~~~

didn't feel like she could cry just yet, but it was good to cling to Patty and not have to explain anything.

"Felicia, she's got dispatch duty tonight. You really think Conrad's been …" Patty leaned back enough to see her face.

"It answers so many questions."

"Yes, well, maybe for you, but I have more by the minute."

"Is that Becca?" Pastor Roy came through the door at the back of the room that led to his office and the treasurer's office and the equipment room. "How are you? What can we do to help?"

"I need to make a phone call, but I think you need to be there, because it's going to hurt and I just don't know if I can find the right words."

"Speaker phone in my office?" He reached out a hand for her. "Come on in. Who are you calling?"

"That's the hard part." Becca took a few deep breaths, trying to pull some clear thoughts out of the spinning that threatened to become a tangled whirlpool soon.

She waited until they were seated around Roy's boat-sized desk. Piled high with sorting racks and jars of candy and two computers and a microphone for his weekly podcast ministry and dozens of other items, somehow it managed to look orderly and neat.

"Okay." Another deep breath. She was glad Patty still held her hand. "Miss Sarah faked her death because she was afraid. Conrad was adopted — did you know that?" She waited until they both nodded. "His twin brother found him. I'm thinking both his twin brothers — triplet brothers — found him, and they took over his life, because they're crooks. Devona and Rufus, and Eden up at the Mug, helped her fake her death and hide. She's down in Columbus, trying to make peace with the family, after Raymond was killed. She needs to know, right away. She's going to need you."

"Bless you." Roy reached across the desk, and she gave her hand into his grasp. "Most ladies in your place would be focusing on their own pain right now. Self-medicating. Which is healthy, a totally understandable reaction, to a point. But not exactly helpful to anyone else," he added with a shrug and a crooked smile that somehow generated one from her.

"I'm too numb to fall apart right now."

"That's healthy too," Patty said.

With their help, she figured out what to do, how to make the call. She texted Rufus, telling him simply that she had bad news to give Sarah. Could he make sure she wasn't alone? He responded immediately. He and Devona and Sarah were back from dinner, at their hotel. They had a suite they were sharing, so Sarah was right there.

Becca gave Pastor Roy the basic information, the simple details, and Rufus's phone number. A few knots in her gut and chest and head loosened as he broke the news gently, with sympathy and sorrow warm in his voice. There was silence on Sarah's end for several moments. Then she sighed, a ragged kind of sound, with a threat of tears, but her voice was calm.

"I knew. Somehow, I knew. That Nick West is a very good liar, but ... a grandmother knows these things. Oh, my poor Conrad ... How? Do they know how?"

"They're still investigating, doing the examinations. I imagine the coroner won't get to work until morning," Pastor Roy said. "Sarah, the important thing is that we know now, and we can trust Allen and the captain to make sure there's justice. But even more important than that, we know where Conrad has been all this time. I examined him when he made his decision. He's home and he's safe."

"I know." She sighed again, a little more ragged. Becca feared the tears would start soon. "But he was gone, and none of us knew it. He was lost!"

"He's found now," Patty said.

"What about Frank? Are they going to find him there, too?"

Becca flinched. She hadn't thought about Frank Fontaine. He had vanished, probably after confronting Steven a second or a third time. Yes, Nick had said that murder wasn't Steven's pattern, that he made his victims take the fall, but if he had killed Conrad in June, and he had killed Raymond just a few days ago ... that was a pattern too, wasn't it? That was his new pattern. So where was Frank?

She listened as Pastor Roy encouraged Sarah and prayed with her and promised to keep her updated whenever something new was learned. He offered to call Conrad's parents, but Sarah said she would do it. She was sniffling, holding back tears, when the call finally ended.

Becca wondered how long it would take until she could cry. Maybe not until all the answers had been found. After Steven had been caught. And Nathan. She thought about the appearing and disappearing scratches, the two different cars, the different tones of voice, and flipflopping between calling her Becks and Becca. There were two men living Conrad's life. Both of them had to be found. And stopped.

She would cry when it was over.

Letting Pastor Roy and Patty counsel her and comfort and sympathize would just bring on the tears. Becca refused to let go and give in. She had the awful suspicion that once she started crying, she wouldn't be able to stop.

She thanked them and assured them she would call if she needed help. Right now, she just needed to be alone, to think. And yes, indulge in a carton of ice cream and maybe an entire package of Oreos. She really wished she had given in to her latest urge to buy a dog, because she could use some cuddling and unconditional loving, without having to talk to anyone.

Driving home, she called her parents. They were fourteen hours ahead, probably just getting back after lunch, at the international school in Tokyo where they worked. Becca knew she was cheating, calling her father rather than her mother. As a math teacher, her father wouldn't have his phone with him in the classroom. It was a school rule. Her mother, as the principal, would have her phone. She could leave a message with her father, he would get it on a break, tell her mother, and they would talk before calling her back. That would save time, and she could have more information for them when they called her tomorrow. And she could brace herself and keep from crying.

Her parents would cry. They liked Conrad. They would expect her to cry and need comforting, and they would hurt for her, because they believed she had been falling in love with him before everything went so strange.

That was the problem. She wasn't really sure how she felt about Conrad. The man she had known and cared about was too tangled up with the criminal look-alikes who had stolen his life and his identity. That would take time for her to straighten out. And right now, she couldn't spare that energy. There was too much else to deal with.

She was just finishing the basic details, relating everything that had happened, by the time she pulled into the duplex driveway. A tiny snort escaped her as she noted that Devona and Rufus's side of the house had lights on timers, to give the appearance of being occupied. Her side was dark. That wasn't smart. Now she really did wish she had gotten a dog. A sign of life in the house when she wasn't there. A dog with a big voice, even if the dog itself wasn't big, to scare away creeps.

Such as Steven trying to get in, like she had caught him trying to get into Devona and Rufus's side? How many times? Was he just looking for that letter Sarah had supposedly entrusted to them, or something else? Passwords recorded somewhere in Rufus's workroom, to let him take down the firewalls and safeguards created for Conrad and the Fontaine business?

Was that Steven sitting there in the shadows of the porch? Why hadn't she thought to at least leave the porch light on when she left to go to the Four Corners meeting? The backyard had never seemed so dark before, with so many hiding places, and obstacles to trip over, unseen.

"Anyway, Daddy, I'm okay, so don't worry about me, okay? I have a promise that I'll be notified when more details are found. I mean, I could be wrong and that's not Conrad ..." Her voice cracked a little and she caught her breath. "I'm heading home now," she lied, and smiled into the darkness. Her father would probably know she lied, with his too-accurate parental radar. "You always lecture me about talking on the phone and driving, so I'm getting off now. I love you both, and yes, I went to Pastor Roy and he and Patty loved on me and offered to let me stay with them if I didn't want to be alone."

Now, she wished she had taken them up on that. It was just her imagination that someone was sitting in the shadows of the porch, right?

"I'll have more to tell you tomorrow when you call. G'night."

She tapped the red button, turned the key in the ignition, and listened to the throbbing of her heart as the engine died. If there was someone sitting on the porch, staying in the car too long might alert them that she suspected he was there.

You're just imagining things, she scolded herself.

A nosy neighbor might have seen the car pull in and would get worried if she didn't get out right away. On the other hand, she could just be imagining that man-shaped shadow among darker shadows.

Becca tapped the phone she still clutched in her hand, nine and then one. She left her tote in the car, slung her purse over her shoulder, and clutched her keychain so the longer keys stuck out between her fingers on her other hand. Careful to keep her thumb away from the second one, she got out of the car. For a moment, she couldn't remember her usual routine, getting from the car to her back door. If she didn't act normally, she could alert whoever was sitting there.

Please, Lord, let it all be my imagination?

A snort escaped her when she decided that if either of the remaining triplets were sitting there, waiting for her, she was keyed up enough to make him very sorry he had messed with her that night.

"It's West," that increasingly familiar baritone announced when she was halfway between driveway and porch.

Becca had half a mind to press the one and let him deal with the consequences. But that would delay getting answers, and she had the feeling that even though he hadn't been there during the investigation, Nick had more answers than the police right then.

"That was you, wasn't it?" she said as she reached the porch steps. She turned her phone around to show him the lit screen and the nine and one waiting to be completed.

"Me?"

"You were working upstairs, pulling up boards, when my club arrived. You found Conrad's body. There were some other loose boards, put back in place. Did you find more money?"

"Oh, yeah. Not all of it. Lots more boards to pull up." He stood up and came out where the weak moonlight could touch him.

More clouds were moving in, threatening another storm before morning, according to her weather app when she checked it that afternoon. An entirely different storm had hit much earlier. She preferred bad weather, thanks very much.

"Will you find Raymond's father soon?"

"I'm going to let the police finish the job." He stepped back, to let her up onto the porch, and turned on the light on his own phone as she unlocked the back door. She thanked him with a nod, opened the door, and led him into the house. "Saundra asked me to check on you."

"She's sweet."

"She's one of the toughest girls I've ever met. I think you're another one, but it might be smart to take her offer to stay with her for a few days. Until we catch the brothers."

Becca supposed she was being stubborn, maybe a little self-destructive, but the more people offered her shelter with them, the more determined she was to sleep in her own bed and face down whatever monsters tried to come out of the closet once she turned off the lights.

"How about using me as bait? Can you adjust the security cameras Eden installed for Devona's side of the house?" She opened the refrigerator and pulled out the jug of milk. She would share her Oreos, but not her fresh carton of mint moose tracks.

"I could just camp on your sofa."

"Thanks, but I really do need to be alone."

"Consider this. If one of them is interested in you, and my bet is Steven, it might push him to do something stupid. Out of jealousy. You did say that one of them talked about you just running away with him. He's tried a few times to get you alone. There's the whole psychological mess of taking over his good, successful brother's life. Not just his money and his reputation, but his girl."

"That's kind of creepy." She took the package of Oreos out of the cupboard and tossed them down on the table. When she took two glasses out of the cupboard and offered one to him, Nick smiled crookedly and shook his head.

"Yeah, well, these are creepy guys, and a whole creepy situation. And you shouldn't be alone."

"I need to be alone. Nobody talking to me." She picked up the jug and filled one glass.

"Let it all out? It's okay to cry in front of other people."

"I can't. Not yet. I'm just relieved that wasn't Conrad all this time, not sad that he's been dead all this time. Is something wrong with me?"

"You're human. Let me send Saundra over, if you won't go to her."

"Thanks, but I just want to be alone. And sleep." She gestured at the pack of cookies with her glass. "Get enough down, I'll go into a sugar coma. Better than drugs."

"If you say so." He backed toward the door. "Saundra said to tell you she's praying for you."

"Thanks. That does help." She dunked the first cookie, holding it by the edge, trying not to leave it in the milk too long, or it would break and go to the bottom of the glass. "You're not really going to leave, are you? Find a place to park and watch the house?"

"You think you have me all figured out?" He tipped a salute to her with two fingers off his eyebrow, then reached for the doorknob.

"No." She pulled the cookie out and held it carefully, to let the excess milk drip off. "Are you a believer?"

Nick paused with the door open just wide enough to step out. He tipped his head slightly to the right, and a slow, crooked smile seemed to cast shadows over his face. Then he shook his head.

"I'm ... not a very good one. Miss Cleo, that's Saundra's aunt ... she'd say I've got my ticket stamped, and that's about it. But I'll tell you something, Miss Rebecca Veronica Sheridan ... if I wasn't one, all the necessary things I've had to do in my line of work would have rotted me from the inside a long, long time ago. I can sleep at night, and that's a gift too many people don't know how to appreciate."

Then he stepped backwards out the door, pulling it closed behind him, and she didn't hear his footsteps on the porch. For all she knew, he settled back into the chair where he had been waiting for her. Becca turned off the kitchen light and went upstairs. She changed into her pajamas in the dark, and came back downstairs, retrieved the glass of milk and Oreos, and settled in a nest of afghans and pillows in the corner of her sofa. She slowly ate one row of Oreos and watched the light filtering through the sheers of her living room windows. She fell asleep before the incoming clouds entirely blocked the moonlight and didn't hear the first rumbling of thunder.

Chapter Thirteen

Wednesday, September 14

Becca woke up with one of those sinus headaches that pounded at the back of her head and threatened to dive-bomb into her stomach. She hoped it wouldn't, because far too many Oreos lingered there, making her dread the thought of trying to eat anything. Definitely, that rain out there was poised to shift into a killer storm. She would have given anything to make a huge pot of peppermint tea and curl up in bed and drowse the day away, reading and napping.

She knew better, though. If she stayed home, anyone driving by could see her car in the driveway. The two-car garage for the duplex served to house all the gardening equipment and the lawn furniture and Rufus's workshop, so there was no way she could hide her car from spying eyes. If anybody knew she was home, she wouldn't be allowed to ignore calls. People would come by, with casseroles and bakery, sympathy and curiosity. She could imagine all the twisted variations on what little bit was known about last night, and all the speculation that would fly through Cadburn.

The safe bet was to park her car in one of the municipal parking lots in town and then settle in for the day at either the library or Book & Mug. She had managed to train most people to understand that if her car was visible in town, then she was working. She wasn't available for gossip, or in this case, interrogation. If someone did have the temerity to call her, she could tell them, "Sorry, I'm working," and leave the assumption that she would be free to talk later.

Not if she could help it.

If she parked at Book & Mug, Eden wouldn't have to call her to update her whenever the police learned something from the body found under the floorboards.

Becca shuddered, thinking about the parties and meetings she had attended at Windows those few times Steven had allowed a group or organization to use the room. How many times had she sat over Conrad's body, enjoying herself, and never suspecting he was there? She had done some demonstrations with members of Four Corners, when people at those parties asked.

Had she danced on Conrad's grave?

Somehow, she thought Conrad might have been amused if he knew.

She had to believe his soul was safe, and he knew what was going on, all his grandmother had gone through, and the steps taken to finally discover the truth. She hoped he had been amused, and maybe he had missed her. Just a little? Could people have feelings like that, watching from Heaven?

By the time she was washed and dressed, and driving through the rain, she decided the root of her headache was the soaring relief she felt to know that the Conrad hadn't changed. Hadn't turned into a selfish, egotistical jerk who abandoned his growing spiritual life. And then the sudden drop of despair, at the awful suspicion that yes, he had been dead, and nobody had grieved for him. People who used to be his friends had written him off, including her. Let him walk out of their lives, thinking badly of him, and never realizing that he was gone.

She really should have been seasick, rather than having a killer headache, with all the up and down and up and down again.

~~~~~

Kai was in the front window of Book & Mug and waved to her as she came up the sidewalk from the Metroparks parking lot at Sackley and Center. She had parked there in the hopes of a short walk at lunchtime, if this lull in the rain held. Of course, with those darkening clouds coming from the north, that might have been a foolish choice. She should have brought her pocket umbrella.

He met her as she came in the front door. "Conrad is still missing."

She nearly corrected him that they knew where Conrad was, currently lying on a table in the morgue. Then she realized he said it for the benefit of anyone who might be listening and didn't know all the events of last night. Especially Conrad's brothers who had stolen his life and identity.

"Meaning ... no one could find him last night, either?"

Just how soon did Steven, or Steven and Nathan together, find out about the police activity at Windows? Before she called him, thinking she was reporting trouble to the real Conrad?

"Well, they sent someone to his house last night, after ..." He tipped his head toward Windows. "Nobody home, no car. Checked the office. Checked all the buildings that have vacant spots, in case he's hiding out there. Nothing and nobody. Allen said they've already got alerts out, highway patrol, police departments, the airport, any port where someone could get a boat and cross the lake. Hard core stuff."

She managed a nod of thanks when he told Olivia to give her the house special, on the house. Then he walked away. He did have a business to run. The special turned out to be a warm cinnamon roll the size of her hand, and a cinnamon cappuccino. Both of which she feared she wouldn't be able to taste, much less enjoy.

Becca settled in the far back corner, behind the bookstore, where she
~~~~~

wouldn't be visible and the sounds of people having a better day than her wouldn't intrude on what promised to be sketchy concentration, at best. She got through checking her email and declined two text message invitations to meet up. One was a client, another was yet another bozo, probably a pervert or a politician, who addressed her as Theresa. Although in the case of the second text, "declining" meant blocking the caller. She sometimes played with the notion of responding and asking whoever had spammed her this time to go find whoever gave them the false information and punch him or her in the mouth for being a liar. There was no Theresa at her number and never had been. Today was one of those days when she was in the mood for a nasty fight, calling names, and making threats. She just didn't have the energy.

"Hey." Eden slid into the seat facing Becca. "How are you doing?"

"Sugar hangover." She gestured at the half-eaten cinnamon roll. "Helps, but doesn't help at the same time. News?"

"Just confirmation of what we suspected. Doc Williams gave the coroner the serial number of the plate put in Conrad's ankle when he broke it in college. Southfield turned over the dental records at 8:30 and they confirmed the I.D. by 9." She rested a hand on Becca's. "You gonna be okay?"

"Sarah knew." Becca looked around in case anybody was trying to listen. Had they been speaking too loudly? Everything seemed too loud, lately.

"Yeah. Rufus emailed, let me know you called last night. And your pastor. That was really nice. I wish I'd thought of it."

Becca shrugged. It didn't seem like very much help, but was all she could think of at the time.

"How long do you plan on hanging around?"

"My whole day is free." Her phone pinged with another text. "If people would leave me alone."

"Word hasn't really spread yet, but I expect a flood. Friends and snarks. Want to take refuge upstairs?"

"Could I? I won't get in the way?" Becca closed her notebook even as she spoke.

"You're part of the team, as far as I'm concerned."

"Is West here?" She slid all her gear into the tote bag, slung it over her shoulder, picked up the tray, and followed Eden.

"Him?" Eden shrugged as they headed through the coffee shop to the stairwell. "Why?"

"I think he camped outside my house last night, in case one of the brothers showed up."

"Huh. Not as much of a smirky know-it-all as I thought." She shuddered. "Boggles the mind."

"He's not that bad."

"No." She unlocked the door to the stairwell. "Saundra wouldn't put up with him if he was bad news. There's just something about him that makes the hairs stand up on my neck. He knows things. He has this look in his eyes when you catch him watching you. Like he knows a secret and he's just waiting for you to break down and beg him to tell you."

Becca managed a chuckle. She wouldn't have put it that way, but yes, she could see that aspect in Nick West.

Troy was just moving a cushioned leather reclining office chair in front of one of the unoccupied workstations when she followed Eden into the office. He nodded to her and bowed, gesturing her to the chair. That little bit of foolery made her feel better. Becca put her notebook and the tray down, then settled into the chair.

She soon discovered that the freedom from worrying that every movement, every sound was someone approaching, ready to pounce with questions, made it easier to concentrate and get some actual work done. Eden made three calls, and each time she said essentially that Becca was spending the day at the office, so whoever she was talking to could know where to find her. If that was to screen calls from nosey people, or let the proper authorities know where she was, Becca appreciated the consideration. She relaxed a little more. Maybe she could relax enough to fall asleep soon? The office chair was comfortable enough, she wouldn't mind napping in it. That would certainly help the day pass quickly.

Several times, Troy reported in a low voice, probably speaking just to Eden, that he had gotten another call from someone asking what they knew about last night. Eden's phone buzzed several times an hour. Each time, if Becca looked up, she saw Eden glancing at it but not answering. It was safe to assume that as a private investigator, and a neighbor, she was being asked what she knew about the incident at Windows.

Ignoring calls on her own phone didn't seem to discourage anyone from trying. Maybe the gossips and busybodies didn't share information with each other. Eight more came through in the next hour, all supposedly people from Cadburn. She couldn't be sure because they were all marked with North Olmsted as the location on her screen. Becca let them go to voicemail. Cadburn Township was lumped in together with North Olmsted.

Four calls came from friends, people whose names did appear on the screen. She let them go to voicemail too.

She almost ignored the call from her parents. Eden must have been watching, and saw the totally baseless panic before Becca realized that was the fluttering and chill rising inside her. She offered the use of her apartment if Becca wanted some privacy. Becca did. Even after half an hour with her parents offering advice and quoting scripture and apologizing for not being there for her, she still couldn't cry. It was a relief to let them go, and return to the quiet of the office. Yet she did feel much better. Sharing pain did help, more than she had expected.

Then Allen Kenward called to let Eden know he was on his way over. She went downstairs to meet him and bring him up to the office.

"I'm sorry," he said, as soon as he walked into the office and his gaze landed on Becca. "It's official now, documented, murder, not an accident, and …" He raked a hand through his wet hair. "We got called by the FBI office downtown. Not knocked off the case but working under their supervision. Turns out they've been moving in on the brothers for a while now … And you knew some of this," he said, his gaze narrowing as he stared at Becca.

"To be fair," Eden said, "we both did. Another investigator got me involved because I'm local and my mentor sent him to me, and Becca got involved when we realized there were doubles of Conrad running around. So, what are the Feds doing?"

"Over a million dollars hidden in the floor and walls at Windows, and still counting … and another body."

"Frank Fontaine?" Eden said. "Wow. And this used to be such a quiet little town."

That got a snort from Allen.

"So what are you doing now?" Troy said.

"Now that we have some help? Focusing on finding the brothers. We're hoping they're still around here, because no news from highway patrol or any other ways out of town."

"What about the lake?" Eden said. "How hard would it be to rent a boat and cross over to Canada?"

"With the condition the lake is in right now? Have you looked outside in the last two, three hours?" Allen hunched his shoulders.

In the brief pause, the wind moaned past the glass block wall at the front of the office. Becca flinched, hearing the rattle-slap of heavy rain. She thought of Steven on the choppy lake and couldn't make herself feel sorry for him. The Conrad she knew had love the water. He organized at least two canoe trips to Mohican every summer. Until recently. He had taken every opportunity to go water skiing on Lake Erie and learn sailing. He had loved just sitting on the top deck of the ferry to South Bass Island or Kelly's Island, when the Singles group had outings, watching the water. If Steven and Nathan managed to get themselves drowned, or at least capsize and get caught by the Coast Guard, then Conrad would have been avenged by the lake he loved. That would be poetic justice.

"I know TV shows cops doing a lot of things they can't really do, but what about activating the GPS in his phone?" Troy said.

"We actually can do that." He nodded to Eden. "The chief wanted me to ask you, officially, to keep digging. You've got some connections that we can only gaze at with longing—" That got a snort from Troy, and he grinned in response. "She's willing to look the other way if you want to share any classified information from slightly questionable sources."

"I can do better than that. Is Nick West one of the Feds who got involved?" Eden snorted when Allen's mouth dropped open for a few seconds.

"Yeah, he is."

"He got me involved, opened up a lot of records I couldn't legally get into. I'll send over everything I know. Hopefully something will give us that boost we need to catch the brothers before they get too far way."

"Amen," Allen said. "For Miss Sarah, if nobody else."

~~~~~

The theme for Darth Vader blared from Becca's phone, making her nearly jump out of her chair and spill the maple spice cappuccino Kai had brought up for her to try nearly half an hour ago. She stared at her phone, unwilling to believe the call was coming from the person marked by the music. That didn't do much good because it was face-down on the workstation.

"Okay," Troy said, "do we want to know who you hate so much you assigned them that ringtone? Of course, I do want to know why you have someone like that in your address book to begin with."

That question kicked her brain back into gear. Becca reached for the phone and turned it over. The question was if she should answer before it went to voicemail.

"Simone," she said, and slid her thumb across the screen to open the connection. Eden and Troy both got up from their chairs and took a few steps closer.

"Well, there's the old rule about keeping your enemies closer," he remarked. Eden slapped his arm, but she smiled.

"Hi, Simone," Becca began, bracing herself for a volcano of vitriol, blaming her for the trouble the brothers were in. If Simone even knew yet they were brothers, but not Conrad. "What's—"

"You have got to help me. Please, Becca! I know you probably hate my guts but—I don't know anybody else I can call. I mean, you've gotta help me, right? All that church stuff you do, that kind of means you have to help me, even though you hate me. Right?"

"I don't hate you, Simone."

Loathe. Despise. Hate is too strong. It takes up too much energy. There was a time Becca would have laughed at such hair-splitting reasoning.

Eden raised an eyebrow in question. Becca put the phone on speaker.

"I'm here at Finders with Eden and Troy. The police are looking for Conrad, did you know that?"
~~~~~

"Yes, I know that! I'm in jail! They're threatening to get me on accessory charges and murder charges and theft and false documents. I don't know what's going o – o – on!" Her wail shattered into sobs.

"Where are you?" Eden said.

"Oberlin." She snapped out the word as if the place was poison. Or maybe she expected them to know her location automatically. There was no telling with Simone.

"Why are you in Oberlin?" Becca asked.

"Conrad had me come here to empty out his safe deposit box. The big, stupid—" Simone made noises like she had either blown a brain circuit, or she couldn't figure out words vile enough to suit her feelings.

"Why?" Eden asked. "Why does he need to empty his safe deposit box?" she hurried to say while Simone made gulping noises.

"He said Steve is trying to kill him. We need to get out of town before he catches up with us."

"Steve?" She glanced at Becca, eyebrow raised.

"His brother! I didn't even know Conrad had a brother until last night. The big gorilla nearly kidnapped me. And then he threatened to kill me for messing up things. And then Conrad rescued me. And they had this horrid fight and now I'm in ja – a – ail! I didn't do anything wrong!"

"So, who is she working with?" Troy said, his voice pitched soft enough it probably couldn't be heard on Simone's end, over the sobbing, gasping, sniffling noises she was making.

"The other one is Nathan," Becca said. She didn't even try to soften her voice.

"Simone, did Conrad tell you that he was triplets?" Eden said.

"No, he's twins! There are two of him. His scuzzbag brother found him. And he's been blackmailing him for years. And now he's gone wacko. And he's going to kill Conrad. We have to get away before he does something worse!"

Eden made circles with her forefinger and pointed at the phone. Becca guessed that meant she was supposed to keep Simone talking. She nodded, and Eden stepped over to her desk and picked up her phone. She hoped Eden was calling Allen.

"Worse than what?" Becca asked. Well, that seemed like the logical next question.

"He killed Conrad's cousin. And he threatened to put all the blame on Conrad if he didn't play along."

"To do what? Do you know what Steve was planning to do? What has he been making Conrad do?" Becca felt like her brain had frozen up. What other questions could she ask?

"How am I supposed to know? Can you believe the nerve of him? He slapped me around. He told me he'd break my face if I ever gave you a hard time again. I mean, what is with that? Of course, it just figures you'd get the psycho boyfriend."

There was a sound like Simone spat. Becca wouldn't have been surprised. A man's voice came through the phone, distant and warped, but sharp enough Becca guessed he was telling Simone not to do something.

There was probably a law against spitting on city property or at least indoors.

"Look! I am having a really rotten day. I'm sorry! I'm choking on something." There was a brushing sound. Simone kept talking, but the words were muffled. She had probably put her hand around the pickup in her phone.

On the other side of the workstation circle, Eden was listening and nodding. Her gaze met Becca's and she gave her a thumbs up. The brushing, scraping sound repeated and the man's distant voice sounded a little kinder. Still hard to understand what he was saying.

"So this Steve thought you were giving me a hard time? Why would he say that?" Becca asked, when the man stopped talking.

"I don't know! Like, right? I was just protecting Conrad. He asked me to keep people away. But the big jerk has some kind of crush on you. What's with that? Just like in school with JD! Anybody with any brains could tell you didn't want anything to do with him. Which was really stupid of you, because come on, JD was luscious!" Simone broke down sobbing, gasping for breath for a few moments. "How come you get all the really good ones? I mean, okay, let's be honest, something has gone seriously wrong with Conrad. Why do I always get the broken ones?" Simone wailed, and there was a sharp sound that Becca suspected was her stomping her feet.

Troy sank down on the workstation next to Becca's computer, slowly shaking his head, an incredulous smile twisting up one side of his mouth. "Takes one to know one," he whispered.

"But we gotta get out of here. They had a really bad fight last night. Conrad's scared to death. Steve is trying to kill him. He's gotta hide. He asked me to clear out his bank accounts and get his safe deposit boxes."

"Where are you supposed to meet him with all the money?"

"At the ferry docks." Simone gulped and sniffled. "Tonight. We're staying on the island to hide out. Only I don't know how we're going to get across the lake with that big storm coming in. That's where Conrad is right now, getting us a boat."

Eden came back to stand by Becca. "Where are you, Simone? FBI office, or police station, or where?"

That raised a shriek from Simone.

"I'm in one-horse-town stupid Oberlin! This place is barely big enough for a real police station! What makes you think the FBI would get involved?"

"Because there's a state-wide APB out for Conrad," Eden said. "A dead body was found under the floor of Windows, and both brothers are the prime suspects."

"No!" She broke down in sobs, muffled, like the phone was partially covered. "Conrad wouldn't—"

"Simone? Simone, let me talk to the officer in charge. Simone?"

From the clattering sound, Simone dropped her phone. Becca doubted she was coherent enough to have tossed it down.

"This is Sgt. Bradley of the Oberlin police. To whom am I speaking?"

Becca had to muffle a giggle. His slow, gravelly baritone certainly sounded like she thought a sergeant should.

"Hi, Sargent. My name is Eden Cole, I'm a private investigator working with the police department here in Cadburn Township. Captain Sunderson put out the APB on Conrad Price, Steven Harris and Nathan Stemple, and anyone matching their descriptions. Officer Allen Kenward is preparing to drive up to Oberlin and take custody of your prisoner. We're just waiting for the paperwork. Thank you for acting so quickly. I don't suppose you heard what Simone was saying?"

"Oh, yeah. You grow them kind of melodramatic down there in Cadburn, don't you?"

"It's been kind of crazy the last few days. The important detail you need to know is that we discovered a dead body under the floorboards of a rental space managed by the suspect. Just this morning, we identified the body as the real Conrad Price. One of identical triplets. Our current theory is that his brothers killed him months ago, hid the body, and have been masquerading as him, and using his business for money laundering. Now they seem to have fallen out, from what Simone has said, and one is trying to kill the other."

"Well, that sounds like a fun little tangle. Does Miss Radcliffe here know?"

"We just tried to tell her, but she's in a little bit of denial."

"You don't say." He gave a dry chuckle. "You said brothers? How does that happen without people figuring something is wrong?"

"The short version of the story is that they were separated at birth. Conrad didn't know he had brothers until they found him and got to work stealing his life maybe six months ago."

"Uh huh. Hold on, I'm getting handed something." The brushing sound muffled all sounds.

"By the way," Eden said, putting her hand over the phone pickup. "Allen is going to stop by here as soon as he gets the paperwork, to have you ride up to Oberlin with him, help keep Simone calm."

"Are you kidding?" Becca choked on another chuckle that might become a shriek. "Have you noticed that she kind of hates me?"

"Hmm, maybe. But why did she call you, when she has to have a dozen other people to come rescue her?"

"He probably wants you because Simone might spill a lot of things to you, when she'd probably just give him the silent treatment," Troy offered.

"Yeah, that sounds like her." Becca sighed. "Honestly, I think I made a big mistake the other day. I prayed that God would help me be a better Christian, especially when it came to Simone. You don't pray prayers like that, because God will answer and give you a lot of chances to learn, the hard way."

"Sorry about that," Sergeant Bradley said. "We just got a fax with the paperwork. We're all set as soon as your man shows up."

"Great. Thanks. I'm curious, Sergeant. How is it you let Simone call on her own phone?"

"She's not really under arrest, we're just holding her in custody as an accessory. She seems to think she's limited to one call, and honestly, I don't feel guilty letting her keep thinking that. I'm gonna put her in our interrogation room, let her have some privacy, while she's waiting for the pickup."

"That would be a good idea. Thanks."

For punctuation, the elevator slid up to the floor and the doors creak-clattered open. Allen stepped out, shaking rain off his cap.

"Officer Kenward is here," Eden said. "Did you want to speak with him before he heads up there?"

Bradley did, and Eden turned off the speaker and handed the phone to Allen. Becca packed up while they were talking, which didn't take long. When they stepped out of the elevator ten minutes later, Kai was waiting with a takeout tray, two tall cups of something that smelled spicy, and a bag that turned out to hold several of the sandwich wedges Book & Mug carried to promote Deli-licious. She and Allen thanked him and he walked with them to the door. Allen's squad car was double-parked right by the door, but Becca still felt at least partly drenched by the time she could pull the door shut and settle in the front seat. She muffled a chuckle at the thought of Simone's hysterics when they put her in the back seat.

Sorry, Lord. I'm not a very nice person, let alone a good Christian. Help me to be a little kinder to her.

Discussing what Simone had told her and speculating on what Nathan and Steven were doing right then took up a large portion of the forty-five-minute ride up to Oberlin. Allen asked her to call Chief Sunderson to pass on the information that Nathan was trying to get a boat to cross the lake. There were several ferry lines he could be traveling on, depending on what island he was going to. Becca and Allen didn't have to talk very long to agree the destination was probably South Bass Island, and the most likely ferry was at the Miller docks. With that ferry line, Conrad could take his car across, whereas other ferries were only for day-trippers and passengers, not vehicles. Passengers on those lines would need to rent golf carts to get around. Nathan probably thought he could leave his car on the island and make it harder for the authorities to pick up his trail. Allen shook his head when Becca suggested that theory. She remembered what Nick had said about Nathan not having a very strong grip on reality.

When they got off the highway, Allen pulled over to make several calls, to share information and catch up on what had been learned so far. Becca huddled down in the car and watched the rain that just seemed to fall even harder now that they were sitting still. Most of the calls were short, as nothing much had changed since they got on the road.

In twenty minutes, they were in the center of Oberlin and easily found the police station. When they parked, Becca followed Allen at a swift jog through the rain to the door of the station and tried to find something else to think about. She was tired of the constant swirl of grisly, headache-inducing questions about Steven and Nathan and their schemes.

"When we get back in the car, I'm going to call Pastor Roy and Patty, to come see Simone. She's going to need someone to cry on when she finally hears the truth about Nathan," she told Allen, as they waited in line at the front desk. The officer on duty was currently taking care of a dripping boy with a shaved head, wearing all camouflage clothes and a Teenage Mutant Ninja Turtles backpack.

"Good idea," he said.

The boy walked away, blowing an enormous bubble with dark purple gum, and Allen stepped up to the desk.

"Kenward, from Cadburn?" the officer said before Allen could open his mouth. "Hope you brought a dropcloth for your back seat."

When he led them to the back room where Simone had been placed, Becca understood what he meant. While Simone's clothes weren't wet, her eyes were swollen and glistening with tears. She looked up, her mouth fell open, then she let out a wail and shot out of her chair. She hit Becca at top speed and flung her arms around her, nearly knocking them both off their feet. She clung to her, whimpering, and dripping fresh tears, but at least she didn't wail. Becca feared if she tried to free herself from Simone's killer grip, they'd get treated to more wailing, probably at a volume guaranteed to make their ears bleed. She resigned herself to sitting in the back seat with Simone.

Sgt. Bradley showed up then, and he and Allen exchanged

paperwork and signatures and talked in some sort of police shorthand. Becca had the feeling the Oberlin officer was commiserating with them for having to deal with Simone, who continued whimpering and leaking and clutching at her so hard she thought she might have tears in her sweatshirt and totally inadequate windbreaker. She caught a few things Allen said and guessed he was filling in some of the gaps in what the local police knew. They had to arrange for someone to take the contents of the safe deposit box into custody, as evidence, and for someone to come up from Cadburn to drive Simone's car back to town. Then far sooner than she had estimated, they were back out in the car, and yes, she was in the back seat with Simone.

Allen asked if she needed something to eat or to use the bathroom before they left. Was she all right with him recording what they said on the way back to Cadburn? Her response was mostly, "Yeah, fine, go ahead, whatever," building up to, "Just get me out of here!"

Becca suspected Simone really didn't hear any of that. Maybe it wasn't nice, but she wasn't going to correct her. Whatever Simone blurted on the trip back home could be useful in the investigation. After all, while she hadn't been romanced by the mastermind of the operation, and probably the killer, Simone must have heard or learned something useful. Even if she didn't know it.

Eden called with a new bit of information just as they were waiting to pull out of the police department parking lot. Becca considered it perfect timing.

"That was Eden," she announced as she put her phone back in her purse.

"Good news?" Allen said.

"Useful. Mostly just verifying what we knew already. A lot of people in the system don't have very favorable opinions about the brothers. Now we know Steven is the oldest, then the real Conrad, and then Nathan."

"What—" sniff "—do you mean by the real Conrad?" Simone demanded.

"Conrad was triplets. The other two brothers, Steven and Nathan, were separated and bounced around the system. They grew up in the same city, so they went to school together and got in a lot of trouble pretending to be each other. Steven figured out the scam of using each other for an alibi, to get away with petty theft. They probably thought they'd hit it big when they discovered Conrad and the profitable real estate business he would inherit someday. Steven contacted him, and apparently sent Nathan here to skulk around and learn about Conrad's life so they could start taking it over."

"No, Steve came here. No Nathan. He threatened Conrad." She lifted her head and blinked tear-filled eyes and looked so utterly miserable,

Becca didn't find it quite so hard as before to feel sorry for her.

"No, both brothers were in on it. And probably when Conrad wouldn't play their game, or he found out they were hiding behind him, using his name and face, they killed him."

"No." Simone drew back, so Becca was able to sit up straight and not feel quite so much like a boa constrictor's next meal. "Conrad said —"

"*Nathan* told you all that." Allen glanced at them in the rearview mirror. "Conrad Price has been dead, hidden under the floorboards of Windows on the River since June. That explains a whole lot of strangeness and the changes in him. Two identical brothers, trying to live one man's life, and not having enough detail to carry off the deception. It was a lot easier to alienate anyone who might notice the differences."

"We noticed the changes anyway, and just wrote him off when he kept acting like a jerk." Becca shuddered, feeling a little sick. "And they were going to kill Miss Sarah, to keep her from figuring it out. I wonder if they'd have gone after Conrad's parents when they came back to town. Maybe his uncle figured things out, so Steven had to kill him, too?"

"No, you're wrong," Simone whimpered. She hunched into the far corner of the back seat and wrapped her arms around herself. "There's just Steve and Conrad, and Steve is trying to kill Conrad."

Becca and Allen exchanged glances in the rearview mirror.

"Suppose you tell us what Conrad wanted you to do for him?" Allen said after maybe ten minutes of silence, when they were back on the highway. The sound of the rain on the windows and the hiss of the tires kicking up water made a slightly soothing background.

"Why should I?"

"You said Steve was after him, right?" He glanced in the rearview mirror, waiting until Simone gave a grudging nod. "How can we catch up with him and protect him from his brother, if you don't help us?"

A loud sigh from Simone and further slumping in the back seat signaled capitulation. In half-sentences, broken up with whimpers and exclamations of, "He lied to me. How could he? He said he loved me," she told what little she knew. Nathan had given her the addresses and account names and numbers in four banks in four cities, along with the safe deposit box in Oberlin. She was supposed to clear them all out and meet him at the Miller's Ferry docks for the last ferry of the day to South Bass Island. In the morning, they would rent a boat and cross to Canada, and get married. Supposedly Nathan was busy arranging for new identities for the two of them.

Now Becca did feel sorry for Simone. She was willing to bet Nathan had no intention of marrying her. He would grab the money and whatever she took from the safe deposit boxes and just run for it. If he was as nasty as he was smart, because yes, he had managed to carry off the deception for months before things started to unravel, he would conveniently lose her keys and phone and wallet, so she was stranded. Before she could get someone to help, Nathan would be long gone, fleeing her and his brother. It was the promise of marriage that blinded Simone to common sense, more than anything else. There was no way Nathan could get new identities for the two of them in just a day, or even two days. Not unless he had had the plan in the works for some time now. Which, when Becca thought about it, made the whole situation even more grim and twisted.

Simone was silent for a few minutes after spilling those few details, then she sighed and sniffled and wiped at her face. The highway sign announced they had just crossed back into Cuyahoga County.

"If you're right ... well, Conrad was telling me an awful lot of stuff about you, and I guess all of that has to be lies. Or at least most of it," she added, her voice softer.

"Such as?" Allen prompted, while Becca tried to decide if she wanted to know what Nathan had said. Or Steven. Or both of them.

"He was always telling me how Becca was chasing him, and she kept telling his grandmother that they were getting back together, and she — his grandmother — planned on them moving in with her, and they'd take care of her." Simone shuddered. "Why did she think she needed anybody to take care of her? She was fine. Scary smarter. Sometimes, I swear she could read my mind. I did not like going near her."

Those lies, Becca suspected, were to keep Simone away from Sarah, stop her from cozying up to the grandmother of the man she thought she had finally caught.

When they reached Cadburn, Allen dropped Becca off at Book & Mug before taking Simone to the police station to make an official statement. She considered trudging through the rain to her car and going home, but the lights were bright and she was cold and too tired to make the effort. Olivia told her to go upstairs. When Bekka made it to the stairwell, Saundra was waiting. She hugged her and kept an arm around her as they went up the stairs.

Rufus and Devona had returned from Columbus and were waiting upstairs. Until Steven and Nathan were caught, the cousins insisted that the two of them, and Becca, couldn't go back to their duplex. They had to stay in the Mug building. There was more than enough room. Rufus would room with Kai. Devona and Becca could sleep on two futon couches in Eden's apartment. She promised they were very comfortable.

Becca willingly complied this time. She had been lucky last night, when she came home to a dark shadow on her porch that was Nick West. She knew better than to press her luck. While Steven might just be hunting his brother to punish him, that didn't mean he wouldn't come after anyone who had frustrated his plans in Cadburn. While that included many people, Becca suspected she was near the top of that list. After all, he had tried to get her to run away with him.

What would he have done when she found out he wasn't her Conrad? Would he ever have told her? Of course, that was assuming she would have let him persuade her to give him another chance. She had the awful feeling that in the glee of knowing Conrad had finally wised up and dumped Simone, she would have ignored all the little niggles of uneasiness.

Becca hoped she wouldn't have been that selfish and self-blinded. And especially, she wouldn't be like so many idiots in too many movies who knew something was wrong and ignored it because they were "in love," whatever that was.

She was still pondering those questions and unable to sleep, going on 1am. She got up from the very comfortable futon, tiptoed past Devona, and left Eden's apartment to go out to the office and try to get some work done on Charli's next research project.

Somehow, she wasn't surprised at all to find Nick West and Rufus, sitting with several monitors lit up, watching images from the inside and the outside of both sides of the duplex.

"If I'm not there as bait—"

She stopped, not even trying to hide her smile when both of them jumped. Rufus glared at her. Nick just shook his head slowly and smiled. He looked tired, and that worried her. He had struck her as someone who would never let himself get tired until the mission was completed. Successfully.

"If I'm not there as bait, what makes you think he'll show up?" She settled in a roller chair halfway around the curve of the workstations, and pulled it across the floor with her feet, to get closer to them.

"Oh, this is just preliminary. We make him hungry, we make him nervous, until he does something incredibly stupid," Nick murmured.

"And if we run out of clean clothes before then?"

"Hmmm … don't tell the boss, but I … liberated a couple packs of cash. Treat yourself to a new wardrobe, on the brothers."

"I believe it," Rufus said.

Becca decided even if it wasn't true, she wanted to believe. She also decided Saundra was pretty lucky, having someone like Nick around to look after her.

Chapter Fourteen

Thursday, September 15

Becca and Charli spent Thursday at the library. Twila had cut back her hours after the whole ugly mess with Carruthers destroying his career. She glared and sniffed loudly when Charli walked in, but didn't make her usual disparaging comments. Becca found it a little easier to feel sorry for Twila now. Maybe because she had so much practice feeling sorry for Simone. Whether the shock of the last few days would leave any permanent change in her attitude and actions was yet to be proven.

The two of them had a relaxing time, investigating the books available in the library relating to Charli's idea for a possible new series of books. They skimmed through, looking at headings and pictures and making notes of references to other people and events and forensic evidence, to add to their slowly growing list of research. They had permission from Mrs. Tinderbeck to eat lunch in the smallest conference room, and Saundra joined them. They didn't discuss anything having to do with Conrad, and his brothers, and the Fontaine family.

The weather was only marginally improved from yesterday, and the few parents who braved the drippy, gray day to come to the library with their preschool or homeschooled children left Becca alone. This was one of the many nice characteristics of most of the people who lived in Cadburn Township. They knew when to leave people alone and give them time to adjust to or recuperate from odd events.

Saundra came to look for them among the shelves at the back of the library, farthest from the door, around 3:30. Becca remembered clearly looking at her watch and speculating on calling it quits for the afternoon, to walk up to Goody Two Scoops and buy something decadent to take back to Eden as a thank-you. Then she raised her head and there was Saundra. She looked just concerned enough to make something tighten in Becca's chest.

"Are you going to be here for a while yet?" she asked, which struck Becca as a strange question.

"Well, I was trying to remember what I had on hand I could whip up for dinner, and invite you two over, and the other girls, and have a brainstorming party," Charli said. "Why?"

"Eden asked me to keep you here, until she could catch up with you." Saundra shook her head. "She doesn't want to make you wait until you get back to the Mug tonight."

They followed Saundra up to the front of the library and had barely settled down around her desk when Eden walked in. She ignored Twila's attempt to flag her down, and only nodded to a few of the people who talked to her as she passed them.

"Do you want me to leave?" Charli asked.

"Just promise you'll wait a couple years before you put this into a book," Eden said. She looked around, probably checking that no one was trying to eavesdrop. "They found Nathan."

"He didn't get to Canada?" Becca knew that was a stupid question as soon as the words left her mouth. "How is —" Her stomach dropped when she recognized that somber light in Eden's eyes. "Did Steven …?"

"Last night, a boat rammed into the breakwater at a marina in Sandusky. The owner was preparing to take the boat down to the other end, to get it out of the water. The engine was running, and he had just shifted into first gear when a man came up from below decks, where he had obviously been hiding, and tried to throw him overboard. While they were fighting, the boat headed out, managing not to hit any other boats or the docks. Just the breakwater. It took the Coast Guard until this morning to get the boat off the rocks, and then they found a body wrapped up in canvas, with cinder blocks tied to it. They identified Nathan about two hours ago. Allen called to ask me to break it to you."

"Thanks." Becca took a deep breath. "That was … nice of him."

Charli wrapped an arm around her shoulders.

"Did they identify Steven as the attacker?" She surprised herself, asking that question when so many more pressed at her tongue.

"Yeah. Solid identification. The owner of the boat freaked out, when the Coast Guard showed him the body, to see if he knew who it was. He swore that was the man he had been fighting with, who jumped overboard and apparently swam away when the boat hit the rocks."

"I know I should feel sorry for him. Or vindicated. Or relieved. Or something." Becca took a couple more deep breaths. She felt crooked, like she was going to tumble sideways and fall off the planet.

"You need to go home?" Saundra said.

"I think I need some air. And to sit down."

Eden and Charli supported her outside. A few spatters of rain kissed her face and the air felt thick and cool, and that did help her feel a little better. She settled on a bench and didn't even care when she felt water seeping through her jeans. They sat with her and held her hands, and she was grateful.

"Is it over?" she said, when that question seemed the most coherent among all the thoughts churning in her head.

"Probably not," Eden said. "Police investigations don't wrap up as quickly as they do on TV. And there's the FBI and a couple other government initials involved."

"Umm, if I take notes, are you going to be ticked at me?" Charli asked.

A snort of laughter escaped Becca. That lifted some of the heaviness in her chest.

"It feels like everything happened so fast, but I know it didn't. It's been building up since spring. And all this time, I've been … angry at Conrad. Angry at what I thought he messed up. But he didn't. That's the worst part, I think. I want to apologize to him, but I can't."

"Why not?" Charli squeezed her hand. "Like Pastor Roy says, he had his eternal life insurance policy all paid for. You'll see him again, right? And maybe, I don't know, maybe it's not good theology, but I like to think that those who went ahead of us, they can at least know what's going on with us."

"At the very least, it'll help you sleep better, to tell him you're sorry," Eden said. "Look at it this way, you helped trip up his killers and finally bring them to justice. That's big."

"Yeah. It is." Becca took another deep breath, and this one didn't feel so heavy.

~~~~~

Becca and Devona were upstairs in Troy's apartment that evening, investigating his amazing collection of home-grown spices and herbs. Rufus shouted up the stairwell. They couldn't make out what he said, but the logical guess was that they had to come downstairs.

When they reached the office, Kai and Eden and Rufus were gathered in front of the same bank of monitors Nick and Rufus had set up last night.

A mottled, dull-wet man-shape walked through the rainy shadows and gloom around the driveway side of the duplex. Becca guessed he was wearing camouflage. That could not be a good sign. The shape walked around the garage, looking in the window of the man-door.

Then the intruder skulked around the perimeter of the yard, ducking under low-hanging branches, around decorative bushes, stepping over the little white picket fence. Until finally it reached the back porch. She felt like shouting, "Get on with it, already!" when the figure crouched down and reached under the second step.

"Uh huh, just what we thought," Nick said.

That startled her because he wasn't in the room.

"Microphone connection," Eden whispered. "They found some sensors placed around the house yesterday when they were setting up the new cameras."

"Steven?" she whispered back.

"The guy is not patient. He's probably going in to wait for you to
~~~~~

show up. Or hopefully he's running out of hiding places, so he's going to lay low with you."

"Ugh."

"Okay," Nick said. "Ready to lower the boom. Let the chief know."

The figure stood up and put a foot on the bottom step. He paused. Raised his other foot to the second step.

Lights flared from the garage and the peak of the porch roof and the second floor, revealing Steven draped in a camouflage poncho, his features bleached out by the brilliance. He raised a hand to shield his eyes, just for a moment, then he turned and leaped into a run.

Nick flew out of the shadows, barreling into him head-first and hitting him in the gut. They went down. Steven's back slammed into the porch post. The sounds were muffled and distant. Becca supposed Nick had left his microphone behind when he went on the attack.

Other figures came out of the rainy shadows. All in dark gear, all with guns.

Steven growled something and swung his legs up, somehow somersaulting backwards and sideways, so he landed in a crouch on the porch steps. He leaped on Nick, who had barely gotten to his feet. They went down, with Nick kicking his legs up in the air, leveraging them so they rolled, out of the circle of illumination.

Seconds later, Steven stumbled backward, with Nick coming at him, spinning on one foot, kicking with the other. Land, twist, kick. Hitting him in the gut, chest, and finally in the face. Steven went down, and the other men moved in, all their weapons aimed at him.

"Wow, the spook sure has all the moves," Kai said.

"Is it over?" Devona said.

"Looks like it." Rufus turned his chair around and reached for his sister. She fell half into his wheelchair as they hugged and held onto each other for several minutes, while the team restrained Steven and led him out of the pickup range of the cameras.

The speakers crackled. "Good job," Nick said. "Remember what I said, Wheels. I can put in a good word for you with a lot of very prestigious places. You've got the chops."

"Thanks, but the kind of stuff you're involved in?" Rufus grinned around at the others. "I'd rather keep that in the movies."

"Smart kid." The sound crackled and died, and the screens blanked.

"It's over." Devona settled into an office chair and wiped a few tears from her face. "I can't wait to tell Mama Sarah. She's safe now."

"You're all safe now," Eden said. She turned to Becca. "How are you feeling?"

"I'm not sure." Becca sat down.

"Hey, let's celebrate," Kai said. "All that fun stuff has put me in the mood for a Bruce Lee marathon. What do you say?"

Becca laughed. And then finally, she could cry.

Saturday, September 24

Sarah Fontaine returned to Cadburn Township after the funerals of Frank and Raymond in Columbus, and many days of getting to know her grandchildren, and great-grandchildren. The healing between her and her remaining two sons would take time, but she seemed content with the start they had made. She asked Becca to come for lunch, the day she returned. For most of the meal she chatted about the grandchildren and all the chores to close down her yard for the winter, decorating for the fall, and the many silly, relieved, and expected angry reactions from her friends and neighbors, after finding out she had faked her death. They were nearly done with the meal, enjoying thick slices of coffee cheesecake in front of the fireplace, when Sarah admitted she had several specific reasons for asking Becca over, alone.

"If things had turned out differently ... well, my dear, you are a part of our family. Julia agrees with me, and she would like you to be involved in planning Conrad's funeral. You will help us, won't you?"

"Of course. You know I'd be happy to. When will she be home?" Becca decided she would offer to pick up Conrad's parents at the airport, and any other errands that needed doing. She could only partly imagine how Julia and Rick had to feel, hearing about what had been happening only after the ruckus had calmed down.

"Monday. Pastor Roy has reserved the church for the service next Friday, in the evening. So as many people as possible can come."

"That's good. I'll contact the funeral committee. Moira Usher should have a good idea of how many people to expect. What colors would you like for —"

Sarah reached to rest a hand on her wrist.

"Miss Sarah?"

"My dear, that can wait. You are indeed part of our family. You have the right to know, to have answers." Sarah looked away a moment, delicately licking her lips. "Devona and Rufus agree you should know, after all you've gone through for us, for Conrad. They are family."

"Oh, if that's what you're thinking of, Rufus already told some of us. He said to keep it quiet, that their mother was a Fontaine, and that's the whole reason you asked Devona to break off with Raymond."

"Is that how he explained it? The dear boy, always protective of my feelings ..." She sighed. "Yes, their mother is a Fontaine. Albert's daughter."

Becca wanted to say no, that couldn't be. Albert Fontaine was too good and moral and kind a man to do something like that, break his vows to Sarah and father a child out of wedlock. And yet, looking into Sarah's eyes, so calm, serene, no sign of tears or anger ... she had to believe her.

"Her mother ... well, she had some emotional problems. She believed she was married to Albert during a period in his career when he had to travel between three different locations. He gave in to temptation, and for a while even blamed his loneliness, being away from me and our children and ..." Sarah sighed and looked away. But not before Becca saw the old pain in them. Even now. Piercing the serenity that normally filled them. "He was going to break it off with her when his employment situation changed, and he could stay home with us. Then he learned she was pregnant, and he took responsibility for the child. Financially. It took many years of God dealing with him before he could confess to me. Laura was twelve when her mother died. Relatives wanted to throw her into a mental facility, positive she would inherit her mother's problems. Albert couldn't allow it.

"When we brought her home and told our children the story, they were hurt. And furious. And embarrassed. Our sons refused to allow Laura into the house. They lost all respect for their father." Her voice cracked. "The more he fought to bring Laura into our family, the more they fought him. And hated him. They hated me for forgiving him. For staying with him."

"And they just didn't come home from college. Yes, Rufus said." Becca caught hold of Sarah's hands. They trembled.

"Oh, it was nowhere near as simple as that." She blinked away threatening tears. "Our sons went to the leadership of our church and made sure their version of events was heard first. They led the pastor and deacons to believe Albert was trying to hide and excuse what he had done. Albert was called up before them, and his fate was already decided before he opened his mouth. People chose sides without hearing the whole story. It was heartbreaking, and it was only by God's grace that our church did not split and our testimony in the neighborhood wasn't destroyed.

"Our sons left the church because they disagreed with the forgiveness offered Albert. We left our church because it was kinder to our daughters, and to Laura, to start over somewhere no one knew the awful family battle that had taken place. Protecting them was our priority. And going somewhere quiet where we could rebuild our marriage, our family. What was left of it."

"That's awful."

"Yes, well, it's been said that most murders are committed by family members." Sarah managed a thin smile. "So now you know our family secret, our pain, our shame." A shuddering breath escaped her. "I can't help wondering how differently all this might have turned out if I had simply confronted Raymond, that first day I saw him with Devona. I was a coward. He looked so much like his father at that age, I knew exactly who he was, and ... I feared finding out what his father had told him about me, about his grandfather. I feared how he would react to Devona, if I told him she was his cousin, if he knew about Laura, what his father had said about Laura. Raymond might still be alive, if he hadn't kept coming back, if he hadn't kept trying to persuade Conrad to help him ..."

"No, you can't think that. Everybody made their choices. Steven and Nathan made their choices. You can't be responsible for everyone." Becca slid out of her seat and wrapped her arms around Sarah. They clung to each other, mostly in silence, with a few tears, as old pain and new slowly seeped away through the air.

What kind of pain had Sarah endured, what lessons had God been teaching her, that she could embrace the daughter of another woman, visible proof that her husband had broken his vows? What kind of love had she learned to live out, every day, that she could endure the pain of her sons turning their backs on her for the sake of their pride and self-righteousness?

What kind of lessons could and should Becca learn from this?

"We're going to be okay," she whispered, and promised Conrad she would look after his grandmother.

~~~~~

Later that afternoon, Becca went walking. She didn't pay attention to where she was going. She just needed to move, to let the revelations, spoken and unspoken, interior and spiritual, shift around in her mind and heart. When she blinked and looked around and found herself strolling down Center toward Book & Mug, she wasn't surprised. This felt right.

She went in and ordered the most decadent item on the menu. Then she sat in a booth and let her mind slide into neutral, while the frozen whip melted and the layers of fudge and caramel and whipped cream merged together. She could have sat for hours, but then the Tweed cousins came in. They were delighted to see her and wanted to hire her to help with setting up their candle shop, Brighten Your Corner. They were a little apprehensive about the previous tenant, who continued to insist that he had been evicted illegally. He had found out that they were preparing to move in, and he had threatened them in front of several witnesses. He promised to make them sorry for trying to steal what was his rightful place. He stalked off shouting about a man having a right to defend his castle.

Melba anticipated a drawn-out struggle with "the old fusspot sourpuss," while Cilla poo-pooed the idea, sure he was too big of a tightwad to do anything that might cost him a dollar. Soon, they and Becca
~~~~~

were caught up in floor plans, making lists of used furniture shops to obtain display cases and shelves and tables, and calculating what renovations needed to be made. They debated if the candle-making portion of the business should be conducted out front, where customers could see what went into making the decorative candles, or if it should be done in back and leave the front for display.

Several other members of the Guzzlers stopped by. Chatted for a little while. Congratulated the Tweeds. Asked if Becca was all right, if there was anything they could do to help, and shared news of their own. Book & Mug in so many ways was the heart of the township. Becca relaxed and felt as if something that had been twisted out of line, out of proper flow, was finally sliding back into place where it belonged.

These were her friends, her family, her home. The pain, the anger, was finally fading away now that she had answers. She would be all right. Whether she would take Sarah's offer to run Fontaine Realty, she had no idea yet. That would take time. But she knew everything would be all right. Eventually. She just had to pray, and wait, and get on with life.

END

THANK YOU!

Thank you for reading this book from Mt. Zion Ridge Press.

If you enjoyed the experience, learned something, gained a new perspective, or made new friends through story, could you do us a favor and write a review on Goodreads or wherever you bought the book?

Thanks! We and our authors appreciate it.

We invite you to visit our website:

www.MtZionRidgePress.com

and explore other titles in fiction and non-fiction. We always have something coming up that's new and off the beaten path.

And please check out our podcast

Books on the Ridge

where we chat with our authors and give them a chance to share what was in their hearts while they wrote their book, as well as fun anecdotes and glimpses into their lives and experiences and the writing process. And we always discuss a very important topic: *Tea!*

You can listen to the podcast on our website or find it at most of the usual places where podcasts are available online. Please subscribe so you don't miss a single episode!

Thanks for reading. We hope to see you again soon!

About the Author

On the road to publication, Michelle fell into fandom in college and has 40+ stories in various SF and fantasy universes. She has a bunch of useless degrees in theater, English, film/communication, and writing. Even worse, she has over 100 books and novellas with multiple small presses, in science fiction and fantasy, YA, suspense, women's fiction, and sub-genres of romance.

Her official launch into publishing came with winning first place in the Writers of the Future contest in 1990. She was a finalist in the EPIC Awards competition multiple times, winning with *Lorien* in 2006 and *The Meruk Episodes, I-V,* in 2010, and was a finalist in the Realm Awards competition, in conjunction with the Realm Makers convention.

Her training includes the Institute for Children's Literature; proofreading at an advertising agency; and working at a community newspaper. She is a tea snob and freelance edits for a living (MichelleLevigne@gmail.com for info/rates), but only enough to give her time to write. Her newest crime against the literary world is to be co-managing editor at Mt. Zion Ridge Press and launching the publishing co-op, Ye Olde Dragon Books. Be afraid … be very afraid.

And please check out her newest venture: Ye Olde Dragon's Library, the storytelling podcast. Each week, listeners are invited to join Michelle on her blog to ask questions, answer questions posed at the end of the episode, and give feedback and suggestions that might earn your name in the acknowledgments in the final published version of the book. Listen to the podcast on your favorite podcast app or listen on the website: www.YeOldeDragonBooks.com, and click on the Ye Olde Dragon's Library link. Then go to her blog to interact: www.MichelleLevigne.blogspot.com

www.Mlevigne.com
www.MichelleLevigne.blogspot.com
www.YeOldeDragonBooks.com
www.MtZionRidgePress.com
@MichelleLevigne

NEWSLETTER:

Want to learn about upcoming books, book launch parties, inside information, and cover reveals?
Go to Michelle's website or blog to sign up.

Thanks for reading!
If you enjoyed this book, would you help Michelle by posting a review on Goodreads?

Are you a member of Book Bub? If so, please follow Michelle on Book Bub, and you'll get alerts when new books are coming out.

As a way of saying thanks, Michelle invites you to the Goodies page on her website. It will change regularly, offering you a free short story, a sample audiobook chapter, sneak peeks at new cover art, inside information on discounts and new release dates, etc.

Please go to: Mlevigne.com/good-stuff.html

Also by Michelle L. Levigne

Guardians of the Time Stream: 4-book Steampunk series
The Match Girls: Humorous inspirational romance series starting with **A Match (Not) Made in Heaven**
Sarai's Journey: A 2-book biblical fiction series
Tabor Heights: 20-book inspirational small town romance series.
Quarry Hall: 11-book women's fiction/suspense series
For Sale: Wedding Dress. *Never Used*: inspirational romance
Crooked Creek: Fun Fables About Critters and Kids: Children's short stories.
Do Yourself a Favor: Tips and Quips on the Writing Life. A book of writing advice.
To Eternity (and beyond): *Writing Spec Fic Good for Your Soul.* A book defending speculative fiction.
Killing His Alter-Ego: contemporary romance/suspense, taking place in fandom.
The Commonwealth Universe: SF series, 25 books and growing
The Hunt: 5-book YA fantasy series
Faxinor: Fantasy series, 4 books and growing

Wildvine: Fantasy series, 14 books when all released
Neighborlee: Humorous fantasy series
Zygradon: 5-book Arthurian fantasy series
AFV Defender: SF adventure series
Young Defenders: Middle Grade SF series, spin-off of *AFV Defender*
Magic to Spare: Fantasy series
Book & Mug Mysteries: cozy mystery series